D1336492

For *all the menagerie.*

Reunion

April 2005

My reunion with you made my legs shake. As I sat by your bed, I clamped one knee hard on top of the other. You called me 'Nessie', the name you'd given me all those years ago. I didn't call you anything. Not 'Genevieve', not 'Jenny', not 'Mrs Brown'. Old habits die hard.

You talked about the old days, harmless stuff. *Ayam zaman*, as they say in the Arabic songs.

'It was a funny old time. A busy time. A lot of *living*, if that makes sense... Especially for you and your sister. Sherine. Everything so new, as it is to children.'

'Mmm,' I said. The sound came out tight and strangulated. A cat crying in my throat. When you spoke again, your voice was so low I could hardly hear you.

'Sorry?' I said, just as I digested your words, and our voices collided in mid-air as you continued.

'Tell me how you remember it all. I want a record of those days.'

A strange resonance in your voice on the word 'record', as if we'd shifted into a place where sound travels differently: a cavernous hall, not a small, sunny room containing a wardrobe, a chair, a bedside table and a bed.

'Memories don't last forever,' you said. 'You'd be surprised what fades away.'

Then you closed your eyes as if to shield yourself from the reply that burst from my lips: harsh, jangling laughter. A bubble of saliva sprayed in a fine mist onto your pale blue blanket.

'Sorry,' I said. 'I didn't mean to spit all over you.'

A grimace passed over your face.

'Sorry,' I repeated, my face turning hot. 'I've still got your letter,' I offered tentatively in the pause that followed, expecting you to ask which letter, but you just nodded slowly, keeping your eyes shut.

When I thought back to those days, it was the image of the fish, of all things, that niggled away at me. A big silver fish lying on a chopping board. Mama screaming and screaming. A doctor dragging her along by her hair... Me and Sherine aged four and eight (or were we five and nine?) crouched by the door. Sherine fumbling to cover my eyes and ears, saying 'Shhh, shhh,' like it was me making that racket. You huddled in the living room with our father, whispering, 'Don't worry, don't worry.'

I wanted to ask you what really happened that day, but I didn't. It was only a riddle, not the main catastrophe. Certainly not life and death.

We talked about other things. Your children's children: the neat symmetry of your daughter's two boys and your son's two girls. Sherine's job; my lack of one. Your time in America and my time in Japan. We kept our discussion of my parents limited to the ungarnished facts.

'When did your mother go back to Tunisia?'

'Eleven years ago – it was eleven years in March.'

'And you said he's semi-retired...?'

We talked wars, wildfires, earthquakes and climate change, not the things that had ripped you out of our lives sixteen years ago. My *I forgive you*s crumbled in my mouth. Who did I think I was to forgive you? I was a bystander, not the victim. And anyway, you didn't look like someone who was waiting to be forgiven. Your eyes were calm, steady, observant. Something unknowable in them. Had it always been there or had time and distance introduced it? You were different from how I'd remembered (or imagined) you.

Relieved of this burden of forgiveness, I felt my diaphragm unclench, and I said, 'So where should I begin this record, then?'

'Start wherever you want,' you said with a little laugh. 'It's your record. What about the day you arrived in London – do you remember that?'

Almost before the words were out of your mouth I replied, 'I remember the kitchen but not the aeroplane...'

Part 1: Exile

1979–1989

Arrival

I remember the kitchen but not the aeroplane. As if Mama teleported us from Tunis to Finsbury Park. We materialised in a kitchen on the top floor of a dark house, where a strange man greeted us. He had a moustache. He looked like a magician. He said, in a voice that made the air vibrate, 'Welcome, my darlings.'

'Who's that man?' I whispered to Mama, trying to hide behind her. Laughing, she said, 'It's Baba, of course – don't be so silly, say hello to him properly.'

Whether or not because of the strangeness of this meeting, we never learned to call him 'Baba' or anything else. To us he was always just 'That Man' or 'him'.

'I've missed you, I've missed you!' he said, gathering me and Sherine into his arms, pressing his face into our hair. He smelt of perfume – Aramis 900, I learned later – and orange peel. The orange smell was familiar: it meant illness, a cough or a cold, anxious voices saying, 'Eat, ya Susu, eat,' fingers forcing squirty fruit through clenched teeth. The Aramis 900 was a foreign language I didn't speak yet.

I'm told it was February 1979. Sherine was seven, I was three. Sherine and Nesrine; our parents called her Nunu and me Susu back then. Waiting for something to happen, we sat at the kitchen table, me nodding off, hypnotised by the chessboard pattern on the red and blue lino floor, Sherine upright and patient. 'What an incredibly poised little girl,' someone said about her once. 'What does "poised" mean?' I asked you, then went running off to Mama in a huff: 'It's not fair – why does everyone think Sherine's so great? It's only because she's older than me.'

Under the dingy light, Mama and the orange man stood by the cooker raising their voices, pointing at a frying pan.

Years later, Sherine told me Mama had tried to fry frozen beef burgers in vanilla ice cream, thinking it was butter.

'So typical of him,' I said. 'Lazy fucker. Why was she the one making dinner that night? Couldn't he be arsed to do it just that one time?'

'I know, I know,' she said. 'And he wonders why she left him.'

Pretending even then, both of us. Old enough to cover my own eyes and ears by then.

*

Is this when it began?

Our first Christmas in London. A party at Mrs Kowalski's – she was our landlady who lived downstairs. Carols on the cassette player; German, someone said. She was German, married to a Polish man. The smell of her baking wafting through the house. Cinnamon and marzipan and something else, hot and spicy. Dark red liquid like a jewel. I saw it boiling on the stove before Mrs Kowalski shooed me out of the kitchen: 'Nesrine, go to the living room or I'll trip over you! So small!'

Someone held out a Christmas cracker, and I toppled backwards off Mrs Kowalski's sofa trying to pull it. As if I was drunk. 'We used to give you and Sherine sips of our drinks when you were little,' Mama told me once. 'It was funny watching you get giddy and silly.' That was back when they drank. Before That Man went on his trip to Mecca.

'Ah, she's so sweet!' exclaimed a man as he picked me off the floor and averted my tears with a nothing-to-cry-about voice. 'Look at those curls. Like a little dog.'

'He called me a dog!' I whispered to Sherine, hurt and embarrassed.

'No, Susu, he said "doll". He's being nice to you.'

She wasn't there any more when I needed the toilet and went upstairs, wanting to go on familiar territory. Not sure yet what kind of toilet I needed. Looking for someone to take me in case it wasn't the kind I could manage on my own.

'Your mother's gone to the corner shop to buy lemonade,' said Marjorie, the old Jamaican woman from next door, stroking my neck when I passed her by the stairs and tugged at her dress saying, 'Mama?'

Upstairs was quiet and lonely, like a stranger's house. On the edge of scary. Shadows that seemed to have teeth. Footsteps that didn't seem mine. Dark except for one light, in our living room, which doubled up as a bedroom. Soft, warm, orange light. Voices talking in English. One talking, one laughing: a low, throbbing laugh that made my heart shake, like music pumping out of a passing car.

'This is how we do it in England,' the talking voice said. 'This is called...' Something. A word beginning with M. A word I didn't know.

I peeped around the door and saw two people sitting on one of the yellow-blanket beds. A hand holding a bunch of green leaves tied in a red ribbon. Two faces leaning in towards each other, their necks doing something strange – a sinuous, wrapping motion as if they'd joined together, become a snake with two heads, while the hand with the green bunch pressed itself against the wall.

I went back downstairs and wet myself on Mrs Kowalski's sofa.

'Why didn't you get someone to take you to the toilet?' said Mama when she reappeared and found me sitting there, sodden and stinking. 'Why did you just lift your leg and go on yourself like a dog in the street? What kind of people will they think we are?'

'I saw a snake upstairs, Mama,' I said, trying to impress upon her the extenuating circumstances.

'Snake? What snake? Don't be so silly – they don't have snakes in England!'

*

And then came the fish, weeks or months later. Don't ask me when – I was too young for 'when'. It's the screaming I remember, and the way the fish lay mangled on the red wooden chopping board, which they kept for years afterwards. The stench of it filled my nostrils; a trail of blood led across the floor to Mama, who was hunched with one hand cradling the other, screaming. A swivelled fish eye glared out from the mess of scales and bones, as if it had witnessed an unspeakable crime. Sherine and I were crouched in the hallway, her hands fluttering over my head, breath hot and hoarse on my face: 'Shhh, Susu, shhh.'

It was dark when it happened. The lights went on, then off, then on again, as if Mama's screams had activated them. You were in the living room with That Man – our father. Hamdi. I think you were standing by the row of windows, whispering. His face was grey. It looked like one of his shirts before Mama ironed them. You were comforting him: 'Don't worry, Hamdi, don't worry… be fine, be fine…'

No one was comforting Mama. She was alone with the doctor who came with a black leather bag and tangled his tongue around her name: 'No, Bouthaina! You have to stop this now, Bouthaina!'

There was a kind of spittiness in his voice. I didn't know the word 'contempt' at that age, but I could hear it. Mama had been naughty. She'd misbehaved. She'd done something wrong, with the fish, and now she had to be punished. That's why the doctor dragged her along the corridor by her hair, which was very long back then. Almost down to her waist. Like Rapunzel's but black. Puffy, when she forgot to smooth it down with black seed oil. She cut it all off soon after the fish.

Costumes

April 2005

I went looking for you in a cupboard, the day after our reunion – the cupboard under the stairs at That Man's house. The final resting place for junk like the broken ironing board and the Hoover that hadn't worked since 1985. The Buddha-shaped candle that my best friend Mariana got me for my sixteenth birthday and which That Man lit during a power cut, without asking me. The crate of Harveys Bristol Cream that a customer gave him one Christmas, which he lugged home huffing and puffing and slammed triumphantly onto the dining table. 'I didn't have the heart to tell him we don't drink, of course,' he'd said, twisting his mouth in pleasure at his newfound abstemiousness.

Pinned under this crate were three tatty plastic bags stuffed with photos. I took them back to Sherine's place and tipped the contents onto the floor, searching for you.

Look at this, you might say with a wry smile if you were poring over family portraits with a loved one, not hunched on the floor on your own, in your sister's spare room, with the door firmly shut. *Isn't it funny how misery always seems to smile for the camera?* Certain misery, that is, for certain cameras. This snap featured four heads of hair shrieking 'Wham!', two sets of teeth displayed like medals awarded for bravery. You were our choreographer, calling out the steps: 'Left a bit, no, right a bit! Move your head that way, Sherine. Stand over there, Hamdi, by the table.' Preserving us from the critics, from posterity's scathing eyes alighting on the ramshackle backdrop: the peeling wallpaper, the stuffing seeping out of the brown velour sofa, the cracked pane of glass that time – and Mr Marchant from the housing association – forgot to fix.

Who's the handsome, heavy-browed ingenue in the middle? White frills creeping like ivy up her throat, voluminous beige culottes bunched into saddlebags, gold sandals leaping for the stars and falling flat on their face outside BHS. That's Sherine, aged thirteen. And who's the sullen little fellow next to her in the shiny red trouser suit? Pot belly at odds with skinny arms and legs, hair dropping a hint of the young Michael Jackson beneath the George Michael. That's me, aged nine, accessorising my costume with a slapped arse for a face because of a spat with That Man: 'Why do you always wear trousers, why do I never see you in a skirt like a respectable girl?' He was the one who'd bought me that suit, a guilt-trip for the last bollocking.

And what about the dazzling prima ballerina in the dark-red lipstick, green eyeshadow and chandelier earrings? That's Mama, draped in the disgusting rabbit fur coat That Man got her in the Harrods sale, final reductions. 'It's cruel, it's cruel,' I kept saying, but neither of them cared. Even back in Tunisia, that coat stayed clamped to her back like an oxygen tank.

And finally, here he is: the leading man, the bargain-bucket Omar Sharif, in a sombre grey suit. Dressed for the role he should've had: lawyer, engineer, high-ranking civil servant. Not a shopkeeper on Edgware Road. Not a man who sold halawa and baklawa for a living. Dressed for a conference of delegates, an ambassadors' soirée, a dinner of dignitaries. In costume for a different performance altogether, you might say.

Are you surprised that he appears as just 'That Man'? When did you ever hear me or Sherine address him by any name? Dad, Daddy, Baba, all those names were fraudulent – just because he was our father didn't make him those other things.

Then there was you. Part of the family but not. Genevieve, Jenny, Mrs Brown, though we rarely addressed you by any name. No, we summoned you with a clearing of the throat, a catching of the eye, a light tap on the arm.

Of course, we had to call you something when we talked about you. Sherine went for Jenny. I opted for Mrs Brown, copying That Man. Nowadays, I find myself thinking of you as Genevieve. Mama called you *she* or *her*, a distinct quality to her voice, a kind of downward swoop in her breath that left no doubt who she was talking about. 'Is *she* coming shopping?' she'd say with that quiet whoosh in her lungs. 'Is *she* dropping you at school?' 'Where is *she*?' 'There's something I want to talk to *her* about.' You called my parents by their names, their real names, not Mama and nothing. Bouthaina and Hamdi. Each time you called them they'd seem to twitch, to give a little start, as if they'd forgotten who they were until you reminded them.

We talked about memory once, you and me, back in 1985. Your face was in profile like a pale Nefertiti as you drove me to school in your blue Citroen Visa. I was ten then. You were ageless as always, standing outside the framework of 'old' and 'young'.

'How fascinating,' you said, when I told you my first memory. 'I wonder how old you were then?'

The memory was nothing for anyone to wet themselves over – just me being rocked in someone's arms in the dark wooden armchair in my grandparents' flat in Tunis. But the luminous beam of your interest transformed it into something mysterious, profound. Under your regal, benevolent gaze, I became a celebrity being interviewed on the news or sitting on a sofa next to Eamonn Andrews (who Mama insisted must be secretly Arabic because he was called Ayman) as he presented me with the big red book of my life.

Carried away with the notion that all my thoughts were important, I decided to share another one: 'You know before we're born?'

'Yes...'

'We're not alive then, are we?'

'No.'

'So that means we're dead. That means we were all dead once, before we were alive?'

'Well, yes,' you said, frowning as you leaned over the wheel to check for traffic. 'I suppose that's right.'

Why were you so quiet after that? Had this thought of death before life disturbed you? Or was it the song playing on the radio, 'Running Up That Hill' by Kate Bush, which always stirred a pleasant melancholy in me too? Leaning back in my seat – next to you in the front, now that I was old enough – I looked out of the window, happy to be quiet too. It was September, a month that brought the smell of new things: exercise books, pencil cases, school shoes, good intentions to do homework on a Friday, not a Sunday. Conkers would appear in a few weeks, secondary school in exactly a year. In four years' time you would vanish from our lives, as if you or we were dead.

*

I didn't find much of you in those pictures; just the odd shot of the back of your head, your profile in blurry motion: 'No, no, let me take a picture of *you*, as a family.'

That's what you used to say, Genevieve. Funny how we could rarely say your name. It was psychological, not physical, this impediment. Don't ask me to explain it.

A rocky start

We didn't get off to the smoothest start, you and me. When I was four years old, I sought to test your limits at every opportunity...

Ice-cream and obscene gestures
'Hey!' I said. 'Can I have an ice cream?'
'We'll see,' you said. 'If you're good.'
'Oi! Where we going today?'
'It's rude to call people "hey" or "oi". Why don't you call me by my name? Genevieve.' You said your name slowly, bringing your face level with mine, pulling your mouth around in the way my teacher did to Casey, the deaf boy in my class. 'Or Jenny, if you like,' you said, offering up a bite-sized bone.
I replied by giving you the V-sign and sticking my tongue out between my two fingers, a handy gesture I'd just learned at school.
'No!' you said. 'You mustn't do that! It's very, very rude indeed!'
It's hard to understand what happened next; the uncharacteristic lapse of judgement that made you decide to grass me up to Mama by tapping her on the shoulder and replicating the gesture when she turned around. I remember Mama's eyes growing into two dinner plates of horror as you waggled your tongue at her from between your fingers. You flapping your hands in distress at the misunderstanding, pointing at me and saying, 'No, no, *she* did it,

she did it.' Was it one of those moments that was awful at the time but made you both laugh later?

The nursery school incident

'Nesrine, how am I going to get this T-shirt clean?' said Mama. 'It's ruined! Who told you to go and roll around in the sand like a street-dog?'

'It wasn't me, Mama, it was Pam! I didn't want to go in the sandpit but she pushed me in.'

'Bam! Bam!' said Mama, charging into the classroom. 'Talk you now daughter *raml*!'

And off we went – a hail of Franco-Arabic bullets slammed into my nursery school teacher, Pam, she of the long black hair and bare white knees and voice as soft and ineffectual as that of her charges. Situation out of control. Crazy foreign woman yelling in foreign. Someone shouted 'Mrs Brown!' and ran across the road to the library to fetch you. It was a hard job but you did it in the end. A grudging 'sorry' extracted from Mama and a shaken 'don't worry' from Pam as the waves of blame shifted to me.

Public shaming

Blame yourself for this one. It was the way you pronounced the word 'Treat' in that top-heavy way as you drove us to the cinema. Too weighty, this burden of enjoyment. It made Mama stare blankly at the screen, occasionally casting anxious looks at you to gauge the right response to this assault by the English language. It made Sherine sit even more upright in her chair than usual and open her mouth to show how entranced she was. If only a fly had dived down her gaping gullet. It made me run up and down the aisles, practising my newly learned English and discovering an innate capacity for voice projection that would serve me well when I became a teacher nearly twenty years later: 'Supermaaan! I'm Supermaaan.'

'Shhhh!' people said, and 'Tuttt,' and 'Someone get that child under control,' giving you the chance to show how much better the English were than the Arabs at disciplining children. Look, no hands! But when we left in disgrace, it was Sherine who was bawling and saying, 'I'm sorry, Jenny, I'm sorry my sister was naughty.'

'What will your father say when I tell him how badly behaved you were today?' you said as you dragged me up the stairs at Mrs Kowalski's house, Mama having abdicated all responsibility and adopted the stance of a sulky child herself.

Boredom washed over me as the lecture continued. What were those shiny sharp things on the kitchen table?

You made a sound that was almost a scream as I threw the scissors at you. Lucky it was only your glasses that got nicked, not your eyeball.

*

But the war wasn't over yet. You had a weapon of your own up your sleeve, or rather printed across your chest. A few weeks later, when you sat on your sofa wearing that provocative sweater, you knew exactly what you were doing, didn't you?

Bug-eyed at your chest, I leapt up and crouched beside you.

'Hello,' you said casually, flicking through a magazine.

What had you done with Mama and Sherine? Sent them to the corner shop while you carried out your mission.

'I like this,' I said, touching the part of your sweater that felt like paper, not cloth, stroking the saucer-eyed brown puppy gazing out from the blue-grey fabric.

'Thank you, thank you.' You touched it too. 'The children got it for me for my birthday.'

What did you mean? We didn't get you that sweater. Ah, of course. You meant Stephen and Amanda. Your children, who weren't really children because they were so much older than me and Sherine.

'What does this say?' I pointed at the letters above the puppy.

'H-U-G M-E,' you spelt out. 'Hug me.' It seemed like it was the puppy saying it. Guiding my senses to things I'd never noticed about you before. Your long, silky hair, spun from shimmering threads that defied anyone to say brown was boring. Your golden skin that was paler than ours though darker than other English people's. Your big hazel eyes that I could barely distinguish from the puppy's. Your smell of Anaïs Anaïs and talcum powder. A disturbing thought arose: what if you weren't there any more? What if you died?

Flinging my arms around you, I hardly knew who I was crying for. Was it you, the puppy, or myself? That's how Weltschmerz tasted to a four-year-old.

'It's all right, Nessie.' You hugged me tightly, as if you understood exactly how I felt. 'Everything is all right.'

That's when you gave me my name.

Ten years later, when you did vanish from my life, I was dry-eyed. Not a single tear. For years afterwards I barely even thought about you.

Tormenting Sherine

Just because I was friends with you didn't mean I had to stop tormenting Sherine. Little Miss Poisehead. Anxious grabber of hands when crossing roads, frowning scrutiniser of timetables at bus stops, never a 'Why' at all the rules you adults seemed to make up as you went along.

'Let's draw pictures,' she said one afternoon, tasked with entertaining me while Mama was in the kitchen. 'If they come out good, we can send them to *Take Hart*.'

'Okay!'

Gathering our pencils and crayons, we settled down at the small white table in our living room in Mrs Kowalski's house. Even though it was a living room, it contained two single beds with matching lemon-yellow blankets: one for Sherine and one for That Man. The double bed in the real bedroom belonged to me and Mama.

'Don't you want to switch with me and share with Sherine?' That Man would say in the early days.

'No, I want to sleep with Mama.'

'Want' – what a pathetic description for the raw craving that came upon me each night for her skin, her scent, the warmth and mass of her legs as I pressed my feet onto them, the burry softness of her nose, which I had to lap at with my tongue in small, rhythmic motions until I soothed myself to sleep.

'What are you drawing?' I asked Sherine.

'Black Beauty.'

The book was open in front of her, turned to the page with the illustration she wanted to copy: a horse in elegant mid-gallop, all sinewy flanks and flowing long mane. Sherine's dream was to go horse-riding.

'What are you drawing?' she asked politely back.

'A girl.' So far my picture consisted of a triangle threatened by a looming ellipse.

Our work continued. A silent labour of intense concentration on her part, a noisy display of physical exertion on mine as I attacked the paper with the crayons, panting and squirming like a sumo wrestler.

'I've finished!' she said, holding out her picture. Black Beauty in all his rippling, muscular glory stood poised to leap his way off the page, through the TV screen and into Tony Hart's heart. Not like my girl, a blurry blob of crayon vomit splattered across the paper.

Without the courtesy of a warning, I snatched the picture out of her hand and ripped it to shreds. The scream of a wounded animal rent the air.

'What's wrong, what's wrong?' said Mama, running in from the kitchen. Sherine rarely cried.

*

The green lorry was a birthday present for Sherine. A special one. I remember a cake with ten candles, one for luck, and some skimpy clapping around the kitchen table before Sherine unveiled it from its packaging. Carefully, of course, not tearing the wrapping paper off in haste as I would.

'Wow!' said someone, probably you. 'What a beautiful lorry!' That subtle stage-direction adults give children to tell them how they ought to be feeling. Wasted on Sherine. Her round doll-eyes and reverent touch showed she already knew.

'Thank you,' she said, breathily. 'I'll put it somewhere safe.'

A normal child would've played with it. Not her. This dark-green mechanistic wonder wasn't a toy to be played with. It was a sacred object to be kept in its box in the bedroom cupboard, taken out once a day after school. Held in both hands, turned this way and that. Transported close to the window or bathed in lamplight, gazed at from different angles, her lips pressed tightly together in a kind of anxious smirk, as if she wanted to kiss the ikon but didn't dare do it in front of greedy, irreligious eyes.

'Can I hold it?' I'd say whenever I saw it. 'Please, Nunu?'

'No. Your fingers are always dirty – you'll make it all smudgy.' Then, seeing my quivering lip: 'When you're a bit older, Susu, not now.' A gentle massage with the muslin cloth That Man had given her for this purpose, then back it would go to the safety of its nest in the cupboard.

Which one of the On-Seas was it she went to that day? On the morning she left home so early with a chirpy 'Byee! I'll bring you all back a present,' while Mama was still snapping at my heels to get into the kitchen? Clacton? Leigh? A school trip that brought her home laden with brightly coloured gifts: a stick of swirly red rock each for Mama and That Man, a huge green and white stripy mint humbug for me, along with a bucket and spade lugged back with her own so I could pretend I'd been to the seaside with her.

'Mama,' I said when she'd gone. 'Nunu said I could take the lorry to school today.'

A sceptical look from Mama as she handed me my bowl of Coco Pops. 'Really?'

'Yes! Miss Ashley said we have to bring in something green, and that's the only green thing we've got, so Nunu said I could borrow it.' A nice touch on my part. English schools were hotbeds of sinister, impenetrable rituals as far as Mama was concerned.

'Something green?' she sighed. 'What will they think of next? All right, then, but you'd better not break it or lose it.'

When I got to school, a boy called Derek caught sight of the lorry and tried to wrench it out of my hands.

'She nicked it off me,' he said to Miss Ashley when she came over to break up the scuffle. 'I wannit back.'

'What's going on, you two? You know you're not supposed to bring toys to school.'

'It's my sister's!' I said. 'I didn't nick it – I have to give it back to her.' Was I saying that? Or was I saying, 'Wah wah wah wah sister lorry me give you wah wah please Miss'?

'She was a little genius with words,' Mama used to boast about me. 'She was speaking at the age of three months old! Her sister, poor thing, she walked early but she couldn't speak until she was nearly three.'

I can't remember how Sherine found out the lorry was gone. Maybe Mama was the bearer of bad news, or maybe Sherine ran to the cupboard and discovered the pillage herself. I remember the green and white humbug, the bucket and spade, the swirly red rock, but the look on her face is gone. I asked her once if she remembered what happened, seeking some kind of blanket absolution for all my sins, but she just laughed cautiously and said: 'Vaguely...'

Did she ever get the lorry back? If she did I never saw it again.

*

Nothing lasts forever. Sherine managed to find a way to get the devil out of my soul.

'Come here,' she said one day, sitting on her bed, patting for me to sit there too. 'I've got something for you.'

'What?' Something red winked at me from her closed hand.

'See this Kit Kat?' She unfurled her fingers. 'It's mine, isn't it? Mama gave me mine and she gave you yours, didn't she?'

'Yes. I want some.' Why didn't Sherine understand that food should be eaten as soon as it landed on your plate, or someone else's?

'Here.' She broke off half and held it out to me. But as I extended my hand to snatch it, she raised it out of my reach. 'Wait. I need to tell you something.'

'What?' My eyes were riveted to the silver paper.

'If you share with people, they'll share with you. If you're nice to people, they'll be nice to you. If you're horrible to people, they won't like you and they'll be horrible to you too.'

Finally she handed over the Kit Kat and I shoved it down my throat, not realising she'd spiked it with a dangerous substance – the first inklings of morality, topped with a sweet sprinkling of self-interest.

Life had been hard since we moved to England. Hard and exhausting. I was constantly in trouble. People were always angry with me. Without being able to articulate it, I knew I was liked by most adults in Tunisia and I was disliked by most in England. I knew this from the sharp glances exchanged over my head, from the edge to people's voices, from the downward cast of their mouths when they talked to me.

Something in the Kit Kat entered my bloodstream and changed me, subtly, gradually. Teachers began to say different things to me at school. 'Naughty' and 'selfish' in early infant school became 'polite', 'considerate' and 'helpful' in my final year. As I entered junior school, I even became 'a little quiet' and 'withdrawn'. That's what Mrs Harris told That Man at parents' evening – and you. You were the one who went with him to those events while Mama stayed home with me and Sherine.

'I had to ask Mrs Brown what this word "withdrawn" means,' I overheard him saying to Mama afterwards.

'Why did the teacher say that? Does she think there's something wrong with her?'

'No, no! She said she'll grow out of it.'

Years later, when everyone had left him and he was old and alone, he brought up what I was like in those early years. I was living in Japan then, on a trip home to London, and we were sitting at the dining table eating the lamb chops he'd cooked and brought sizzling out from the kitchen, shuffling in his new moccasin slippers from Shepherd's Bush market. They made him look like a character from *The Wind in the Willows*.

'Remember when you locked yourself in the bedroom and threw the key out of the window?' he said, laughing and rubbing his cheek, which was grey and whiskery by then. 'Remember when you jumped onto the table and danced all over my breakfast? Remember that time you hid under the bed and we thought you'd run away and we'd lost you?

'You were so naughty then,' he said. 'So naughty and joyful and full of life. Ahhh!' He laughed, sighed. 'Where did that little girl go?' Wheezing a little, he leaned back in his chair and touched his fingers to his eyes. And I found myself crying too, turning away so he wouldn't see, mourning the old man who was mourning the little girl.

Educated women

That Man had a mantra he used to deliver with the zeal of a revivalist preacher: 'My Daughters Will Become Educated Women.'

His dream of education for himself died along with his father, *Jaddi* Mohammed, who had a heart attack during his one and only trip to Mecca.

'God rest his soul!' said one of That Man's friends on hearing this fact, face aglow, practically clapping with excitement. 'How fortunate to die during Hajj!'

'I wanted to be an engineer, but I had to become the man of the house and earn money,' That Man would say. 'Because I was the oldest.'

'If you died early, would Sherine have to become the man of the house and earn money too?' I said once, facetiously.

'Don't be so stupid.'

Denied the thrill of education first-hand, he sought it out vicariously. 'Mrs Brown is an educated woman,' he'd say. 'She must've read every book in the world!'

Were your ears burning?

A shout-out to the Iron Lady too: 'God curse her days. She's a hard, cruel woman like all that type of English woman, she wouldn't cry if her own mother dropped dead in front of her eyes, but still, she trained as a chemist...'

'I want you girls to have a good education, an English education,' he'd say. 'A thousand times better than you would've had at the hands of those insipid French.'

That's why he brought us to England, not France.

'They hate us in France. They think we're just like the Africans, like those stupid, weak people who let themselves be trampled on and colonised.'

No big-ups for Mama. No props from the Finsbury Park massive. You'd never know from That Man that she was an educated woman too. That she had been to college in Tunis and was a bookkeeper before she married him and had us and moved to England. In England she wasn't an educated woman: she was just a brown woman who scoured the shops for bargains, trundling a tartan trolley.

'I want to work again,' she'd say. 'I can't live like this. And we need the money.'

'I know, but what can you do here without the language? It's not easy...'

'I'll work in the shop with you. I'll help you and learn English that way, like you did, then you won't need to employ an assistant.'

'I'm not having you standing on your feet serving people all day! You're better than that. I'll buy you a sewing machine,' he said.

So she could work from home, all on her own, with her mouth zipped shut. That'd solve the language barrier.

'The big shops employ women to finish things off for them,' he said.

'No,' said Mama. 'I don't like sewing.'

To me, she said, 'So I'm too good to work in a shop but not too good to become a monkey on a sewing machine like those women in *Coronation Street*?' She brooded over it, frowning, then she said, 'I have to talk to her about this. I have to get her to help me.'

A few days later, as we were walking home from school, Mama said, 'She's coming round for dinner tonight. Late, when he's home, so don't get excited – you'll be in bed.'

My heart raced in indignation as I scurried alongside her.

'You can't stay up tonight, *hbibti*,' she added, her mouth twisted in amusement as she looked down at my flushed cheeks and pursed lips. 'I know you want to see her, but didn't you say you've got a test tomorrow? You'll need to sleep, otherwise your sister will start nagging at you and I haven't got time to deal with your bickering tonight.'

'It's not fair! Just because I'm the youngest...' I was seven then, a number that counted for nothing in the face of Sherine's lofty eleven.

'This dinner is for me, *azizti*,' said Mama. 'It's not for you and your sister this time.' Something about the emphatic way she said 'me' scared me. Who was this 'me' who had nothing to do with us, her daughters, and who wanted to arrange things all for herself? I waited for her to put her arm around me and squeeze my shoulders, the way she did when she knew I was upset or disappointed, but she kept walking briskly, eyes straight ahead, as if this 'me' was running along in front of us and needed to be watched more closely than I did.

All her special food came out for you that evening: fish lightly fried in garlicky batter, red rice with onions and prawns, tahini and baba ghanoush, an array of salads that dazzled in their multicoloured glory. She made me and Sherine gulp ours down standing up in the kitchen before she shooed us out of the way.

'Hurry up, *ya* Susu, go to bed now – never mind your teeth, one night won't hurt you... Sherine, go and do your homework in your father's room – it's about time someone used that desk he wasted so much money on.'

The desk was rosewood, a Victorian gentleman's escritoire with a green leather writing surface. That Man bought it as a present for himself to celebrate our move to a housing association flat from our rented rooms in Mrs Kowalski's house. Sherine and I were the only ones who ever used it.

'Bouthaina!' I heard you exclaim as Mama brought out the food from the tiny kitchen. 'My goodness! You shouldn't have gone to so much trouble.'

After that, I heard mostly sounds, not words, from my listening post behind the bedroom door. I heard Mama's voice labouring away in a language I knew must be English: jerky, halting fragments, pitched higher than her usual voice, as if her vocal cords were quivering under an unnatural strain, punctuated by rapid bursts that could only be Arabic or French. I heard That Man's voice responding in a low, contained rumble. And I heard your voice, strong and melodious, weaving in and out of theirs, keeping the ensemble in harmony, preventing any ugly notes from creeping in: 'Don't you agree, Hamdi... importance of education... wonderful thing... perhaps become a secretary in due course... equipped... girls with their homework...'

So that's how you delivered Mama to the promised land: Tottenham College of Technology, to learn English and IT.

Waver of wands, weaver of dreams. Mama needed your magic. Her own stopped working when she got to London. If only That Man had found her a rabbit's foot in the bargain bucket at Harrods instead of a fur coat.

Aspiration

I wonder if the catastrophe would've happened if you hadn't been an Educated Woman. If you'd been a different kind of person, like Viola from the laundrette or Debbie from Boots or Sandra the tea lady from the housing association. Someone who didn't speak the language my teachers called 'Nicely', meaning like a presenter on the BBC World Service, which hummed softly from behind That Man's door late at night. None of us were good sleepers.

Imagine if there'd been nothing in your speech for Sherine to emulate. Nothing for her to crank up another notch, like when she'd take your clipped, concise 'no' on a meandering tour around all the other vowels before depositing it at its final destination. Jesus Christ, why did she do it? Didn't she realise we had the blessed freedom to be our own creation? Why couldn't she create herself in the image of the kids we lived next door to and went to school with? I'll tell you why. Because she'd swallowed our parents' hot air. Aspiration, they'd have called it, if only they'd known the word in English. We were better than our neighbours not because of anything we had, but because of what That Man and Mama wanted us to have.

He had a pet saying, triggered by things like the chewing of gum with an open mouth, the wearing of jeans when taken to a 'restaurant' (as he called McDonald's), the sin of staying out too long in the garden with the children from the other flats: 'You're not the daughters of builders or mechanics. You're the daughters of *people*.'

'What people?' I said once, and he raised his hand, making a promise I knew he wouldn't deliver. It was Mama who came at us with her plastic red flip-flops.

We were the daughters of a man who sold powdery tooth-rot for a living and a woman who had nothing to sell, not in this country. We had to aspirate for the two of them because their lungs were too weak. Could anyone have blown any harder on the candles of the upward-mobility cake than Sherine? She started talking like a little English girl the minute we landed in England – none of Mama's mangled Ps and Bs ever came out of her mouth. But she wasn't any old English girl.

'How come your sister's so posh?' my friends would say.

'How come you haven't got any friends any more?' I asked her once, making her face colour up as she stalked past me to the bedroom, barging her shoulder into mine. I had to be brutal. Didn't she realise I had my own aspiration? I wanted to be 'normal', if only I knew what that meant. *Rich man, poor man, beggar-man, thief.* Being any of these things, or none of them, could be used against you. Two boys from my class once spotted me and Mama coming out of our flat, and I paid for it later. All the imposing Gothic Victoriana of our building counted for nothing when they saw the sign outside.

'She lives in this shitty block of flats – it looks like a massive house but it's basically council flats...'

I wanted to be no better or worse than anyone else. No different, though that was a battle that was lost at the outset. You could've counted the number of Arabs at school on two hands, minus the thumbs. Stupid unicorns here in London, not enough to form anything like a 'Community'.

Sherine's revenge came in the form of remedial English lessons each time I opened my mouth. 'It's "want to", not "wanna". It's "going to", not "gonna". It's "I'm going to the toilet", not "I'm goin' toilet". Or actually, don't say "toilet", say "bathroom" or "loo".'

Everyone egged her on, giving the terrier a bone.

'Good girl,' from Mama. 'You teach her the right way.'

'That's right,' from That Man. 'We don't want her talking like that terrible woman on TV.

'Ang ang ang ang!' he said, making a sound like a dog worrying at a ball of elastic bands. This was supposed to be cockney.

Even you joined in when my vowels came out rougher than you liked: a 'today' that belonged in a rhyming couplet with 'die' instead of 'say', a 'tea' that nuzzled dangerously close to 'May', giving its lawful spouse 'me' the cold shoulder. 'Are you Australian now?' you'd say. Your own children spoke Nicely too. It wasn't enough that you'd named me, you wanted to shape me too.

So who was I before you named me? Susu at home with the family, Nesrine on paper, Nazerene or Nes-Rhine at school. A calamity – not like Nessie, the name you gifted me. Nessie was a different kind of girl: neat and friendly, she rhymed with Jessie; even people in England couldn't mess her up. Sherine adopted her, though That Man and Mama hung on stubbornly to Susu. Nessie even had a twin, a girl in my class whose real name was Vanessa. Vanessa, eh... Why shouldn't I have been a Vanessa too? Deed poll was out of the question, but what about a campaign of omissions and half-truths?

Vanessa sang her siren song, but my surname soon muzzled her. Boughanmi, for Christ's sake, the cross we had to bear; the kind of name to send a CV shimmying into the bin before it's barely out of its envelope.

No, Nessie's in it for the long haul. I met another Nesrine at university who went by Nas, like the rapper, or like the boxer Prince Naseem. A skinny-whippet gravel-voiced girl from Salford, rumoured to have a tarantula and a crack pipe in her room. Was

I a Nas? Not really – it felt like her name, not mine. What about Nesrine, as I grew older? No, that was a name for a woman draped in blue in Kandahar. As for Susu, she was for Tunisia, for family, for being a child. For remembering the people who brought her into the world. For bearing the weight of their sadness.

I'm still Nessie. I'm still the person you created.

Unreliable sources

April 2005

When I saw you again after more than half my lifetime, you said, 'Tell me how you remember those days.' And then you said, 'Tell me what you've been up to since we lost touch.' That delicate phrase; it seemed to hover in the air between us. Deferred delivery was what you were after. You didn't have the strength to rake it all up then and there. I didn't have the courage.

'How did it go?' Sherine said with her back to me as she stood making dinner when I got back from seeing you.

'Fine, fine,' I said. 'You know.' And later as we watched TV, I said, sitting on my hands to stop them shaking, 'Did you know…'

'What?'

'Nothing. Doesn't matter.'

What was the point of asking Sherine? She was no use with stuff like that – she even told me the fish was a dream, though I knew it wasn't. The mutilated fish lying on the chopping board, the gaping black hole in Mama's face as she opened her mouth and screamed her lungs out.

Do you remember Mama's scar? It was on her left hand, long and jagged, between her thumb and index finger. It had always been there, as long as I could remember. Part of the things that made up a mother. Didn't every mother have a scar like that? I asked her about it once: 'How did you get that?'

When she held up her hand and looked at it, she seemed to tune in somewhere else, as if she was listening to another question. 'I had an accident,' she said eventually, snapping her attention back to me. 'Soon after we came to England.'

I sensed she would tell me the full story, if I asked. I changed the subject.

I sometimes wonder if it was my fault That Man stopped asking her to share a bed. Perhaps I was a succubus on her. Did I scrape her love for him off her nose each time I clamped my mouth to it at night? Or maybe the repelling force came from him. All that freedom he'd had in London without his wife and two daughters hanging off him like a charm bracelet made of millstones. All that time to meet other people in his shop, before the three of us came over to cramp his style. New people, English people, people like you. Was that what turned the magnetic poles the wrong way up, made them bounce off each other instead of sticking?

Our move from the top floor of Mrs Kowalski's house to the new flat of our own gave us an extra bedroom. Two bedrooms, four people, two of them married to each other. Simple maths, right? But instead, we ended up with an odd, awkward equation.

'Who does that bed belong to?' said my friend Ashmita when she came round one day.

'It's just a spare bed.'

'Oh,' she said, looking at the rumpled pillows and Mama's nightdress on top of the quilt.

'Me and Sherine sleep in it too, sometimes. When we get sick of the bunk beds.'

Inglan Is a Bitch (to Mama)

The rabbit Mama wore on her back died to pay for the sins of England. Its ruffled, light-grey fur still possessed a certain knobbiness, a spiny quality that sang a threnody for the bounding vertebrate it used to be. This coat functioned as reparation for war crimes committed by England against Mama. Thirty pounds splashed on the Harrods bargain bucket paid for the blank faces when she spoke. The words that got stuck on her tongue and curdled in her mouth. The landlady who shouted at her for using too much hot water. The husband who talked to her in a voice that said 'It's all your fault'. The daughters who went to school and left her alone all day, before she started college. It paid for all the washing she had to do by hand in London, city of gold, while her sisters in Tunisia acquired washing machines.

'How many times do I have to tell you,' That Man would huff when Mama complained about the cracked, reddened state of her hands. 'It's the pipes in these old houses – you know that's why you can't have a washing machine. Go to the laundrette if you don't want to do your own washing.'

The rabbit had to sacrifice its life to make up for the permanently distant look on Sherine's face; the air of condescension she adopted when speaking to Mama. It had to die because I refused to help Mama with her college homework, and laughed at her mispronunciations. Yus instead of yes, ben instead of pen.

They taught Linton Kwesi Johnson's poem 'Inglan Is a Bitch' at Mama's college, but that in itself was a bitch for someone who didn't speak English.

'Why are they making you learn this?' I said, batting the paper away impatiently when Mama asked me what 'facktri' and 'crackry' meant. Years later, when I applied to teach English to unsuspecting innocents in Japan, I cited 'a lifelong love of helping non-native speakers, cultivated as I watched my mother struggle to master this often counterintuitive language.'

The bunny had to die for times like this, when Mama was left to go to the supermarket with only me, then aged eight, for protection.

'Please can we have three-bean salad?' I said in that whiny voice that pissed everyone off but her, looking wistfully over at the delicatessen counter.

'Go and get it, then.'

'No.'

'Please, *ya* Susu.'

'No,' I said again, glaring at her, rooting my feet to the spot.

Mama was the adult, not me. *She* could go and open her mouth to other adults.

Sighing, giving me a look, she wheeled the trolley over to the counter, leaving me loitering in the confectionery aisle eyeing up the Bounty bars, Lion bars, p-p-pick-up-a-Penguins. What was I going to wheedle her into buying me? Hearing her voice rising to a pitch that signalled danger, I dragged myself away from the chocolate and tiptoed towards the delicatessen.

'Sree Bin Zalade!' Mama was saying stridently to the girl behind the counter. 'Sree Bin Zalade!'

Her finger pointing at the salad – wasn't that what you might call a clue?

Skitter skitter I went. One step forward, two steps back. Finally, a tub of salad got wrapped in a cellophane bag and handed over. Mama wasn't crying – it was just her hay fever. Out of my shaking hand went a jar of Sharwood's relish and onto the floor in a bloody explosion. Trolley in a tailspin, my arm in a vice and we were out on the street.

Sherine came home from athletics starving and irritable. 'Nothing for after dinner? Why didn't you go shopping?'

'Ask her,' said Mama.

Please, I said with my eyes.

Looking at Sherine, she said, 'This one left her school bag behind so we had to go all the way back to get it, then it was too late to go shopping.'

After dinner, I got up from the table and stood behind her chair, stroking her earlobes. She knew what I was saying. And I knew what she was saying when she stiffened for a second and then shivered and gave a soft laugh that seemed to catch in her throat.

You

Did we ever 'meet', you and me? We must've done, but I don't remember that day. You were just there, like the rest of them. A treasured possession once we got over our rocky start, though I had to share you with Sherine. You taught us songs, like the one that went: *Hullo, hullo, what's your little game, don't you think your ways you ought to mend, if it wasn't the girl I saw you with in Brighton, who-who-who's your lady friend?* You had the two of us in stitches at the way you sang the hullos.

It wasn't all high jinks. You were my fire-fighter too, extinguishing the flames that leapt out of the TV and into my anxious brain, spreading like wildfire.

'She can see me, she can see me,' I wailed, after I stuck my tongue out at the presenter of *Play School*, and, for reasons I'll never understand, she wagged her finger at the screen and said, 'No.'

'She can't see you, Nessie,' you said. 'The people on TV aren't really there. You can see them but they can't see you.'

Toxic smoke billowed daily from *The Six O'clock News*. 'No, Nessie,' you said. 'The government aren't going to come into your bedroom at night and shoot you. The troubles are happening in Northern Ireland, not here.' '"Indigestion" just means a bad tummy,' you said. 'It's when you eat something and it doesn't go down properly. It definitely can't kill you.' That one puzzled you. 'What made you think it could?' you asked.

'I saw it on *The Six O'clock Show*,' I insisted. 'The woman with the gargly voice said it.'

'Hmm. That must be very unusual indeed. It's nothing for you to worry about.'

Smoke crept into real life too: spiders under the bed, a mouse in the cold-water tank in our communal hallway. A macaw parrot in a cage at London Zoo that fixed me with a cold, beady eye and said, in the voice of someone who'd been dead four hundred years, 'I want to be your friend. I want to be your friend.'

'Why?' I sobbed to you. 'Why?'

Sherine didn't need all this reassurance. She knew the TV was just the TV, spiders and mice were more scared of you than you were of them, parrots were there to be admired, not feared. 'You're such a baby,' she said scornfully, after the zoo.

As we grew older, our outings became separate, no longer a receptacle for a single mass of child. Sherine got whisked off to the Natural History Museum and the British Museum, places that sounded boring and stuffy to me. Madame Tussauds was my far superior treat, which Sherine, seeming to miss the point, dismissed as 'fake'.

'I saw Prince Charles and Princess Diana today!' I told That Man afterwards. Unusually, he was taking more interest in my day than Mama, who'd vanished to the kitchen after a cursory 'Did you have a nice time?'

'That's good,' he said. 'You always have a good time with Mrs Brown, don't you?'

'Yes.'

'Good, good.' He was nodding. 'That's good. You like having her as our friend, don't you? You want her to carry on being our friend?'

'Yes,' I repeated, feeling the excitement turn into a gnawing in my stomach. Why was he asking these questions? He might as well have asked if I wanted Mama to carry on being my mother or Sherine to carry on being my sister or him to carry on being my father.

'Good,' he said, his needle caught in that groove. 'I hope she'll always be our friend.'

Could indigestion be caused by words as well as food? I wanted to ask you, but I couldn't. You might have said, 'What made you think that?' and then I'd have had to tell you.

*

What did you do with your days when you weren't entertaining us? You had loads of other friends: teachers, health visitors, social workers, people like that. You had your hobbies, too: books, films, art, plays, 'the' ballet and 'the' opera, as you called them. Then there was your sister – Gabrielle? Gabriella? – though you didn't see much of her. She lived in Cornwall, at the tip of the map, and you told me once that the two of you 'weren't terribly close'. Most importantly, you had your children, Amanda and Stephen, whose visits were a special occasion now that they didn't live with you.

Once, when you said, 'The children are coming this weekend!' I asked, 'Why do you call them "the children"? Aren't they grown up now?'

'Your children are always your "children", however old they are.' You smiled in a way that seemed a bit sad. 'You'll find out, Nessie, when you have children of your own.'

This idea made me chew my lip and frown. 'I don't think I want to have children of my own.'

Your surprise showed on your face, though your voice was neutral. 'Really? Why not?'

In all honesty, I wasn't sure why I'd said it. Maybe it was because you'd said 'when,' not 'if,' as if it was something that would definitely happen, but I knew it didn't for some people –

Aunty Aicha, for example, my grandparents' neighbour in Tunis. Mama and her sisters called her *messkina*, 'poor thing', as if it was a title like 'esquire'.

'Thank God I met your father and had you before it was too late like Aunty Aicha, *messkina*!' Mama would say sometimes, burying her face in my neck.

Aunty Aicha didn't seem *messkina* to me. She laughed a lot and played cards with the neighbourhood children whenever we asked her to and never raised her voice. It seemed to me that Aunty Aicha could do all these things *because* she didn't have a husband and children – that was, after all, what made her different from other adults.

'Because,' I said to you, grasping for the right words. 'I want to have my own bedroom, and eat dinner when I want, and go to bed when I want.'

Laughing, you replied, 'But you can still do all those things when you have children! You'll be a grown-up yourself then, not a child.' Then, more to yourself than me, you said, 'Children give you purpose. They give you fresh eyes to see the world. They sustain you.'

I'd recently learned the word 'sustenance' in assembly at school. It had stuck in my head because of all the Ss, like how a snake might talk.

'Sustain like sustenance? Like food?'

'Yes, that's right, Nessie – you're becoming very good with words now that you're reading so much. And yes, it is like food, in a way.' You sounded pleased with this comparison.

My frown deepened. 'But what if you don't want to be someone else's food?' I was only dimly aware that I was arguing about the injustice of being a child, not having one.

'Not like cannibalism!' you said, sounding as if I'd accused you of this crime. 'Not like *eating* someone.' And then, seeming to forgive me for my obtuseness, you said in a softer voice, smiling,

'Mary, Mary, quite contrary, that's who you are sometimes, aren't you, Nessie?'

The conversation left me feeling small and deflated. What if I never grew up? What if, by some unlucky twist of fate, I remained a child forever like Peter Pan, shackled to other people's rules for the rest of my life?

When Stephen and Amanda came to your flat, filling it with their laughter and stories and big duffel bags, I knew what would happen. Your face would light up and your cheeks would turn pink as you listened. You would nod energetically and wave your hands around. I can't say when it struck me, but at some point I became aware that this was exactly how we behaved when you came to *our* flat. Voices barging into each other in our haste to tell you our news, feet tripping over themselves in the rush to bring you a cup of tea (fresh mint, no milk, no sugar, just like That Man and Mama drank it). You received our offerings with gracious smiles, warm *thank you*s and no favouritism. All of us were important to you. None of us was important enough to make you blush and wave your hands around. You were our sustenance in so many ways, feeding each of us what we needed – and you seemed to know what that was better than we did – but if you were our sustenance, what were we to you?

*

The lingering after-effects of That Man's questions made me ask some questions of my own. 'How do we know Mrs Brown?' I said to Mama one evening when she was in the kitchen making pastilla.

'Ask him,' she said brusquely, rolling out the pastry, going back to muttering a prayer or calculation under her breath. She only seemed to do this for pastilla, which was harder than shakshouka or tagine and therefore needed intervention from God or science.

It was Sunday and he was home early, slouched on the sofa flicking through prayers and antiques on TV: one two three four, then back to the beginning again.

'How do you know Mrs Brown?' I said.

Finger on the remote control, he paused and looked up at me. 'We met her in the shop. A long time ago.'

'You and Mama?'

'No. Mama hadn't brought you here yet. Mrs Brown came in the shop with her friend and we found out we both lived in the same area. She gave me some useful information to help me when you came – schools and doctors, things like that. She very much wanted to meet you girls when you came.' Putting the remote down on the side-table, he picked up his prayer beads and started flicking them instead, a habit he'd recently acquired after his trip to Mecca, September 1984. A lads' holiday with Uncle Youssef and Uncle Karim, his two youngest brothers. He came back with a shaved head, a white towel around his shoulders and a pious look on his face, which slipped into annoyance when Mama asked in a barbed voice if they had all had 'fun'. I wished he hadn't discovered the prayer beads: the sound grated on my ears like someone clipping their toenails.

'And did she want to meet Mama too?' I asked.

'Yes, of course!' He switched to his don't-wind-me-up voice. 'Go and get me some nuts and ask your mother when dinner's going to be ready, I'm starving.'

'You know, Mama,' I said, as I counted out twelve monkey nuts – the quantity I judged would stop him from moaning about how long the pastilla was taking and then complaining about how full up he was when it did come. 'You know, Mama, if you said Mrs Brown's name in French, it would be *Madame Marron*.' I laughed at my own joke, prepared to be the only one laughing – even I knew it was silly and not very funny – but then a sound bubbled out of her. It started off as a soft chuckle before mutating into something else: a giggle of the kind she always told me off for, saying it made me sound stupid or mindless or crazy. The giggle trickled on as I put the nuts into a bowl and took them out to That Man.

A few years later, for reasons I chose not to think about at the time, I asked you how you'd met him. We were talking quietly in the library I always thought of as 'yours' though it belonged to Haringey council. You were getting ready to finish your shift and drop me home. Do you remember how you told me the story almost as he did, smiling and lowering your voice to a whisper? You touched my arm, as if you were about to tell me a secret now that I was old enough. Then you said, still in that whisper, 'My friend thought he was ever so good-looking, Nessie. She kept saying he looked just like Omar Sharif!'

Something in the air

In 1985, the twisting needles of fate gave both my grandmothers a stroke in the same week.

'Go, go,' you said to Mama. 'The girls can stay with me – you must go and see your mother.'

Speaking in English, slowly, making a point after That Man stopped hiding his fidgets and frowns whenever you and Mama spoke French. When you told Mama your evening classes were bringing it all back, that learning a language was like riding a bike, she laughed and clapped her hands as if you'd made up that expression yourself.

'How are you going to learn English if you keep speaking French?' That Man said to her when you left, and her face folded back into the lines that had ironed themselves out while you were there.

At first I didn't realise what was different when we stayed with you for those three weeks. We'd been to your flat loads of times before. We'd washed our hands with your pink Camay soap, which oozed luxury and femininity, unlike the shrivelled, scummy bars of no-brand stuck together on the edge of our sink. We'd played in your garden, which was bigger than ours and had a swing on the lawn and trees with branches low enough to climb. We knew the children from downstairs and upstairs and across the road who came spilling out of the red-brick Victorian conversions at six o'clock on the dot every evening in summer. When I was eight, one of them told me I was sexy before my soft-perm went bad, then he decided I was ugly and threw stones at me. We'd never slept in your spare rooms before, but so what, a bed was just a bed – apart from the novelty of having our own rooms, a taste of heaven that wouldn't be repeated until I was eighteen and Sherine twenty-two.

But it was different being with you for that extended period. The luxury of time made me notice something. An absence of a thing in your flat that was always there in ours. A presence in the air, invisible, that wailed like a banshee at the four of us when we sat together in our living room, drowned out only by the TV, when it decided to protect us. Something that shoved shoulders down into hunched resentment, grabbed lips and twisted them into sneers of grievance, slammed doors in violence disguised as accident, and set the clock ticking for an explosion that was always worse than the one before. It's hard to describe how words that sound comical in English can feel like blows in Arabic. Animal, donkey, daughter of this, son of that. The worst were the ones we didn't understand. Rigid on the sofa, Sherine and I would watch and listen, pretending it wasn't happening, that we couldn't see each other's blotched, stricken faces.

All this was confined to the four walls of our flat. The escape route was barred to other people's ears, even yours. Talking about it would've made it even more frightening. But you knew what went on, didn't you? You must've known.

In your flat, nothing like that ever happened. The air was clean. Even the TV could breathe easy. It knew it was just a TV, not a life-support machine.

*

Mama was lucky: she got to say goodbye to her mother. That Man was too late – *Jadti* Ramza died three days before he was due to fly back to Tunisia. Not our grief, we barely knew the woman. It was the other grandmother we cried for: *Nana* Latifa with her headscarf tied under her chin like a babushka, gentle hands that smelt of parsley and onions, soft heart that made her cry whenever her grandchildren did, over nothing. But rest in peace too, *Jadti* Ramza. Thirteen children to raise on her own; no wonder she always looked so stern and forbidding. What would she make of my life, and Sherine's? Spoiled brats of the western world. Both grandmothers were felled by sugary peasants' diets. Both were married at thirteen, mothers a year later, dead before sixty.

That Man greeted us with red eyes and a puffy face when you took us round to our flat to say sorry.

'They buried her yesterday,' he said. 'I'd bought her a Moulinex blender.' He waved his hand at a big square box in gold wrapping paper on the dining table. 'To give her when she got better.' Voice breaking, he raised his hand to his face to hide the tears we'd never seen before. His head jerked down to your shoulder, stopping just before it got there, waiting for you to do the rest. And you did, bringing your hand up and his head down. 'Oh, Hamdi, I'm so, so sorry.'

What was going to happen to the blender? Was he going to give it to Mama now that *Jadti* was gone? I couldn't look at him like that. Naked. Even worse than the times I'd accidentally barged in on him in his tighty-whities.

He didn't cry for long. When it was over he said, 'Are you girls staying with me or Mrs Brown tonight?'

What was Sherine going to do? Always me looking at her, never the other way around.

'I'll stay here,' she said, and he put his arm around her and hugged her to him.

'What about you, Susu?' he said.

Now it was you I looked at. Your face said, 'You do whatever you want, Nessie.' It gave me the courage to say, 'Maybe I'll go with Mrs Brown?'

'Okay, my love,' he said in English, nodding hard as if that was only what he expected. And then he reached out with his other arm and hugged me to him too.

*

In case you were wondering, the blender made its way to Tunisia after all – That Man gave it to *Amma* Zeinab, the oldest of his eight sisters, a gruff-voiced woman with thick, powerful hands, indicative of an ability to fracture a swan's wing with a blow from a finger. In the absence of a swan, she broke the blender instead, demoting herself from Very Capable Woman – his highest accolade after Educated – to Stupid Girl. This girl was two years younger than him.

Much later, a couple of years after Mama left him, That Man brought up the subject of the blender one Saturday night when I was home for the weekend from university. The two of us were eating shawarma sandwiches that he'd brought home from Edgware Road, when he said, apropos of nothing, 'She was ungrateful, your mother. Nothing I did was ever good enough for her. Even the Moulinex blender, she didn't want it when I tried to give it to her. Never mind, it went to someone who deserved it. A woman who actually cared about her family.'

'Maybe Mama didn't want a "present" that kept her chained to the kitchen,' I said sharply.

'Ha! You think I kept her a prisoner in the kitchen? She wanted to be there! Even the first night you arrived in this country, she insisted on making a mess instead of eating the food I'd prepared for you.'

'What food?'

'Everything you can think of. A feast, as if it was Eid. I stayed up until dawn cooking for you the night before, and then she says, "No, the girls don't like this, the girls don't like that, let me make something else for them." What was I supposed to do?'

'Of course, you always took her side,' he went on, as I looked down at the tablecloth, running my fork around an ancient food stain in the shape of Australia. 'You and your sister always think everything's my fault.'

'Mama liked the fur coat you got her,' I said, steering the conversation away from this treacherous territory he was leading us into with his wheedling voice, his moodily jutting head, his cheeks puffed full of air. 'She still wears it every time she goes to a wedding,' I said cajolingly. I could've left it at that, but then I added, 'And I'm sure she appreciated the thought itself. It wasn't even her birthday, was it? She must've been so happy to get a present like that, just because you felt like it.'

Out of the quicksand and into the swamp. What was it that made me say it? Pushing and testing like someone running their tongue around an old abscessed tooth.

'Yes,' he said, sinking his teeth back into his sandwich, shifting his eyes to the right as they say people do when they're remembering. Or is it what they do when they're lying? I forget which way round it is.

Identity crisis

I wonder how well you really knew That Man, or realised you didn't know him. Did you ever catch a whiff of the things he suppressed in front of you? His fixation with all things English – 'English' being a code for the diseases he worried we'd catch in this country: promiscuity, fecklessness, atheism, cold-heartedness, lack of family feeling. 'Don't you dare think you're English!' he'd say to me and Sherine whenever we broke one of his arbitrary rules. He should've saved his breath – we knew full well we weren't lucky enough to be 'English'.

So what were we, then, if 'English' was a prize out of our reach and 'Tunisian' was the mask we wore at home? Nothing, really. It was easier to be nothing than to try and fail to be two things.

I remember once Stephen – your son Stephen – played me an old video of X-Ray Spex, laughing at the ten-year-old me wincing and covering my ears as they sang about an identity crisis. 'Who *is* that girl?' I said. Marianne Elliott-Said. She looked like she could be one of my cousins. The illusion was shattered when she opened her mouth.

Your children weren't really English either, but they never seemed to be in crisis. Constant smilers: at each other, at you, at us, apart from an odd little something between Stephen and That Man. Speakers of the language called 'Nicely'. A father I never heard you mention by name. The mysterious Mr Brown.

According to Stephen, he was from Trinidad and he liked pork chops and Brussels sprouts. Was he dead or did he get kicked out or run away? To this day I don't know. Once, when you saw a woman crying on TV, you said, 'It's very sad when someone leaves you for a younger person.' Looking at you expectantly, I waited for more details that never came.

As for me and Sherine, the question of identity rattled at my door long before it started bothering her.

'Miss Hunt,' I said to my teacher in junior school. 'You know this talk on Friday for African and Caribbean pupils? Shall I go to it, because I'm from Africa?'

'Of course you can go, Nessie.' She put my name on the list.

Why were those two girls staring at me in the assembly hall? Karen and that other one, Lydia. Looking at me, then away, then looking again, giving exaggerated shrugs. Not my friends. Just two girls in a different class. The arrival of the dance troupe at the end made me forget all about them.

'It was really good!' I said to Sherine, back at home. 'They were wearing these costumes and the stage was shaking from the drums – they had it in the infants' hall. And we got to skip film time!' I meant the marathon medley of 1970s public information broadcasts that someone decided to inflict on the next generation each Friday afternoon. Children losing their fingers while playing with plastic, or their lives while crossing roads, interspersed with mini-documentaries about metallurgy and the Swiss dairy industry.

'Why did you go?' said Sherine.

'Huh?'

'*We're* not African. African people are black.'

'So what are we?' I said, feeling the belated realisation of my mistake creep over my face.

'White!' she said, pointing at her brown forearm.

Other people agreed...

Some girls singing in the playground, 'Frankie' by Sister Sledge, making it sound like something I'd never heard before.

'We're singing in a white girl's face,' said one of them.

'Good. Teach them how to sing,' said another.

No one else in the vicinity. The white girl must've been me.

...And others didn't.

'Ooh, look,' said a dissenting voice – a customer in a shop. 'A little coloured boy.'

It was when we went to stay with your sister in Cornwall, our first ever trip to the countryside, and you took me and Sherine to the gift shop to buy postcards for our friends. I was looking at snow globes while you and Sherine were over by the freezer getting ice cream.

'Everyone thinks I'm a boy,' I sobbed to Mama when we got back to your sister's place.

Stroking my hair, the recent victim of a Tunisian hairdresser who'd turned it into an angry ball of candyfloss using a technique called 'the lion cut', she said: 'Don't be silly, *azizti*, of course you don't look like a boy. I'll get you some nice clips to wear in your hair and then you'll look like a girl again...'

*

I never told you what that man in the shop said to me. Without having consciously heard the word 'coloured' before, I knew what it meant. I knew what he said would upset you.

Stephen, your Stephen – I wanted to marry him when I grew up, in the most innocent way possible, like children holding hands in a forest. I wanted him to build us a treehouse and play tapes up there, just as he did in his old bedroom in your flat when he came to visit. 'Have you heard this?' he said once, putting on a tape of dark, discordant music as we lay on our stomachs in front of the cassette player.

'It's weird,' I said. 'It sounds like someone banging saucepans together.'

'It's The Human League,' he said. '"Being Boiled".'

'Or, or, I bet you'll like this!' he said, playing 'Mirror Mirror' by Dollar, which was much more to my taste.

Who cared that he was more than ten years older than me and Sherine? He was still a boy, a playmate, in league with the children against the real adults. Not like his sister, Amanda, who could only be described as a lady.

'Hi, my love,' That Man would say, lighting up whenever Amanda walked into the room with her warm smiles and handbags, her car keys and occasional migraines, just like you had. None of that with him and Stephen. That was all awkward silences and strained conversations about what to watch on TV, curled lips when Stephen chose something like *The Young Ones*.

Mama smiled at Stephen, but it was Amanda she beamed at, putting her arm around her and saying, 'Ma chérie...' Graceful Amanda with her hair in long plaits, her voice that always sounded on the verge of sympathetic laughter. Her boyfriend, Max, gazed at her like he couldn't believe his luck. He'd speak to me and Sherine in silly, babyish voices, looking at Amanda the whole time, making it obvious that this display was for her, not us.

Taller than even you, Amanda was like a tree you could lean on. You seemed to let yourself flop around her, saying things like, 'Oh, would you? Could you?' And she'd say, 'Yes, of course, Mum, it's no trouble at all.' With Stephen, once the initial rush of delight at seeing him had passed, you stayed upright and alert as you did with me and Sherine, on guard for things that could hurt us; ways we could hurt ourselves.

'No, Caroline,' I heard you say once when a former girlfriend of Stephen's phoned the house. 'You hurt him very badly. I don't think you should try to see him again.'

Before the Cornwall incident, you told me a story about Stephen, something that had happened to him when he was around my age. 'He fell onto a piece of glass and slashed his knee open when he was playing tennis. He ran down the road looking for help, but no one would open the door – they looked out of their windows but nobody came.' 'He was wearing his new white plimsolls,' you said. 'They were ruined, I couldn't get the bloodstains out.' It was on the word 'plimsolls' that your voice seemed to wobble for a second. 'This is where it happened,' you told me soon after, when we drove through a road in Finchley. I knew that road. That Man made us all walk up it once to look at houses he'd never be able to afford, saying 'Why is it I work like a dog and yet I'll never be able to have one of these?'

'He had to limp all the way home,' you said. 'Five stitches.'

I turned my head away to hide my tears. How could anyone do that to Stephen, my Stephen? From those tears sprang a fantasy... We were running in the forest, me and Stephen, Stephen with his squirrel-boy eyes and skinny-boy legs and bashful, bunny-rabbit smile, and some hunters came with guns and I protected him by flinging my body in front of his. It was him they'd shoot first, of course. No one had to spell out why.

*

Identity didn't get to Sherine until much later. It got her when she went for a job interview aged twenty-two and some Rupert or Guy said, 'Do you have to queue up at the airport with all the other brown people?' That's how she found out she wasn't white. Personal, not political, her awakening. Gulf War I didn't do it. Broadwater Farm certainly didn't – it had the opposite effect. For me, it was friends who didn't come to school the next day. Ayse's house that burned down, caught in the middle. Olivia's nan who knew the policeman who was hacked to death, Delroy's nan who knew the grandmother who was scared to death. For Sherine, it was a chance to baste her face in talcum powder: 'Why don't black people take some responsibility and stop imagining everyone's racist against them?'

Where were you while the debate was raging? Sitting on the sagging brown sofa in our living room, arguing with Sherine, looking appalled. At Sherine, at That Man when he piped up on her side, using your children as ammunition: 'Amanda and Stephen don't have this bad attitude, this, this what do you call it, chip on their head...'

I kept quiet though I was on your side. Ten-year-olds didn't count. Neither did Mama, sitting sullenly at the dining table, letting the waves of English wash over her like a form of low-grade torture. She was a ten-year-old too, at times like that. Just like a child, she mimicked you afterwards, when you'd gone home. The swoops and intonations of your voice. The way you sometimes put an extra 'eh' sound into the word 'bedroom'. Your unsatisfactory explanation when she'd asked you why it was 'Marks & Sparks' but not 'Lady Diana Sparks'. Your habit of saying things she didn't understand. 'These English women,' she said, leaving the rest of the sentence dangling.

*

What about your identity, Genevieve? Who were you? Who were your parents?

'She was on the stage,' you said, as we sat at your dining table looking at bits and bobs from your childhood, and you produced a black-and-white picture of a woman in pearls, eyes cast beatifically up at something to the right of the camera.

'On the stage,' I echoed, in awe of this term that conjured up images of diaphanous ladies tap-dancing with ghosts, golden liquid sloshing around ice in chunky glasses. Agatha Christie, tinkly pianos, the jazz age. Women with glittery bands across their foreheads and emerald pendants at their throats.

As for your father, his picture made me do a double-take: those eyes, that moustache…

'He looks a bit like your dad, doesn't he?' you said, laughing at my reaction. The coincidence became even spookier when you said, 'He was an engineer – he worked all over the place… Hong Kong, Peru, America… he was once sent to Afghanistan, before this terrible situation with the Russians, to build a dam in a place called Helmand. My goodness, Nessie, the things he used to bring back! I wish I still had them to show you. They all seem to have vanished over the years.'

An engineer! That's what That Man had wanted to be before he was plucked out of school and forced to become the man of the house.

It was funny to think your dad looked like mine. This unexpected connection gave me licence to imagine you as a child, something I'd never done before. You as a tall, slim girl with long brown hair and a dreamy look on your face – in my fantasy you were wearing a pinafore too, like the pictures of Alice in Wonderland – waiting for your dad to come home bearing exotic gifts.

Curious whether this image matched the reality, I said, 'Haven't you got any pictures of you when you were little?'

'Mmm… somewhere.' You had a quick rummage. 'Not here.' With a pensive expression, you said, 'I didn't really like having my picture taken when I was a child. I always felt like something of a misfit. Seeing myself in these poses that my mother liked to arrange us in – they were so very *mannered* – just made it worse.'

'Mannered' was something I could only guess at, but misfits were my specialist subject. How could you have been a misfit, though? Just as I opened my mouth to ask, you shook your head vigorously and made a kind of 'rrrr' sound, as if shooing away a fly.

'Anyway,' you said. 'Here's a picture of my grandmother on my father's side. She was Indian. Did I ever tell you that?'

You produced another black-and-white picture, this one of a wavy-haired beauty with liquid dark eyes.

'Oh!' I said excitedly. 'That's why Mama says...'

'Says what?' You were smiling.

'She says you look Spanish.' I reined myself in, improvising wildly.

'Spanish,' you repeated in a murmur, for a moment looking just like a Spanish woman, the upward tilt of your head signifying the opening move in a flamenco dance.

What Mama had said was less specific: foreign blood... nicer skin than an English person... white but not too white. Not like milk.

He never commented on your appearance, of course. That would've been inappropriate.

Disappointment

I was eleven when you caught me red-handed in the murder of innocents. They died swimming in their own shit, mouths agape at a betrayal they couldn't remember.

'Oh, Nessie,' you said, your voice full of reproach. 'What a shame.'

I looked down at the carpet, away from their corpses, feeling the word 'shame' burn into my skin.

You'd only bought them for me because I was so desperate for a pet. Because our parents said a dog, cat, rabbit or even hamster were out of the question in our flat, and I was so envious of my best friend Mariana with her new guinea pig, Cochon Dan.

'Now, you will look after them, won't you?' you'd said when you handed them over to me in their plastic bag, having used all your powers of persuasion on That Man and Mama and bought me the tank yourself.

'Of course I will,' I'd replied. 'Of course!'

So why did I murder them through neglect? I don't know. I can't explain it any more than I can tell you why I nagged Mama to buy me a geranium from Woolworths, then let it shrivel and die unwatered on the windowsill. Something in me can't keep things alive. Is that why I lost interest in babies as soon as I stopped playing with dolls? Aged eleven, I knew I'd never have children:

'Oh, can I hold her, can I hold her?' said Mariana when we were at our friend Rachel's house and she produced her baby sister to say hello. The baby slotted perfectly onto Mariana's hip, as if she was born to stand in that position, a tall, proud ship bearing precious cargo. 'Do you want to hold her?' she said, offering her to me.

'Okay,' I said, knowing that was what I was supposed to say, feeling the baby squirm almost as soon as I touched her. How could this thing that was so small weigh so much? What if I dropped her and she cracked her head open? 'Is this right?' I tried to hoist her up as Mariana had, forcing her legs apart like a wishbone on the verge of snapping.

'Kind of. Shall I take her back off you?'

You didn't say much more about the goldfish. The dark-red flush on my face was proof of my self-punishment. But the disappointment lingered between us. You'd set me a test and I'd failed it.

*

Was disappointment a peculiarly female phenomenon? That's how it seemed sometimes. The smell of it pervaded the air like a heavy perfume when Mama and her sisters sat in the living room of the flat in Tunis, gossiping in the dark. Keeping the shutters closed to block out the heat, they'd murmur in the corner while lizards made amorous sounds from behind the grandfather clock that seemed to tick slower than any clock in England. The lizards' kissing sound cheered me up – it was a brazen riposte to the hushed, confidential tones.

'...And I said to him, "Aren't you going to come and see her in hospital?" and he said, "I'm afraid she might die," and I said, "Are you scared of death?"'

'...He said he doesn't want to... what can I do?'

'...Never mind, *hbibti*, it's your fate, what can you do...'

'...Nothing but blood for six weeks, she said she's getting sick of the sight of it...'

Their disappointment sucked the oxygen from the air and made it hard to breathe. Why did they do it, this gloating, secretive gossiping in dark rooms? Why couldn't they be like men, shouting in the open air, getting angry in broad daylight, saying what they really meant? I didn't realise then that men can shout about things they don't really mean, keeping the real things quiet and festering.

As they became aware of me pretending to read in the dark, the whisperers would try to draw me into their circle of disappointment, which seemed to be a synonym for woman: 'It's hard being a woman, Susu, you'll find out when you're older.'

You were disappointed too, I learned. Not just by my piscicide. By a *he*. Not my father, but a nameless man of your own, presumably the mysterious Mr Brown. You and Mama once sat on a bench in Finsbury Park talking quietly in a mixture of French and English that seemed to comprise only negatives. 'He wouldn't...' you said. 'He couldn't... He didn't...' A rapt concentration on Mama's face as she listened to you, as if you were reciting a poem she'd written, word perfectly, without skipping a single beat.

*

What about the times you disappointed me, Genevieve? Rare, but so what? Their rarity only made them more disturbing.

I was six the first time it happened.

'You'll never guess what she did at school today!' Sherine said from her throne beside you in the car, her voice shrill with righteous indignation. 'She was going round saying, "We want France" in the playground when everyone else was saying, "We want England"!'

'It wasn't everyone!' I said, raising my voice back at her. 'Imtiaz and Nina and Jasna and Mei-Ling wanted France too!'

Your face was hidden from my view – I was relegated to the back seat among the shopping bags – but you sounded stern when you said: 'Why did you do that, Nessie? You're supposed to want England to win at football, if you're English.' The back of your head looked stern too. Your hairdresser's fault – she'd put something on it that had made it look like a shiny sheet of metal, stiff and unyielding.

What did I know or care about football, or about being English? Roughly as much as I knew about the Suez Crisis or the brewing of moonshine during Prohibition or the intricacies of Hegelian dialectics. All I knew was that I wanted to be on the small, beleaguered, raggedy side, not in the goose-stepping army bellowing 'Ing-er-land!' as it advanced across the playground. Unable to explain this, I slouched in my seat and seethed at you for not understanding; for telling me off and ganging up on me with Princess Poisehead.

What I think of as the sequel to this incident happened five years later, when I was at your flat planning my costume for a Halloween fancy dress party to be held at the library. You were one of the judges. We'd decided I would go as a witch. Mama would brush my hair out into a frizzy halo – we'd already done a dummy run – and you would borrow a black robe and a witch's hat from your friend who had a daughter my age, and draw black warts on my face with eyeliner. 'Although,' you said, with a teasing tone, 'You could always borrow your mum's fur coat and go as Cruella de Vil instead?'

'Eurgh,' I said. 'That's horrible. I'd never wear it. I wish she wouldn't either.'

'Why?'

What kind of a question was that? What did you mean, why? 'Because it's cruel, of course!' I said, looking at you, aghast.

'But doesn't your mum deserve nice things?' Your voice was different from usual; you sounded as if you were talking to someone else, not me. 'Isn't it more important she does what she wants than what you want?'

'But what about the poor little rabbit?' I felt my ears getting hot.

'I don't really like fur either, but we knew she'd always wanted a fur coat. That's why we got it for her, as a surprise.'

It's hard to say what made my moral outrage slip into something less comfortable. An unease... a sense that something I didn't understand was being said. Perhaps it was the word 'we', with all its connotations of complicity, of alliances that didn't make sense. I'd thought it was *he* who'd got her the coat, not *we*. The *he* I could always blame, because that's what he was there for. Or maybe it was the set of your mouth as you spoke, something unusually thin and hard and cold about it, rather like the blade I pictured slicing into the rabbit's neck as its mouth went slack and its lifeblood ebbed out of it. As if you'd suddenly become someone I didn't know either. Someone who wasn't on the same side as me, which was always the side of the underdog. France, not England. Rabbit, not fur.

'Anyway,' you went on. 'If your mum hadn't ended up with that fur coat, someone else would've done. I'm afraid the unfortunate rabbit was a goner in either case.'

'But...' I thought hard, sensing victory around the corner if only I could formulate the words correctly: 'Isn't that like saying it doesn't matter if we buy fruit from South Africa because someone else will, even if we don't?'

'Not at all. It's nothing like that.'

'That's ridiculous,' I muttered, slinging one of your pet phrases back at you, and you said, sharply, 'What was that?'

'Nothing.' I was scared enough to make my voice meek and conciliatory. 'I didn't say anything.'

When you pulled up in your car on Friday evening and summoned me with your usual 'beep beep', that's when I made up my mind: 'I can't go, Mama. I feel sick.' We were in the bedroom. I was already in my witch's outfit, with only my makeup left to do. That was supposed to be your job, in the office at the library.

'What is it, *ma perle*?' She stroked my hair that she'd spent ages brushing out, putting her other hand on top of my head to steady it and stop me wincing and tearing up as she pulled. I was her pearl as well as her *hbibti* or *azizti* – dear one. Sherine was just Sherine, once she grew out of Nunu.

'I don't know. I just feel sick.'

She looked into my eyes as she kept stroking the black cloud on my head, until I turned away. She was dressed for a quiet evening at home with Sherine, wearing a faded pink house dress that I hated because it made her look lumpy. Her hair was freshly washed and wrapped in rollers, like Hilda Ogden from *Coronation Street*.

It was supposed to be just you and me that evening. Our special time. You were the one who'd witness my glory if I won first prize, which was a five-pound gift voucher from WH Smith's. We'd already started talking about what books I'd buy if I won. Top of the list was *The Dark is Rising* by Susan Cooper, which I kept borrowing from the school library. I wanted my own copy. I wanted to own it, to have it next to me and be able to touch it any time I wanted. To be able to copy the text using the red fountain pen I'd bought from Woolworths with my Eid money, the most expensive pen on the shelf, almost pretending I was the one who'd written this story that kept playing in my head like a film. 'Only if I win,' I kept saying. 'I know I might not.' You were the one who understood this physical craving Sherine and I had for books. Not as a stepping stone on the path to becoming Educated Women, but a necessity in themselves.

The beep-beep came again, louder now. Urgent and impatient. Menacing. I started to feel genuinely sick.

'All right,' she said with a sigh. And then in a faintly grumbling tone, 'Now I'll have to go downstairs and talk to her. I'm not in the mood for pointless talk tonight.' When I said nothing, gripping the pink sleeve of her dress, she started stroking my head again and said, in a voice that made her sound further away than she really was, 'Maybe I'll send Sherine down instead. She can tell her you're not well.'

Little pigs

Much of this is familiar to you. You witnessed it yourself. You heard it from one of us. You inferred it from our silence.

Some of it you don't know, even though you were there. You don't know how the perfume of womanly disappointment seeped into my own nostrils around the age of twelve, and how I learned to disappoint in turn. I hid this from you: it was something to be shared with people my own age, people who understood the rules of our particular type of disappointment. People like my best friend Mariana, until her own disappointment put mine in the shade.

Did I ever mention Calvin? Possibly, in passing, in a 'that boy in my class who does this or that' kind of way. He toyed with me first before he disappointed Mariana. Before he blew her house down.

He got me in the science lab in the Nelson Mandela wing. Double science on a Tuesday, our teacher, Slaphead, droning on at the front.

'Boys!' said Slaphead, raising his conductor's baton, a black marker pen he had a habit of fellating nervously when he thought no one was looking. 'Boys, sit up straight. Ajay! Stop throwing paper or I'll send you outside.'

'Girls!' he went on. 'Why do you girls always sit at the back and let the boys take over? Don't you think it's time to lay these stereotypes about girls not liking science to rest?'

'Oi, sir,' said someone. 'When did you last get laid?'

Slaphead's waxy white dome turned crimson. Must've been catching – some kind of infrared wave pulsated through the room, penetrating my face and neck. Why did I care? He was just my science teacher, a balding, middle-aged, ascetic-looking man with a dark-red beard.

No one knew this, but he'd come to me in my sleep the night before, in a swimming pool that was also the sea, contained somehow. It was dark. There was no moon but I could see his body very clearly, illuminated by some other source. He stood waist-deep in the water like John the Baptist, sombre and abstracted, while I floated in his arms, baptised in a sequence of movements that could only happen in a dream: my body in his arms, his head moving down it, his mouth on my skin, bumping over my clavicle, gliding over my chest and stomach, completing the ritual with a single hard kiss between my legs. The memory made me jerk violently in my seat.

'What?' whispered Mariana, jolting upright from her stupor.

'Nothing.'

Yawning, stretching, she tapped Calvin on the shoulder. 'Borrow me an eraser.'

No one said rubber any more, just like no one said laid. Why didn't she borrow my eraser? Because she had nothing to erase but her boredom. The two of them teased each other, flirting quietly. 'Who do you go round with outside school?' he said. She reeled off a list of names, then added, 'And Nessie, sometimes.'

I didn't hate her for it. That's just how it was. I was the reluctant junior accountant with my starched white collar sticking out over my jumper, my sensible shoes that had to be polished every Sunday night, my jeans that I ripped at the knees in a moment of daring rebellion and then humiliatingly had to fix with two cheap patches from Woolworths while That Man supervised from the sofa. Legs tucked sideways under his arse, he'd barked like an angry seal: 'Why did you do that to your jeans that I paid good money for? Do you want people to think I'm a beggar?'

The bouncer had spoken and my name wasn't on the list. You had to say the right thing when you fancied someone, I got that. Mariana hadn't told me she fancied Calvin, but it was obvious. Did I fancy him too? Not in the least, even though he was beautiful. Everything I'd have picked if I had to assemble a boy from scratch. A face begging to be sculpted for an art project, each feature chiselled and defined, curly hair that was softer and thicker than mine, the kind of brown skin that has red in it not yellow, always bright, never grey and sallow even in winter. A prime specimen. Not like Slaphead. Mariana liked other things about him too.

'He punched James Haley in the head the other day for laughing when he tripped over,' she told me once, admiringly. 'He punched Sam Jones the other week for asking in front of everyone if his mum and dad got divorced.'

All this punching made me nervous. I didn't understand why an unpredictable temper was something to chase after. Mariana had a dad like mine, but that didn't seem to have put her off this quality in others.

'You look like Jane from *Neighbours*,' Calvin said to Mariana, caressingly.

Mariana did look like her – blonde hair and creamy skin, blue-green eyes I'd have killed for. If compliments were going free, I wanted one too.

'Who do *I* look like?' I said, thoughtlessly, offering my throat up to the knife.

He looked at me, considering. I lowered my eyes bashfully, not realising what I'd done.

'You look like an alien,' he said eventually. 'An alien with green slime dripping out of its cunt.' In the same voice that had said 'You look like Jane', he whispered some more about my cunt. The exact shade of green slime coming out of it, the quantity, the consistency, the toxicity to anyone foolish enough to get close to it. Mariana sat silent, twirling the eraser between her fingers like a baton. It looked like she'd been infected by the infrared wave too. A small, bright circle high on each cheek, like rouge.

'Ha!' I gave a vulgar guffaw. People turned round and looked.

Slaphead drifted over saying, 'Shhh.' The dome of his forehead offered the sanctuary of a cathedral. We don't get to choose who slips into our dreams. You of all people must know that.

Not long after this, I had another dream, this one about the fish. It lay on the chopping board in all its degradation and, this time, the swivelled eye seemed to smile from the wreckage of the body. I knew it was happy to hear Mama's screams. In some way I didn't understand, the fish had won, even though it was dead and she was alive.

*

Calvin The Great Disappointer didn't act alone. Sometimes he was joined by two others whose names I can't remember – let's call them the three little pigs. They liked to play games, like the one they initiated on the coach during a school trip to a farm in Essex.

'You're a slag,' said Calvin, pointing at a girl.

'You're frigid,' said pig number 2, pointing at another girl.

'You're a slag,' said pig number 3, and on they went, working their way down the rows.

What did the girls do? Not much. Kiss their teeth. Bury their heads in *Just Seventeen*. Giggle sometimes, as long as it was slag they got, not frigid. No one wanted frigid. Pigs and their molls. Our teacher was dozing at the front, oblivious or pretending to be.

'You're a slag,' Calvin said to me.

A split second of relief that I didn't get 'frigid', and then I launched my response: 'Well, you're a stud.'

'I know I'm a stud,' said Calvin, in the voice of someone who'd been given exactly what they wanted for their birthday. 'I know I am.'

People laughed, even Mariana. I cursed the English language for having no male equivalent for slag.

*

What can you do but be a disappointer too? Spread the green slime. Maybe all disappointers were disappointed once. I did it to the ones I liked, like Tinoosh, the fresh-off-the-boat Iranian boy in our class. We'd only exchanged a few words, but we had a bond. Us swarthy types, you know? That's what some of the teachers called those of us who weren't white but weren't black or Asian either.

Tinoosh and I would exchange shy smiles when we ran into each other by the wastepaper basket. I liked him. I knew he knew. I knew he wouldn't use it against me. Not that kind of boy. He was the type teachers praise for being 'mature'. Clever too, or at least he would have been in his own language. He looked a bit like Prince, the eyes, the lashes, the mouth. 'Alphabet Street' was in the charts that summer. Each time I watched the video I thought of Tinoosh.

'Why are you smiling?' said Mama once.

'Nothing. I just like this song.'

The first time I disappointed him was when he came up to me in maths to ask a question. 'Nesrine,' he said, holding out his textbook. 'You know this word in Arabic? Maybe same in Farsi.'

'No, sorry,' I said brightly.

Mariana did the snigger and nudge thing as he turned away.

'Nesriiiine!' I squealed, getting in there before anyone else could, watching the backs of his ears turn red as he walked away.

It was the second time that put a stop to our shy smiles. An end to all conversation. I got him during PE when a bunch of us walked past the boys as they were warming up for football. We were the unsporty girls, ambling along eating Hula Hoops off our fingers when we were supposed to be running cross-country. My friend Ashmita said, 'Hi, Tinoosh!' All my friends knew by then, not just Mariana.

'Hi.' He smiled and waved, not realising hi doesn't always mean hi in English. Not when you're twelve.

'Nessie wants to say something to you,' said Ashmita, nudging me. 'She wants to say you've got a nice—'

'Shut up, shut up!' I clamped my hand over her mouth.

He smiled again, not quite looking at us, the giggling gaggle. We watched them move the ball around. I watched him move himself around. His back, his shoulders, his legs. He was tall and broad. Much older-looking than the other boys. More like fifteen. Maybe he was older and they put him in with us twelve- and thirteen-year-olds because of his limited English. A serious expression even when he was playing football. Showing off a bit when he got the ball, the way boys do when they know they're being watched. In a nice way, not arrogant. Someone did something wrong with the ball and he exclaimed, 'Handball!'

His voice sounded ugly, raised like that. As if there was something wrong with his tongue. Clotted and thick, like rancid milk. Why didn't speakers of Swarthy ever learn? Why couldn't they keep their mouths shut until they learned English properly, instead of embarrassing themselves like that?

'Handi-bollll,' I shouted from the sidelines, exaggerating his accent, cupping my hands so it carried as he turned to look at me. Everyone else joined in, making a football chant out of it.

That's what 'hi' meant in English for Tinoosh. It meant being cut down to size. It meant becoming a cringing little boy on the grass when he was a tall almost-man just a minute ago.

*

Tinoosh only stayed a couple of months at our school, then David came. That one was manslaughter, not murder, and it backfired on me – David had a weapon that Tinoosh didn't have. He was a white English boy, fresh off a car from some other part of London.

What was it I said to him in the corridor? I can't remember. Something awful. Something that ignited gleeful hisses from the people around us, a frenzy of finger-slapping and 'Man, you gonna take that from her?' with an undercurrent of 'fight, fight.' I was only trying to be funny because I liked him. I liked his short brown hair and geeky glasses and dry, sarky sense of humour. I was aiming for sarcasm too, but it went wrong. Like when people fire jubilant rounds of live ammunition at a wedding and end up accidentally killing the bride and groom. Not in England, of course. In Swarthy-land.

David's self-control was unnatural for a thirteen-year-old. Keeping his face impassive, he said, disappointing the crowd baying for blood: 'I have to tell you something, Nessie. You're really not a nice person. I don't understand how anyone can pretend to like you. You're the kind of person who goes round solidly running other people down.'

It was the redundant and awkwardly placed 'solidly' that I fixated on afterwards. 'Why "solidly"?' I kept saying to Mariana. 'What did he mean by "solid"?'

'Don't know – who gives a shit? Don't keep thinking about it.'

That night in bed, I planned my apology, luxuriating in the warm glow of anticipated redemption. I *was* a nice person. How dare he. I didn't go round running people down, solidly or otherwise. I'd show him.

'I'm really sorry I said that to you,' I told him at school the next day, opening my eyes wide to show my sincerity.

'It's all right,' he said, with an indifference that made me want to shoot him again. Properly this time.

But why would she choose to be raped?

You handled my ambushes well. I'd developed the habit of quizzing you about sex when I was about ten, a couple of years before disappointment set in. Your only hesitation came the time Michelle from *EastEnders* got pregnant and I asked you how she knew who the father was.

'Well… well, because she just does.'

The book with the red cover appeared in my school bag soon afterwards. A silent, tactful gift. By Dr Miriam Stoppard, I think. *Sex Talk*. Or was it *Let's Talk About Sex?*

The probing phase didn't last very long. Prudishness and secrecy soon took over, even with you. Ten-year-old knicker flasher became eleven-year-old wimple wearer in the blink of an eye.

It was hard for me to get my head around the concept of sex. Rape coalesced first because it was one of those words you heard on TV all the time. 'A woman was raped while doing such and such… A girl was raped while going to so and so.' Male rape didn't happen back then. Eventually I said to That Man, 'What's rape?' and he said, 'It's when a man assaults a woman.' I think he used the word 'bottom', in English. 'He puts his bottom in hers.' His face said, 'Don't ask me anything else.' That was fine, I didn't need to. My cousin Amani in Tunis, who was two years older than me, filled me in. Like a teacher coaching a remedial pupil, she told me what rape was at the same time she explained what exactly sex was.

'But I don't understand,' I kept saying. 'Aren't they the same?'

'No,' she said, patiently. 'One is when the woman chooses to do it. She chooses to go to sleep with the man's penis inside her.'

'But why would she choose to be raped?'

'No...'

Something in my brain just wouldn't get it. Only for a bit. Weeks or months, not years. Rape and sex were the same, technically. Weren't they?

I wasn't the only one. Other people suffered the same confusion. It lasted longer for them. It came out as an answer, not a question.

*

Contrary to how the fairy tale goes, it was the three little pigs who huffed and puffed and blew Mariana's house down. It happened in the third year of secondary school, at a party I wasn't invited to, that I wouldn't have been allowed to go to anyway. I never told you what happened.

I spent that night watching TV with Mama and Sherine. Feeling bored and resentful, as if life had passed me by. Thirteen going on seventy, a dried-up old woman. Mariana was fourteen, nearly a year older than me; she was the oldest in our class, I was the youngest.

I read Clive Barker's *Weaveworld* before bed, only half absorbing the sex and violence. I felt jealous of Mariana for not being under the same kind of lockdown as me. I wished I was Greek instead of Tunisian. Wished I was her instead of me.

When she rang me the next day and said, 'Can we meet?' it was in a coldy voice. 'Not at my house,' she said. 'Not at yours.'

The bite marks on her chest came out in McDonald's in Wood Green, in the toilets. The same McDonald's where she'd been chatted up by two seventeen-year-olds the month before and got us their digits. The Turkish one for her, the Greek one for me. Mixing it up. Saying fuck you to 1974, to the war that brought this bit of the Mediterranean to Green Lanes, Wood Green, Palmers Green. My telephone lover lasted a week. I drove him away without ever meeting him. He must've got a whiff of my starched collar, even down the phone.

'Everyone saw,' she said. 'They saw me.'

The tears were all mine, not hers. She was calm, how people are when someone they love has just died and it isn't real yet.

'Didn't realise...' she said. 'So drunk... thought it was Calvin. Didn't realise it was the other two too.' 'Two too,' she repeated, not really there. Normally I would've said it too, simultaneously, then we would've said 'Jinx!' and made a wish.

'What are you gonna do?'

'Don't know. Could be pregnant, could've caught something.'

'You have to tell someone.'

'Not them, he'll kill me...'

She meant her dad. Her father who would kill her before killing the three little pigs for what they had done to her.

'I had to pretend,' she said. 'I had to stick my finger down my throat and get it all out in the toilet and then go home and act normal. I can't get undressed in front of my mum. She'll see the bites.'

Her tears came on Monday, to our form teacher. *Pregnancy test, STD test, we'll take care of all that. Are you willing to tell your parents, Mariana?*

I can't, they'll kill me.

Sorry, then, nothing much we can do.

Word spread, as it always does. Who did Mariana become then? Not the charismatic girl who always knew what to do. Not the one who didn't give a shit about 'eurgh, you're a lesbo', who told her friends she loved them and held their hands when the occasion called for it. Not the fourteen-year-old who thought she was on the verge of being loved by another fourteen-year-old. No, she became That Girl. That Girl who got pissed and got herself raped. That Girl who should've been more careful. That Girl who really reckoned herself just because all the boys fancied her and she wasn't even that fit anyway. As for the three little pigs, who did they become? None other than who they always were: studs.

Good Friday

'Catastrophe' isn't the right word for the event that drove you out of our lives one rainy Tuesday in July 1989. It's 'nakba'.

Don't get me wrong. I'm not trying to equate what happened to the real Nakba, capital N. I've done my bit for the Palestinians: I've written essays about them for GCSE this and that. I've worn a black-and-white kaffiyeh, when everyone else was doing it, so I wouldn't look like the Arab who was making a big deal about being an Arab. I've shot down my bimbo cousin Mohammed when he said, all Bambi eyes and inane grin, eyelashes filling the void where his brain should be, 'Why are we always doing things for the Palestinians? Why do they never do anything for us?' No, I've done all I can for them, short of giving them a state myself.

By nakba, I just mean the point at which it becomes official. The point that marks the end of any self-deception. There's another Arabic term that's also apposite: *gomma al hazeena*. I learned it from an album of Lebanese Easter songs sung by Fairuz: it means sorrowful Friday, which means Good Friday. We had our own sorrowful Friday – a Friday the 13th, no less – but I didn't understand the significance. Our sorrow was on a slow-release mechanism. No one rose triumphant on the Monday.

*

Our Good Friday came on 13 January 1989. It began with a phone call in the evening, a bring-bring that brought good tidings.

'He's going to France for the night,' said Mama, putting the phone down and coming into the living room, where Sherine and I were watching TV.

'France?' came the chorus.

'Yes. He's got a problem with a consignment of dates he was expecting. He has to go to France to meet the supplier. On the ferry. He'll be back tomorrow evening after he's sorted it out.'

Looking from one of us to the other, she knew what we were thinking. We knew what she was thinking. Had three people ever extended such warm regards to France? *Vive la France!* France with her permanently enraged farmers and constant blockades of sheep, her supply chain problems that had delayed That Man's consignment of dates, nasty, cockroach-textured fruit that they were. And he'd gone on the ferry, she said... how did the Zeebrugge disaster happen again? *No, no, I didn't mean it! Please bring him back safely, God.* The God I didn't believe in until I wanted something. But not before we'd enjoyed our juicy morsel of freedom, sweeter than any bumper pack of Deglet Noor.

He was a night owl and a social butterfly. With his friends, that is – we got the moth, not the butterfly. Things kept him out late. Chatting to people at the shop, going for coffee and shisha pipes with his Lebanese friends, having a bite to eat with his assistant. But he always came home, eventually.

That phone call gave us a whole evening's reprieve from him. It promised a night we could watch TV without someone walking in and saying, 'All you girls ever do is watch trash, why don't you read a book and improve your minds?' A night we could read our books without someone glaring and saying, 'Each one with her nose in a book, always. Don't you know it's rude to sit there ignoring other people when they're in the same room as you?' A night we could exchange the odd word with each other or with Mama without someone saying 'Shhh, I'm trying to watch the news!' A night free of the clicking of fingers on prayer beads, teeth on pumpkin seeds, clippers on fingernails, each sound a micro-explosion of rage at something we were oblivious to and yet was clearly our fault.

'Maybe we can watch *Working Girl* tonight,' said Sherine, casually. 'I have to take it back to Blockbusters by Sunday.'

'Why not,' replied Mama, with studied nonchalance. 'How about some chocolate trifle, girls? I've got a fancy for something sweet.'

An even more daring idea came to me. 'Shall I ask Mrs Brown if she wants to come and watch the video too?'

'Yes yes, ask her!' said Sherine. 'I know she wants to see it – we were talking about it the other day.'

'Okay,' said Mama, in the same casual way she'd talked about the video and the chocolate trifle. 'Ask her.'

I let the phone ring until it cut off, then tried again a few minutes later in case you were in the bathroom. When I went back to the living room and said, 'She's not there,' Mama just inclined her head upwards.

'Oh, that's a shame,' said Sherine. 'Ah well.' She put the video in and we hunkered down, me and her on the sofa That Man normally colonised, Mama in her usual chair.

What was up with her? Was it a rule that at least one person in our living room had to have their face all scrunched up at any given time? Would the universe implode if not? What did she have to be miserable about anyway, that night of all nights?

'Don't you want your trifle, Mama?' I said.

'No, no, you can have it.' She pushed it towards me. As the film skipped along, she gazed with us at Melanie Griffith's toothy grin and Sigourney Weaver's shoulder pads and Harrison Ford's 'Ah, women, whaddya gonna do?' expression. She laughed almost when we did. You had to be paying attention to notice the time lag.

*

A week or so later, a box of clotted cream fudge sat on our coffee table. You'd brought it back from your trip to Somerset to see Amanda, the same weekend That Man went to France. Your hand and his reached out at once, collided, jumped back as if they'd had an electric shock.

'Sorry, Hamdi,' you laughed. 'I don't know why I'm in such a hurry to try them when I got them for all of you.'

'Not at all.' He gestured for you to go ahead.

A flush crept up his neck. Was he embarrassed because he'd forgotten to lift the box and offer it to you first? He would've shouted at me if I'd done the same, like he did when the man from the housing association came round and I let slip in front of him that we only had one can of Coke left. Or was he simply overcome by your presence? He shimmered and fluttered for you, always. Butterfly, not moth. Pronouncing your name the French way on the odd occasion he plucked up the courage to say it. Gallant, I think the term is. He'd have kissed your hand if propriety permitted it, Sir Lancelot to your Guinevere. The best jumpers came out when you were there – the ones with diamond patterns and matching socks.

But the blush was unusual. That was a disease that usually afflicted only me in our family. My face erupted into blotches at the slightest provocation, my skin not dark enough to hide it. Stony-faced, the rest of them, unbetrayed by their own blood.

Mama came out of the bedroom to greet you – three kisses as usual, left then right then left again. I remember she was wearing a new top that day – a dusky pink blouse from C&A that looked like silk but was made of something synthetic that trapped her sweat and wafted it into other people's noses. You were in a knee-length black skirt and an olive-green jumper that Sherine had once told me was cashmere. It would've looked drab on most people, but it seemed to warm your skin and bring out the golden flecks in your eyes and hair. I don't think I ever saw you in trousers – Mama never wore them either, but that was because she thought they emphasised the width of her backside. Her pink blouse made her look soft and girlish next to you in your severe, army-like colours. She looked exposed, like something that had been peeled.

'Tell us about Somerset,' Mama said. 'You never mentioned you were going.'

'It's a beautiful part of the country,' you replied. 'Closer than Cornwall. Perhaps we can all go sometime.'

Mama looked at That Man, seeking permission as always.

'Inshallah,' he said coolly, master of our destiny once again. The butterfly unleashing tornados and earthquakes with the flapping of his wings.

The making of a moth

Was it mine and Sherine's fault, how That Man was? Did we turn him into a moth when we forgot to give him a name?

'What do your daughters call you?' Uncle Ali asked him as we had Ramadan breakfast with him and Aunty Noura and their son and daughter. They were family friends – Lebanese – not real relatives: all the real ones lived in Tunisia.

It was April 1989. I'd given up on fasting by then. I was thirteen years old, and nothing came between me and the toffee crumble ice cream I bought for lunch every day from the Tonibell van parked outside the Nelson Mandela wing at school. No one at home knew that though: I brushed my teeth as soon as I got in from school so they couldn't smell food on my breath.

'Do they call you Baba or do they say Dad or Daddy?' asked Uncle Ali. 'These two used to call me Baba when they were little, but now they think they're English so they say Dad.'

With the usual Arabic confusion over vowels, he pronounced Dad and Daddy as Dead and Deady. The two kids twinkled and dimpled at their own outrageous Englishness.

'Nothing,' replied That Man. 'They don't call me anything.'

He gave us a look from under his eyelashes as he shovelled rice into his mouth. A lurch of something like shame joined the lentil soup, tabbouleh, moussaka and rice already churning round my stomach. Grilled meats and lasagne still to come, followed by dessert – crumbly, sticky, honey-soaked cakes served with cream, or ice cream if you liked – and then fruit. So much for the month of abstinence.

How was Sherine dealing with the red-hot rings of aggrievement emanating from him? By eating steadily and keeping her eyes cast down at her plate, that's how. It was left to me to blush and squirm. Mama was nattering with Aunty Noura down the other end of the table.

How long had That Man known he didn't have a name? In birthday cards, he was simply *Have a Lovely Day! XXXX*.

Uncle Ali started talking about the Israelis in the way that English people talked about the weather. Light, conversational. Lebanon. Their antics there.

'It's disgraceful!' said That Man, spitting flecks of rice across the table, sounding more pissed off than Uncle Ali, who was Lebanese. 'Why don't these sons of dogs care who they hurt?'

You didn't accompany us to breakfast that night, not being an observer of Ramadan. We never really talked about where you stood on matters of the soul, did we? You handled the issue with the delicacy you applied to all your dealings with us. Picking around the dangerous bits like a cat filleting a fish. But I remember that time… A couple of months before the Ramadan breakfast at Uncle Ali's, in those strange days when a mob on TV burned a book they'd never read. When graffiti appeared on a wall at school misspelling the name of the book's author, turning him into an oily fish, and someone scrawled in spidery green ink beneath it: 'I'd rather be a bible-basher than a Koran-basher.'

One Thursday, after double science and before lunch-break, our religious education teacher Mr Tanner, a thin-lipped, desiccated man who looked ninety-five but was probably in his forties, said something about Muslim women being forced to wear the veil. I put my hand up and said, 'Some of them choose to wear it.'

'How can it be a choice?' he spat back, his long, narrow head trembling as if hoisting up a mental barbell. 'How does "choice" come into it with a group of people who roam the world saying, "become a Muslim or we'll chop your head off"?'

'But it's true, sir,' piped up a white English girl called Kate whose mother was a psychologist and father something big in the music business. 'Some of them do choose to wear it.'

And now Mr Tanner leaned forward to listen, trembles subsiding, hands behind his back and a twinkle in his eyes because God knows, everyone loved a girl with spirit, as long as her spirit belonged to us, not them (or did I mean them, not us?).

Back at home that night, Mama's eyes shone at the TV with a liquid brightness that made you look down at the plastic tablecloth, your non-committal noises fading to silence. That Man sat next to her at the dining table, giving you a glimpse of the face he normally reserved for us. Moth, not butterfly. The two of them were opposite you. Sherine was studying in the bedroom. I was hunched on the couch with the hood of my lilac sweater pulled up, covering my hair, being a moth too. How can it be a choice, how can it be a choice?

'No, I won't have any coffee, thank you,' you said, and made your excuses. Your early departure didn't bother me. So what if your dad was half Indian? So what if the mysterious Mr Brown was from Trinidad? So what if your kids were mixed-race, as you'd taught us to say when other people were still saying half-caste? That didn't mean you knew what it meant to be them, or us. Drab, brown, unwelcome invaders, fatally drawn to your light.

Nakba

Just before the nakba, one evening in July 1989, Mama and I were standing in the kitchen. For reasons I can't explain, I said, 'Why do English women always say Arab men look like Omar Sharif if they think they're good-looking?'

'Which Arab men? Which English women?' Her questions hit the air almost before I'd finished my sentence. She put down the knife she was using to chop the salad vegetables and spun round to face me.

'N-no one.' I turned hot under her scrutiny. 'Just, you know, on TV, when you hear them say things like that, in general.'

'Huh?'

That crappy fridge we had then. Nearly as old as me. Powerless against the furnace raging in my cheeks as I opened the door and stuck my face inside, pretending to look for something. 'It's nothing, Mama!' I injected attack into my voice. 'It's just a general thing people say sometimes, not even women to men, men might say it to other men or to women, it's just a thing I've heard sometimes.'

'Men might tell women they look like Omar Sharif? What are you talking about?'

Kissing my teeth was something I could only get away with when you, Sherine and That Man weren't around. I did it then, as it was only Mama. Funny how you seemed to hate it even more than the others, saying it set your teeth on edge.

'It was nothing, Mama! It was just a comment. *Ya Allah*! I just think it's funny that the only good-looking Arab man people can ever think of is Omar Sharif. He's not even that good-looking!'

'So who would you choose, then?' She picked up the knife and turned back to the salad, her back looking squarer than it did minutes earlier.

Who would I choose? What famous Arab men were there apart from Omar Sharif, Yasser Arafat and Colonel Gaddafi? This was 1989, remember, a year before Saddam Hussein burst onto the celebrity circuit.

Ah, ah, there was someone! What was his name again? A dark-skinned, feline face; high, pointy cheekbones…

'Sadat,' I said. 'Sadat wasn't bad. Maybe. Before he got shot. When he was young. If he'd had more hair.'

'Sadat!' She laughed as if reassured by this proof of my silliness. 'Can't you think of anyone better than that?'

'By better, I suppose you mean lighter-skinned? You Tunisians are so disgustingly racist,' I said, picking a fight, trying to make her forget what I'd asked.

*

Would she have gone hunting in That Man's wardrobe if I hadn't put the idea of Omar Sharif and his admirers into her head?

Nakba day was a rainy Tuesday. It started off like any other. I went to school and came home. Sherine went to school and then to a friend's house to study. He went to work. Mama went to college. What was different was that when she got back, she went into his room and came out with a crumpled scrap of paper in her hand.

'What's this?' she said, holding it out to me.

'What is it? Where did you find it?' I took it from her and smoothed the creases.

'In his pocket. His grey trousers.'

Faded and bedraggled, the words had a power you wouldn't expect. Conductors of electricity and heat, they seemed to dance off the paper and scald my hand. They kicked my heart into a chaotic rhythm and squeezed my windpipe into a narrow straw.

Cats. Friday 13 January.

The night he was in France. The night he went to meet his supplier. Mama could read those words too. She knew what a theatre was and what a cat was. She knew what January was and what the number thirteen was.

'I don't know.' I gave the paper back to her with a trembling hand.

'What's this?' she said again, thrusting it into my face as if I were to blame, shaking like the electric current had slammed into her too. 'What's this, what's this, what's this?'

Swatting the paper out of her hand, I ran to the bedroom and locked the door. I didn't come out until Sherine got back from her friend's house, and then I stuck to her for the rest of the evening.

*

Thursday came – your usual night – but you didn't. I knew you wouldn't, but still. It's one thing to imagine the apocalypse, another to have it unfold on you.

It was the Why that got me when I asked where you'd gone.

'Where's Mrs Brown?' I said to That Man when we hadn't heard from you for a week. Still hoping I was wrong. Still hoping the apocalypse was in some book, on TV, in my feverish imagination, anywhere but in real life. Asking Mama was out of the question. She was contaminated, unclean. Her eyes red and swollen, her nose bulbous, her face twenty years older overnight. 'Tell her to go back to her own family!' I heard her hiss, venomously, to That Man one night in the living room. Who was *her*, Mama? Please not who it always was. It mustn't be. Being alone with Mama was dangerous, to be avoided at all costs.

'She's gone on holiday,' he said.

'Oh. Where?'

'America.' He hesitated for just a second before replying.

I asked again a week later: 'When's Mrs Brown coming back from America?'

'Why?' he said, daring me to kick the chair from under us all, knowing I wouldn't, and I said meekly, 'No reason.'

'She's gone away,' he said. And then, 'She doesn't want to know us any more.'

It was your name that haunted me. That summer, when Mama, Sherine and I went to Tunis for the holidays and I hardly thought about you, a bad sweet potato sent me to bed for a week and delirium slipped in with the bacteria. That's when you came and visited me, or rather your name did, tiptoeing delicately through the mushrooms draped in fur and cats with purple eyes and big kettles hissing like snakes.

'Why Genevieve?' people used to ask you, meaning 'Are you foreign?' or 'Who do you think you are to have a name like that?' And you'd say, 'No reason, they just liked the name.'

Why Genevieve? Why Genevieve? They just liked the name; why Genevieve...?

'What's she saying?' said my cousin Amani to Mohammed, as they perched on my bed playing cards.

'Slike the name,' said Mohammed. 'What does that mean?'

'Slike the name, slike the name,' said Amani, plucking the rhythm from my head, repeating it obediently, as if you'd whispered it to her too.

I got your letter back in London, in September. It arrived at school in a blue airmail envelope, handed over by my teacher with a joke about a secret admirer all the way from America. A reference to a Joan Armatrading song that I didn't get for several years until I heard the song for the first time on a mix-tape a friend made for me at university.

Dear Nessie,

I hope you're well and looking forward to the new term. Fourth year already – how time flies! I hope you had a nice summer holiday in Tunis, if you went this year.

I'm very sorry I didn't get to say goodbye before I left. You may already know that I've gone to California for a year on a job exchange for librarians – something like a busman's holiday. I applied for it a while ago but didn't expect anything to come of it, and then it all happened so quickly. Everything is very different here, but I'm starting to get used to it. It's good to give ourselves a change every once in a while, before we get too set in our ways.

I do hope you and Sherine and your mum and dad are all well. You're all incredibly precious to me, Nessie. I hope you always understand that. You take care and look after yourself. My address is at the top of this letter.

Your friend, always.

Genevieve

Once I'd read it in a quiet corner of the playing fields, I folded it up and shoved it into the pocket of my jeans. Back at home, I transferred it to the pyjama case where I kept the things I didn't want anyone else to see: my diary, sanitary towels, the only Valentine's Day card I'd ever got, from a boy called Imtiaz. Joseph to my Mary in the school nativity play of 1983; two Muslims bringing down Christmas from within.

Our old landlady Mrs Kowalski told me a year later when I ran into her that she heard you'd met a man in America; that you'd married him and you were staying out there. 'It was a whirlwind,' she said. 'Pouf!'

No one else ever saw the letter or heard of its existence. When I left home and moved to a different city it came with me. When I moved to a different country it came too, still in its envelope. On occasions when I travelled back to England to see Sherine and That Man, it waited patiently for me, tucked away in chests of drawers in tatami-floored bedrooms, shaken by earthquakes every once in a while. Packed up and moved from village to city, one bedroom to studio, life alone to life with another and back again. When I went to Tunisia to see Mama after she left That Man, it waited for me still, asking me to reopen it, to read between the lines for different meanings, different truths. The nakba was worse than I thought it was. Things are not what they seem.

But I ignored it. Even when delayed adulthood finally prised my hands away from my eyes and forced me to confront a fact I'd always known about you, something too big to face in childhood, I ignored it. Even when I came to understand why people can put the things they love through a mincing machine, and why your act of destruction was perhaps an act of self-preservation, I still ignored it. Only after I saw you sixteen years later, when you looked up from your bed and said in that strange, carrying voice, 'I want a record,' did I finally open the letter again, exposing my eyes to the implicit admission of guilt. To the neat blue biro that made my stomach clench and my heart race as if I'd been sent something pornographic in the post. Not a letter from a friend, all the way from America.

Part 2: Aftermath

1989–1997

Self-harm

I didn't know back then that it was called 'self-harm'. That wasn't how I thought of it. Each time I dragged my nails across my stomach or scraped a fork up the insides of my thighs, I was harming That Man, Mama, the world. Not myself.

It began soon after the nakba. My face was what I was itching to get at – what better way to punish That Man than to throw the imprint of his crime right back at him, in the form of vivid, throbbing tribal scars? But each time I came close, something stopped me: the image of the scar on Mama's left hand, between her thumb and index finger. The memory, or dream, of a mangled fish lying on a sideboard, and of you whispering, 'Don't worry, don't worry.' The knowledge of a line that had been crossed, though no one had ever told me what that line was.

Cowardice pulled me back by the scruff of my neck each time I tiptoed too close to the edge. I didn't want some doctor dragging me along by my hair – it was bad enough when anyone else tried to brush it. Only I was allowed to cause myself pain. No, I knew how to play the game without getting caught. Until the day Mama caught me.

*

We were invited to Uncle so-and-so and Aunty somebody's house in South London. A late dinner on a Friday. I ran the outfit I was going to wear past Mama before I put it on, and she said, 'Yes, it's fine.' A red silk blouse and black-and-white polka-dot palazzo pants that Mariana's mum had bought in the wrong size and given to me instead. Black, fake suede loafers with bows on them. Mama had bought them for me from the market in Wood Green Shopping City. They were made of something like Velcro and acted as a magnet for every speck of dust within a five-mile radius. I felt like a fifty-two-year-old secretary. I felt good. Relaxed, to the extent possible before a family outing. Safe from That Man's scowling scrutiny that night. Confident that I'd covered my arse, in more than the literal sense. This was the type of 'good girl' outfit I was supposed to wear when we went out to meet other Arabs. In the absence of stylish and gleaming, frumpy and inoffensive would have to do. Nothing that made me look like a 'punk' or a 'witch' as he said about my black lace-up boots and fringed blue skirt that I'd bought from Camden market, or like a 'street-child' as he described my plimsolls from Woolworths, which I only owned because he was too tight to buy me some new trainers when the old ones fell apart. I had to try much harder than Sherine not to piss him off with my clothes. Being Miss Poised automatically conferred good-girl status on her – in that respect, at least.

I only met the so-and-so family that one time. They were Algerian. The father was a doctor – That Man had met him in the shop and they'd exchanged invitations, which meant that we had to go to their place. We were still in the flat in Cranfield Gardens, which was out of bounds to other Arabs. How could we act like *people* with the damp patch on the ceiling and the peeling section of flocked wallpaper tittering at our pretensions?

Uncle so-and-so was quiet and smiley. Aunty someone was tiny and glazed-eyed. They had a son and daughter called Adam and Sarah; nice, neutral names that wouldn't get them bullied at school, unlike the Punjabi boy in the year above me called

Kamaljit, known almost universally as Camelshit. The names must've been Uncle so-and-so's work – he seemed plugged in, aware of these things, the type who wanted to make life easy for his children. The mother didn't look like she lived on this planet, let alone in England.

Adam was a beautiful boy a couple of years older than me. Doe eyes and curly, flicky lashes like his sister's. I had to ignore him because I couldn't talk to him without blushing. Sarah was beautiful too. Silky hair. Half my size. She was twelve, two years younger than me.

But I liked her. You could tell her life was dysfunctional too. Some kind of high-pitched hum that seemed to hover in the air between her and her mother, at a frequency only other miserable people could hear. I looked over at Mama, and found myself smiling at her once or twice. Despite the fact her eyes were shrouded in dark shadows and hadn't opened properly ever since you left, I was relieved she was my mother.

When we got home, That Man waited until I was about to follow Mama and Sherine into the bedroom before he took me by the arm and steered me back into the living room. It came out calm, measured, not too loud, as if he'd been rehearsing it all night while he'd been nodding thoughtfully at Uncle so-and-so or smiling at the kids and asking what subjects they were studying at school or tossing his head back and giving that loud, bellowing laugh that only ever came out in public: 'Shame upon the family,' 'Devil in your heart,' 'Humiliated me in front of other people, those good, decent people,' 'Ashamed to look at you next to his daughter in her nice clothes,' 'You look like a beggar'...

What had triggered it? The black shoes – what else? Paraded in front of the so-and-so family, they'd set off a siren in his head. The cheapness, the lintiness, the way the silly little bows at the top had gone scraggly and mangy around the ends, the fact that they didn't even have proper hard soles but something rubbery and thin...

I waited until he'd gone to work the next morning before I replied to him. Formally, you might say. In writing, of sorts. Sherine had gone to the library and Mama was in the kitchen when I took my jewellery collection out of its container – a plastic Safeway's bag – and rummaged around for the present you'd got me for my thirteenth birthday. A chunky, old-looking dark silver bracelet with a lapis lazuli stone in the middle. Gemstones were my obsession that year. Their magical, healing properties. Sitting cross-legged on the woolly blue carpet in our bedroom, next to the bottom bunk bed that was mine, I rolled up the sleeve of my red and blue tartan pyjamas and used the sharp tip of the bracelet to carve a series of lines into my left forearm.

'What are you doing?' said Mama, appearing in the doorway. How could I have not heard the door opening?

'Nothing.' Letting the bracelet flop to the floor, I covered my arm with my other hand.

She came over and peeled my fingers away. I looked out of the window as she gasped. When she started making a keening noise, I grabbed a pillow from the bed and buried my head in it.

'Why did you do this, *ya rouh qalbi?*' I think that's what she said as she rubbed my back the way she did when I was ill, her breath coming hot and ragged onto my neck. *Rouh qalbi* means soul of my heart. You heard her say it – I know you did – but did you ever know what it meant?

When I didn't reply, she said, in a shrill, trembling voice, almost shouting, 'God forgive me for what I did!' Then, her voice sinking to a whisper, 'I was ashamed... What do you have to be ashamed about?'

'What did you do, Mama?' I mumbled, knowing she wouldn't hear me with my face pressed against the pillow. When she said 'What?' I didn't repeat it.

I kept my head buried in the pillow until she took her hand off my back and left the room. Before she went, she said, 'Put some

Dettol on your arm and don't let him see it.' Then she closed the door behind her quietly, as if reluctant to disturb whatever was going on in there.

*

Was I punishing you too, Genevieve, with those sharp objects? It would've made perfect sense, wouldn't it? After all, the crime was yours as much as That Man's.

But it didn't work that way, for the simple reason that there was no 'you' left to punish, even in the privacy of my own mind. As if through spontaneous combustion, you'd all but vanished from my consciousness, leaving only a formless, throbbing sense of shame. A pair of shoes and a pile of ashes would've been easier to deal with. Physical detritus can be swept away, at least.

And yet... was it just a coincidence that the one time I used your bracelet to slash my skin was the time Mama caught me? Some people might think there was more to it. The kind of people who say, 'There's no such thing as coincidence.' The kind of people who believe that dreaming about a dead person means you're going to die soon, or decorating your doorway with an evil-eye amulet means your new washing machine will be protected against your next-door neighbour's jealous gaze.

Mama was that kind of person. She believed that kind of stuff. And she'd seen your bracelet lying on the bedroom floor, after I'd finished my work with it. Did the lines on my arm form a bloody circuit board connecting her back to you and your crime?

But if you and That Man were the culprits, why was Mama the one in the shit with God? And in those months after the nakba, why did the waves of disgust that rose up from my stomach lap over her as much as him, the convicted criminal? None of it made any sense.

Curtain up

After the nakba, against the backdrop of the bigger production, Sherine and I began to act out a play of our own. This play was staged abruptly, without warning even for us, the leading ladies. No time to learn our lines or check our makeup. Once it started, it started. All we could do was run with it.

The theatre was our new house, which you never saw; Mama always called it 'his house'. We moved there in March 1990.

On this occasion, the scene took place in our bedroom, the curtain rising as the two of us sat on our beds doing our homework. Or rather, Sherine was doing her homework; I was reading *Flowers in the Attic*, concealing it inside my big blue ring binder. The play-within-a-play went like this:

Sherine's character [scribbling in her notebook]: Have you had a shower today?

My character: Yes.

Hers [giving mine a probing look]: No you haven't. Go and have a shower.

Mine: No. I don't need one. Anyway, it's too late now. I need to finish my homework.

Hers: You're disgusting.

Mine [interior monologue]: La la la la, I can't hear you. [Concentrating on the words in front of me, pressing my whole being

into the book, away from her voice.] Rat poison... Donuts...
Cory dead.

Hers: Why don't you want to have a shower?

[The answering silence is a provocation.]

Hers: You're disgusting. I'm ashamed to call you my sister.

Aged eighteen, she wasn't just Miss Poised now. She was
something else. Her eyes glittered with a dangerous energy.
She was sinewy and muscular, sharpened and hardened by all
the sports she did. She was a coiled spring ready to flip, to
turn this play into something unsuitable for family viewing.
Don't blame her, blame the dust. The dust we dragged into this
theatre along with the props from our old flat, where you'd
stood by the front door and said, 'I'll see you on Thursday,
Nessie,' before you vanished.

There was a subtext to this play. Sherine's character wanted
mine to help her. She wanted mine to stick a finger down her throat
and help her cough up the dust. But she was asking the impossible.
That kind of catharsis wasn't in this script. She had to stop. She
had to learn she couldn't improvise like this. Recklessly.

I stared fixedly at the words in front of me. After a while she
turned back to her homework.

Desperate to escape this play, to become myself again and
make her herself, I waited for the pounding in my ears to subside
and then I started telling her a funny story about something that
had happened at school. My voice was weak and quavery. It lacked
conviction. It needed to take it again, from the beginning: once
more with feeling. It trailed off before the end when I realised
she'd put on her headphones, 'Tango in the Night' seeping out of
her Walkman.

She ignored me for the next three months, a new phase of this
play. As we went about our lives, she glided past me, looking
through me, as if each of us was a ghost. The ghost of the sister

we used to have. And the dust swirled around us all the time, choking us.

*

He only bought that house for us. That's what That Man always said. He would've been happy in a flat, a shack, curled up on a straw mat, as long as we had the things he'd never had.

The vocabulary of home ownership was unfamiliar, and a source of pride, to him. 'I'm thinking of doing a "loft conversion",' he said to a friend once, injecting a faintly interrogatory tone into the words, as if the very existence of loft conversions was up for debate. When the friend was out of earshot he told us to forget about a loft conversion, it was too expensive, he couldn't bankrupt himself any more than he already had.

Everything was a 'Don't' in the new house you never saw: Don't drag your dirty shoes on the new carpet. Don't leave your books lying round. Don't spill food on the tablecloth, it's new. Don't lean against the wall, you'll smudge it. Don't knock against the elephant on the mantelpiece, it's very valuable, Aunty Amira and Uncle Farouk bought it for us from an antiques shop in Kensington. (Funny how they had three of those antique elephants in the storeroom of their shop.)

But the biggest Don't was this: Don't leave the bathroom in a state – The Brand-New Bathroom.

Youth and vitality weren't on the side of the previous owners of our house, which was a 1930s terrace in Bounds Green. Before decamping to Eastbourne or Hastings or wherever it is old English people go to die, they left us with some unwanted gifts, including a filthy pink toilet brush and a pair of mouldy cricket pads. But that wasn't the worst of their crimes.

'These English people,' said That Man. 'They like to pretend they're so clean, but you can tell what they're really like when you walk into their bathrooms. Carpet in a bathroom! What kind of animal would put carpet in a bathroom?'

Like an anthropologist exhibiting the relics of a barbaric civilisation, he preserved a bit of the carpet to show us during the renovation, holding a sodden corner of it gingerly in his hand, turning his face away from the stench. 'Look! Can you imagine what this carpet's seen in its lifetime?'

Anyone who bathed or showered in our Brand-New Bathroom had to leave it cleaner than they found it. Soap scum had to be scrubbed off the bathtub, the surface rinsed clear of all cleaning fluid, the tub rubbed dry of even the tiniest drop of liquid. Each time someone came out of the bathroom while That Man was home, he went in to inspect it. If it hadn't been cleaned to his satisfaction, this is what happened:

'Who last had a bath?' he'd say, standing on the landing outside the bathroom, hanging over the banister if everyone else was downstairs.

'Me,' I would say. He knew it was me. It was always me.

Nodding in acknowledgement of this fact, he'd say, 'Come over here and look at this.'

Time to perform my part in another of our theatre productions, the Ballad of the Brand-New Bathroom (call and answer):

Him: Why are you so ungrateful?
Me: I'm not ungrateful.
Him: Don't argue with me!
Me: I'm not arguing.
Him: Why do you think I bought this house?
Me: For us.
Him: Yes, for you – not for me. I was happy to stay in the flat, but no, you all wanted a house, so I got you one. And now none of you wants to clean it! I'm the only one who ever cleans it!

[Silence.]

Him: Why are you so stubborn?

[Silence.]

Him: Why don't you answer me when I'm talking to you?

[Silence.]

Cue the solo performance, ratcheting up ten decibels with each line (bankrupted myself for you/lucky if I don't have a heart attack before I'm sixty/other people's families don't do this/that useless woman downstairs who never teaches you anything), reverberating through the house and bouncing off the walls until Mama came running up the stairs with a pinched look on her face and a scouring pad in her hand and went into the bathroom and slammed the door behind her.

–Don't slam the door! would come the crescendo.

Usually, without making my intentions explicit, I timed my showers right before Mama's so she could clean the bathtub for both of us. I was normally a stowaway on the ship of other people's labour. But on the evening Sherine dragged me into her play, that ship had already sailed – Mama had been in. That was why I didn't want to have a shower.

So why didn't I tell Sherine? Because that would've meant breaking the pledge. The unspoken pledge we had not to talk about what had happened, and what went on happening: about your disappearance and the fact that none of us ever mentioned you again; about That Man's rages, which only got worse once you were gone, once he'd established that none of us would ever speak of his crime; about the doors that slammed even harder in the new house than they had in the old flat; about Mama's habit of jumping and screaming when the phone rang, as if the day of judgement was about to descend with a telephone call from God; the way her face seemed to clench when she thought no one was looking, how it seemed to close in on itself and say, 'Is this all there is?'

Sherine knew all that. What was she playing at? What was she thinking by asking me a question that started with 'Why', even in a play?

Winners and losers

Our lives might've taken a different turn if you hadn't vanished. For one, you might've waved your magic wand for Sherine's sake, just as you did for Mama all those years ago when you helped her enrol in college. In your absence, That Man's extremes went unchecked.

'No daughter of mine is going to live away from home doing God knows what!' he said, when Sherine told him she'd been offered a place at Bristol University. 'No daughter of mine is going to leave my house until the day she gets married. Forget this Bristol business. You'll go to university here, in London, and sleep in your own bed!'

If you'd still been around, his desire to look like an enlightened man in front of you might've triumphed. You understood these things. I'd heard you talking about them with Sherine, the year before: 'There comes a time in every girl's life when she needs to get away and be her own person... I felt like that, and so did Amanda,' you'd said. 'I'll talk to him, nearer the time.'

And you'd put your hand on Sherine's arm and given it that quick little rub that meant 'Don't worry, everything will be okay.'

But never mind you. Why didn't Mama stand up for Sherine instead of lurking in the background like a shadow? An imposter in that house, not an inhabitant. Doing nothing, saying nothing, leaving Sherine to fight her own corner, night after night: 'Why did you bring us to England if you expect us to live like we're in Tunisia?'

'Ha! Yes! I brought you to England and now I wish I hadn't, all it's done is put the devil in your heart, giving you these ideas… you'll stay here in your home, madam, don't you dare think you're English just because you live in this cesspit of a country.'

'But all my friends are going away—'

'Your friends! Ha! Don't talk to me about your friends, those cheap, easy girls… And don't you dare think you're going to leave home and take up with someone the way those girls do, some "John" or "Dave" or "Steve"…'

The two of them fighting downstairs, shuffling from the living room to the dining room to the kitchen – forget the loft conversion, he'd converted the whole ground floor into a boxing ring. Me and Mama listened upstairs, from our hiding places under the covers. When I thought of her in the little room next door, I wanted to jump up and drag her out of bed, switch on the light, expose her ruined face and slap it into action, make her do something for once in her life instead of always letting things be done to her, and to us. Passing headlights flashed like lightning into the room, syncopation to the thunderclaps downstairs and the thudding of my heart. No proper curtains on our windows – no one ever bought them. Just flimsy nets that left us all lit up like shadow-puppets at night, on show to passers-by. No real curtains in the old flat either, or the top floor of Mrs Kowalski's house. Curtains were the final frontier, representing some kind of permanence that our parents weren't ready to accept. An acknowledgement that this country really was our home, not a blip in our family history.

When the beaten boxer staggered upstairs and collapsed onto her bed, she got no encouragement from the crowd. No 'Well done' or 'Keep trying' or 'It's your life, Sherine, keep fighting for it'. What she got was a lump in the bed a foot away from hers, keeping as still as it could. Pretending it couldn't hear the shuddering sobs Sherine was trying to muffle by sticking her head under the quilt.

*

Perhaps to make up for forbidding Sherine from going to Bristol, That Man let me go to Cyprus with Mariana. Just for a week – a half-term trip, to stay with her nan and grandad.

That holiday was our last-chance saloon, in a way. Mariana was off to a different sixth form next year. 'Where no one knows my name,' she said, alluding to what the little pigs had done to her, and I missed the chance to say, 'How are you, Mariana?', not knowing how to ask the question.

I got to let my hair down in Cyprus, literally and metaphorically. My ponytail could finally stand down: no father around to have a fit at the hair texture with too much Africa that he passed on to me. Starched collar got to rest its weary bones, too: I wore T-shirts on that holiday. In clothes borrowed from Mariana, I looked almost like a normal girl.

Daylight hours in Cyprus were for the family: Mariana's little brother and sister, uncles, aunts and cousins. The beach, the mountains, houses and flats. I discovered that family could be comforting, like a soft, warm blanket, as long as it was someone else's family. One day we passed a scorched mountain in the car on the way to Paphos and an uncle said, waving his arm at it: 'The British.' An army training exercise gone wrong. It was October 1990: they were practising for Operation Desert Storm.

At night, Mariana and I would get dressed up and go out to the bars in Limassol. Early, before the crowds came out, before her grandparents started fretting. As we paraded up and down the same strip of road, Mariana would peer into the windows and doorways of bars, a dissatisfied look on her face. 'There's no one around,' she'd say. One day there was, a guy in his early twenties who she knew through family. They had an intense conversation in Greek while I sipped two Malibu and Cokes, wondering why I wasn't feeling carefree and light, as alcohol was supposed to make you feel. When he got up to leave, he ruffled her hair to say goodbye and she swore at his back – '*poushti malaka*' – then laughed to me: 'He thinks I'm still six!'

We got what she was looking for in the cab home, but from the wrong person: a middle-aged taxi driver who ran his eyes all over us before parking them down her turquoise wrap-top and up my black ten-denier tights. 'I feel like I have to have another shower now!' she said, making puking noises when we got out of the taxi. 'Fucking dirty old man.'

I was already holding her hand when she started crying. We were lying on two mattresses shoved close to each other in the covered balcony we were sharing with her little brother and sister. Their peaceful sleep-breathing merged with the sound of the sea in the distance.

'I don't know who to trust any more,' she said, and I gripped her hand tightly and said, 'Shhh, shhh.' She cried, with her hand in mine, until we fell asleep. In the moments before I drifted off, I remembered a secret I needed to tell her. Something buried. Something that made me feel dirty too. But it was gone by the morning, along with her tears.

*

As for Mama, perhaps she wouldn't have bothered making a new friend if you'd still been there.

She met him a year or so after the nakba. When her face had repaired itself, to the extent it ever did. When she'd created a new mask for it. This friend was a man at her college, Greek but raised in Egypt. Small, baldish, slightly tubby. He looked like anyone's Greek dad. They talked in Arabic and English. Mariana and I ran into them once in Turnpike Lane, and Mariana chatted away in English and Greek, and Mama said to me later, 'Why can't you be friendly like Mariana?'

Her new friend would call her at home sometimes, in the late afternoon or early evening before That Man got back. They'd chat about college, their children, what was going on in the world.

'My youngest daughter, Nesrine, she's doing her EGCEEs this year. She says she wants to be a psychologist, I said to her, "Why do you want to spend your life listening to other people's problems, haven't we got enough problems of our own?" The oldest one, Sherine, she's at university now studying law... no, no, here in London.'

She talked in a voice that was low but not a whisper, from the phone in the hallway downstairs. All out in the open: nothing that would make her go into That Man's room and shut the door like Sherine and I did when we talked to our friends.

One Saturday afternoon, Mama arranged to meet her new friend for a coffee. I was the only one in the house when she came into our bedroom to say goodbye: Sherine had gone to the library and then to do the shopping in the second-hand car That Man had bought her when she passed her A-levels. Two As and a B. The weekly shop at Safeway's came as part of the package. That was her consolation prize for giving up Bristol.

Mama had a new, orangey lipstick on. She was wearing a light-green dress and a pair of orange shoes we didn't see very often.

'Tell him I've gone shopping with Sherine if he phones,' she said.

Nothing unusual. All of us were always telling That Man we were somewhere other than where we were, for no particular reason.

'Okay!' I said, head full of Joan Miró. 'Have a nice time.'

Our art homework that week was to draw the alphabet in the style of an artist of our choice. I'd chosen Miró not because he was my favourite artist but because his squiggles looked easy to shoehorn into some kind of alphabet before the *Brookside* omnibus came on at 5pm.

When I got to the letter 'M', I looked out of the window and saw Mama walking slowly back up the road towards the house.

M for mother, a nice coincidence. She looked different – smiling slightly, lips parted, walking in a way she didn't normally walk, swinging her arms, swaying her hips. When was the last time I'd seen her like that? I knew when. A flashback, gone in a second. Free and unburdened, not a care in the world, not my mother, not my letter M. She should've been careful. Bang bang went my heart, hurting like someone had smacked it for the sins of another. A funny taste in my mouth. The paint went wobbly and indecisive, even more than usual with watercolours. Hated them, should've used acrylics, my alphabet was a pile of shit. I threw my paintbrush onto a piece of newspaper and rushed downstairs to greet her.

'That lipstick makes you look like a fat clown,' I said as soon as she opened the door, before she'd had a chance to say hello.

She turned away as if she'd been slapped. I ran back upstairs to the bedroom and bit myself as hard as I could on my left arm, stopping when I saw traces of blood. Then I went back downstairs and showed her the bite mark. 'I'm sorry, Mama.'

We hugged each other tightly, our bodies clenching and unclenching as we cried without a sound. Anemone, I thought, for no particular reason.

The Gulf between them

There was a brief period when it seemed they might make it. Hope rolled into our house on 2 August 1990, the day Iraq invaded Kuwait.

We were in the middle of a heatwave. Mama and I were at home, both on our summer holidays.

'Go to Vinay's and get us an ice cream. That new Mars one for me,' she said, fanning her face with a bit of cardboard ripped off a tissue box. 'Then come back and tell me what they're saying.'

We were standing in front of the TV, watching the news that had interrupted some other programme.

When I got back from the corner shop, she was talking to someone on the phone in the hallway.

'What about the United Nations?' she was saying. 'And the Americans? That son of a dog Saddam, he's going to set the world on fire. And they don't care either, as long as they get their oil.'

Her voice was relaxed, animated – no hard, sulky edge to it like when she talked to That Man, or cautious formality like when she spoke to Sherine.

'Who were you talking to?' I said, handing her the already melting ice cream on a saucer when she put the phone down and came into the living room.

'Baba. There's not much work going on in Edgware Road today... They're all watching the news. He told me not to bother cooking in this heat. He'll bring home shawarma if you don't mind eating late?'

'No, that's fine.'

An unfamiliar impulse came over me – I actually wanted That Man to come home. Sherine could hurry up and get back from her summer job at John Lewis too. For the first time I could remember, I wanted us all to sit together, as a family, and watch the show unfold.

When the others came back, we ate the shawarma on trays in front of the TV, our conversation flowing with an ease I'd never witnessed before in this room. Saddam Hussein's moustachioed, jowly, pockmarked face seemed to have achieved a miraculous feat: it had made us forget about ourselves, and each other. It had turned us into a normal family. So we could do it too, when the stars were on our side.

Something of this spirit infected the start of school in September. Something bigger than timetables and homework diaries and new desk configurations. A columnist wrote an article for *The Sun* denouncing British women married to Iraqi men for their disloyalty, talking about their 'hideous husbands' and 'unattractive children', and I used it for a media studies essay on racism in the media. I can't remember where I got the article from. Maybe a friend or teacher came across it and cut it out for me, knowing I was interested. Or maybe I went looking for it myself, scenting concrete proof of something I'd always suspected: that it wasn't a good thing to be 'an Arab'. Filthy rich or just plain filthy, violent fanatic or oppressed member of a harem. Hook-nosed, mendacious – lucky us, sharing stereotypes with our cousins, 'the Jews'; though we were never typecast as being overburdened with entrepreneurial spirit or intellectual prowess. There was a certain satisfaction to be had in seeing these sentiments expressed without reserve, or with only the thinnest veneer – something validatory and bracing about it.

It didn't last long, the change that swept into our world. Defeated by the mundanity of everyday life, Saddam Hussein faded into the background. School was still school; home was still home. Things went back to normal – our normal, not the normal normal. Even when Operation Desert Storm began, the impact was subdued, rather like the war itself, or so it seemed. Cold, technological, precise. Like a video game, as people kept saying. None of the gruesome viscera of wars I'd read about or seen in films. Nothing to inspire a Wilfred Owen or a Siegfried Sassoon, whose poems we were studying for GCSE English.

'Sons of dogs,' our parents would say sometimes, watching a flashing white star punch the sky open above Baghdad, but more to themselves than to each other.

Then they bombed a bunker full of civilians, and Mama couldn't stop crying. '*Haram, haram,*' she kept saying. 'What did those people do to deserve that?' According to the Americans, it was largely their own fault. Something to do with Arabs not respecting the sanctity of life, even their own. Allowing themselves to be put in that bunker by Saddam.

I cried a bit too at first, but then it became too much. Melodramatic. Affected, almost. '*Yezzi, ya Mama,*' I said. Enough. 'Don't upset yourself, crying won't change anything.' Feeling sage and pleasantly world-weary. An adult comforting a child who didn't understand the ways of the world, who hadn't managed to cultivate the necessary immunity to its cruelty.

Ignoring me, she flicked from channel to channel throughout the evening, watching the same footage of women in black wailing for their dead, her eyes darting back and forth across the screen as if looking for someone she knew in their midst. 'They won't even show us the bodies,' she said. 'The criminals.'

I woke up just before midnight that night and saw the hall light still on. Some instinct told me she wasn't in her room. She normally went to bed right after the 10 o'clock news. Was That

Man home yet? Opening the door quietly, tiptoeing into the hall, I heard her in the living room. She was crying again, quite loudly, saying, 'Haram, haram, why should they have been killed like that? Like insects, as if their lives didn't matter.'

He was home. It was him she was talking to. He said something about dogs and God, and then as she kept sobbing, I heard him say in an odd, muffled voice, 'Forgive me, Bouthaina.'

What did he mean? It wasn't him who'd bombed that bunker. He said something else I couldn't hear, and then, 'Forgive me, forgive me, forgive me.'

When I realised he was crying too, I crept back to the bedroom and got into bed, my heart slamming against my chest. Sleep was out of the question. I tried to cry too – and why not? This seemed to be the night for it, after all – but the tears wouldn't come. Something heavier than sadness was stifling them. In the bed next to me, Sherine was sound asleep, snoring gently, her eyes covered with the mask she used to block out the street lamps. Trying to move without ruffling the air around me, I reached for her new copy of The Unbearable Lightness of Being, which I'd already read twice, unbeknown to her. Sliding it under my quilt along with my torch, I flipped through the pages until I found what I was looking for: the bit where Tereza's dog dies.

Not long afterwards, a deep, luxurious sleep enfolded me, coaxed out by the shivery release of tears. It's easier to cry when you know what you're crying for. When the reasons are laid out for you in black and white.

Significant. Other.

June 2005

So that's what you left behind. Is this what you meant by a 'record'? Or was I supposed to compile a redacted version – one where the nakba never happened?

You asked me a question when I came to see you the second time. You said: 'Do you have a significant other?' Your choice of words kept echoing in my head. Significant. Other. Wasn't that what you'd been to all of us? I twisted my mouth into a smile of sorts and said, 'Not at the moment.' And then, my voice ringing into the hush of your room, I said, 'My first relationship was an open relationship.'

Perhaps you didn't realise that this was a card laid on the table – that I was offering to tell you who I was now, if you would tell me who you were.

Even if you did understand, you weren't playing. Your reply, so quiet I had to strain to hear it, seemed nothing more than the frayed edge of a wispy trail of thought: 'Simone de Beauvoir...'

I wanted it then, the thing that had scared me when it became a real possibility – the idea of 'closure'. I held my breath, thinking I was about to get it when I said, 'I've made lots of mistakes,' and your lips parted as if you were about to reply, 'So have I.'

But all you said was, 'We all make mistakes.' The finality of your words forced my shoulders into a slump as I exhaled.

What was it that stopped you from going any further? Was it my air of quivering anticipation? Or were you waiting for me to state my intentions plainly, like an adult? To stop pattering around the elephant in the room like a five-year-old waiting for someone else to take charge? How much effort did it take me to be as cowardly as I was then, knowing that experience had formed bridges and callbacks between your life and mine, and wanting so much to say things to you…?

My heart thudding from the force of all we weren't saying, I sat next to you averting my eyes from your thin, exhausted face. From your hair that had lost its brown and your skin that had lost its gold, as if I'd drawn you from memory but had forgotten to colour you in. I looked out of the sash window that almost touched the ceiling and grazed the floor, at the summer sky and the muddy white trunk of the silver birch in the garden: at all the things that still belonged to me but not you. When the pounding of my heart subsided, I said, 'It's such a lovely view from here, isn't it?' And then, as I closed the door of your room behind me and texted Sherine to tell her I was on my way home, I told myself, 'Next time. I'll talk to her properly next time.'

*

When the next time came, I sat hunched in the chair by your bed, crying. Holding a crumpled piece of tissue to my nose, I let my tears drip freely onto the grey tiled floor, and you were someone different again: not 'Genevieve' or 'Jenny' or 'Mrs Brown' or even the gaunt woman who'd replaced them, but someone else altogether.

'Ask me anything you want,' you said, your tongue finally loosened by my shameless abandonment of dignity, and I said, 'I think I saw you on the bed at Mrs Kowalski's house when I was four years old… You had mistletoe in your hand.'

When I said 'mistletoe', you flinched as if I'd hit you.

Cake and eat it

If you thought my open relationship came about from a desire to be Simone de Beauvoir, you misunderstood. It was driven by practical considerations – a simple cost–benefit analysis. Why should I break free of my prison at home only to enter a new one at university? Why should I tie myself down at the age of eighteen, leave myself open to betrayal and disappointment like Carly from Nuneaton who'd cried in her room for a week after she'd caught Dave, her new boyfriend, fingering Lisa, her new best friend, in the hall of residence next door?

I didn't want any of those things, but I still wanted a boyfriend. I wanted to be normal, to finally kiss goodbye to my junior accountant persona with her starched collar and a poker up her arse. I wanted closeness, companionship, sex and someone to argue with in a way that could easily be forgiven and forgotten – not like family arguments, which carried a whiff of danger akin to unscrewing the lid on a jar of tarantulas. My closest brush with a relationship so far had been a double date at the Ally Pally ice rink with Mariana and two cousins she knew from sixth form.

'I've told Stav how gorgeous you are!' she'd said as we made our way there on the W3 bus, sitting upstairs at the front. 'He can't wait to meet you!'

'Shut up, shut up!' I'd said, lapping it up as she threw compliments at me like roses. I'd made an effort that day: I'd put

Vaseline on my lips so they wouldn't crack and bleed in the cold, and borrowed a light-green corduroy jacket from Sherine that had pinged a button when I'd tried to do it up.

When we got off the bus and Mariana dragged me towards the two boys, I heard Mariana's one say to mine, 'Cuz, man! Don't fuck things up for me! You can't just leave. I swear I didn't know she was such a dog...'

Away from London, up north at university, I pitched the idea of an open relationship to my new boyfriend – or rather not-a-boyfriend – Michael, as he drove us out to the Peak District in his second-hand VW Golf. His driving was smooth, confident, easy, like how a real adult drove, someone who'd been driving for much longer than a year. This bestowed a maturity on him that almost made me forget he was my age and a virgin too. I'd been hoping for someone older, who knew what they were doing.

'What's the point of putting each other in chains like that?' I said as the car chugged up another twisty corridor of swaying fir trees. 'It'd be different if we were twenty-five and ready to settle down, but we have to be realistic. Nothing lasts forever.'

On the cassette player, Massive Attack's downbeat registers whispered their agreement. Like Massive Attack, Michael was from Bristol, or rather from somewhere 'near Bristol'. Everyone at university seemed to be from near somewhere, not the place itself. It was his accent that had drawn me to him. *Gurrrl. Wurrrld.* I wanted to eat it.

'Some people meet when they're eighteen and stay together all their lives...' he said.

'Yeah, but what are the chances? Anyway, those people don't have our family shit to deal with, do they?'

Right on cue, the miniature Virgin Mary in the windscreen gave a little rattle. I'd christened her Our Lady of the Dashboard, which pissed him off. 'At least she didn't marry a nine-year-old,' he'd said, and I'd felt my face turning hot, as if he'd just called one of my uncles a paedophile. I'd bitten my tongue, though. He'd already accused me of hypocrisy for calling myself an agnostic-slash-atheist but going into meltdown when I found a stray morsel of pig in my cauliflower cheese. 'It's only a bit of bacon,' one of the dinner ladies in the canteen had muttered, rolling her eyes when I'd taken it back and asked for something else instead.

'I mean, we know it can't last after college, don't we?' I said. 'Seeing as your parents expect you to marry a Catholic and mine expect me to marry a Muslim.'

'It's out of order,' said Michael, changing gears with an uncharacteristic abruptness. 'You hardly even know any Muslims, do you? And your parents know you're not religious, don't they?'

'Yeah, but we all have to pretend. Me and Sherine have to pretend to believe in what they believe, and our mum and dad have to pretend to believe that we believe, so they don't lose face.'

'What would they do if they found out you were an atheist? Would they have you stoned to death? You know, a whaddyamacallit, an honour killing?'

'Shut the fuck up!' In my indignation, I accidentally spat on the Virgin Mary's head. 'What kind of savages do you think we are? They'd just be really upset, that's all. They'd feel like they'd failed us as parents, by bringing us to England and then letting our souls drift into ruin.'

The word 'soul' drew a rumble of recognition from Michael. Souls were something he understood. He'd had them shoved down his throat since childhood, and seemed to have digested them better than I had. He wore a miraculous medal tucked inside his T-shirts and went to Mass every Sunday – Wednesdays too sometimes, and other days as well if it was a holy day of obligation. He'd once walked three miles to return a packet of envelopes he'd absentmindedly slipped into his coat pocket in the post office. 'Well, I couldn't just keep them, could I – that would've been stealing!' he'd said, when I asked him why he'd bothered over something so trivial.

'I don't want to lie to you,' I said. 'You know how I feel about you, but I don't wanna be with just one person right now. I can't put myself in prison again when I've only just escaped.'

'Why is it prison if you love someone?'

'Because… Because things always end up being prison. Isn't it better to be honest about what you want than to lie and cheat and demean yourself and other people in the process?'

He made an indeterminate noise that I chose to interpret as assent.

When we got to the little village we'd picked out from his map book, we sat in a coffee shop eating Bakewell tart and talking about how funny it would be if I pretended to convert to Catholicism and he pretended to convert to Islam.

'Then we could be together, properly, forever,' he'd said, throwing up his hands in mock horror, and I'd pinned one of his legs between mine, nearly upending our wobbly table in the process.

So what did an open relationship mean in practice? Probably nothing much different from what most relationships mean to most eighteen-year-olds. The occasional exchange of kisses and drunken fumbles with other people, sometimes resulting in ruffled feathers, wounded egos and sulks. The sporadic burning desire to be with someone else or to be free of relationships altogether. Several long patches where nothing much happened and life ticked along as usual, like it does for old married couples.

I only really realised what was different when Lisa, the scarlet woman from the hall next door, said to me, 'I heard you got off with a Welsh nationalist plumber at Innuendo the other night and Michael was devastated about it.'

'Oh yeah? Who told you that?'

'Michael told Dave. He says he can't stand this open relationship business but he puts up with it because he doesn't want to lose you. I hate to say it, Nessie, but I think it's a bit cheeky – it kind of seems like you want to have your cake and eat it.'

'Fucking bitch!' I whispered later to my new friend, Amy from Hounslow, as we sat in the library making notes. 'Who does she think she is to lecture me about relationships? I wanted to say to her, "Listen, darling, wasn't it a bit cheeky when you let Dave finger you when he was still going out with Carly?"'

'That's how people are,' said Amy. 'They want everyone else to behave like them because it makes them feel better about their own choices.'

'I don't care how dysfunctional our relationship might seem to other people,' I said as I copied an R-squared equation into my notepad. 'That's between me and him. At least I'm not lying and sneaking around. How dare she, the fucking cow, with her have your cake and eat it!'

I must've raised my voice too much when I added, with a touch of the Simone de Beauvoirs, 'I'm not gonna live a lie to satisfy societal norms. I might have to lie and sneak around at home, but I refuse to do it in my personal life. I need to live a truthful life!' That's when people looked up and said shush.

I'd learned something from Lisa, though. I'd learned that society didn't really care if you wanted to have your cake and eat it as long as you ate it just like everyone else: sitting on a picnic blanket woven from secrets and lies.

In dreams

I started dreaming about you soon after I went to university, as if my subconscious could only process you from a safe distance. Away from That Man and Mama and Sherine and anyone else who'd ever known you.

The dreams came sporadically, when they felt like it, separated by months or years. Catching me out when it seemed you'd almost slipped out of my brain. They buckled under the weight of a symbolism that would've had a psychologist weeping into their hands at my lack of originality: the one where we were in your car, parked outside the gates of my primary school, and I suddenly realised I was naked. The one where my teeth fell out as we sat at your dining table eating those weird green balls made of sugar and food colouring that I once saw on *Saturday Superstore* and begged you to let me make at your flat. The one where I had to take a book back to your library, but a small turquoise man wearing a sombrero in the shape of a Californian sunset kept snatching the book out of my hands.

The unusual thing about these dreams was that in them, I was me *and* you. I inhabited your form even as I observed it. Your thoughts were mine and so were your emotions, experienced with a keenness that gave me the sensation a hand was using my heart as a stress ball while I slept.

'Why are you crying?' Michael asked me once when I woke up with tears streaming down my face. All I could say was, 'Because it felt so sad.'

'Do you miss her?' he said when I tried to explain, and I shook my head, unable to convey what I'd been feeling. 'Not exactly,' I replied, brushing the dream and the conversation aside.

In case you were wondering, people knew about you – people I was close to. I explained who you were and the circumstances of your disappearance at least once to each of my inner circle. It was one of those facts we feel compelled to disclose about ourselves to explain certain aspects of our personalities. My mistrust of monogamy. My ability to pronounce certain words I had no right to even know, my parents being who they were. My visceral aversion to Andrew Lloyd Webber and musical theatre more generally. My determination not to pollute the life I'd chosen for myself with deceit and subterfuge. Your existence and your actions were no secret. I created an avatar of you to present to the world, using words like 'librarian', 'English', 'theatre ticket' and *Cats*.

'We had a friend,' I would say. 'A family friend...' And sometimes I would say: 'Her name was Genevieve.' Why only sometimes? Because naming you made me feel like I was making you up: fabricating a story about a woman called 'Genevieve Brown' to make my childhood and my family sound more interesting than they were. It turned you from an uneasy memory into an improbable fiction – like the fantasies Mariana and I used to concoct that we were adopted, and that the proof lurked somewhere amid the piles of junk that ran like a mountain range across all our houses and flats, those of us whose parents came from somewhere else.

'What was she like?' Amy asked me once. 'She sounds like a right sneaky tart – making out she cared about you when all she was interested in was getting her end away with your dad!'

'No,' I said calmly, dispassionately, as if we were discussing a character in a TV programme. 'She wasn't like that... she wasn't some kind of... I don't know... *strumpet.*

'She was tall,' I said lamely. 'Elegant, everything about her was *elegant*. I don't know how else to describe her...'

'Elegant!' said Amy, laughing because it was the kind of word we only ever used ironically, in village-idiot voices, like 'dainty' or 'sophisticated'. I laughed too. How ridiculous was it that even if I turned you into a soap opera character, I still didn't know how to describe you?

Tall. Elegant. English. A librarian. A woman who once took a man to the theatre to watch *Cats*. A woman who'd said she was our friend. They were the clues I dished out for other people to make of you what they would.

It wasn't a conscious decision to conceal other, perhaps more pertinent facts about you. Things that might've explained the crushing sadness that crept into my sleeping brain. They were still hidden at that point, even from me. Buried in a place that goes deeper than dreams, if such a place exists. It would take time, and the mess I made of my own life, to dig them out and finally give them the recognition they deserved.

Leaving where?

When I told the story of my parents' marriage in later years, the chronology sometimes caused confusion. 'Five years!' someone once said to me. 'Why did it take your mum five whole years to leave him after she found out he'd cheated on her?'

Mama's bombshell came charging up the M1 on a blustery day in March 1994. It burst through the double doors of my hall of residence and into my ears when I least expected it. It blew my wheels off.

I was eighteen years old, two hundred miles away from home. Gliding round bossing my day into submission. About to leave my unhappy marriage to Business Studies, the drab suitor That Man had set me up with, for my heart's desire of English Literature and Linguistics – unbeknown to the matchmaker. And what would That Man think if he knew I'd secured a part-time job in the kitchens downstairs? Wearing a uniform! Serving people! Slopping food scraps into pig buckets! Nothing the daughter of *people* should be doing. All this had been arranged with uncharacteristic calmness and efficiency. I felt like I was evolving into the kind of person who might one day be trusted to operate heavy machinery, like Sherine, who could drive a car *and* ride a bike; so far, I'd never learned to do either.

The note was lying on the floor of my room when I got back from rearranging my life. A scrap of yellow paper folded into a strange, jagged formation, like an origami bird of ill-omen. *Ring your sister at work*, it said. *URGENTLY*. I started to cry. Someone was dead. Someone had died. What else would be so URGENT? At least it wasn't Sherine, if she was the one who'd left the message. Grabbing a handful of coins, I flew downstairs to the phone box on the mezzanine floor, the only one with a semblance of privacy.

She answered with a terse 'Sherine speaking.'

'Who is it?' I snivelled.

'Huh?'

'Huh?'

'What do you mean, who is it? You phoned me and I said my name – you know who it is.'

'What is it?' I said, taking it from the beginning. Her snappy tone had brought my galloping heartbeat back in check. It couldn't be someone that important if their death had given rise to annoyance rather than devastation.

She sighed heavily. 'Listen – before you phone home today, there's something you need to know: Mama's leaving and *he* says it's all our fault.'

'What do you mean – leaving? Leaving where?'

'England. Him. She says she's had enough. She wants to go back to Tunisia.'

'But what... I just spoke to her two days ago. What...?'

'Are you honestly that surprised? You surely can't have been deluded enough to think they had a happy marriage?'

Something about the clipped, brutal way she was speaking made me wince. Why was she being like this? Her voice vibrated with irritation, as if the whole thing was a massive pain in the arse, like the last-minute meetings people kept asking her to organise at the places where she temped while she looked for a permanent job. An inconvenience rather than the rip to the heart those words had caused me. Mama leaving? How could that be? And why hadn't she said anything herself the last time we'd spoken?

'Yeah, I know.' I forced myself to sound as unburdened by sadness as she was. 'But I don't get it. Why now?'

'I suppose there's nothing here for her any more,' she said. There was a sharpness to her voice that pierced through my own turmoil.

'Shit.' My throat constricted. 'But why's he saying it's all our fault?'

A grim snort this time. 'Oh, you know him – always looking for someone else to blame. He says we were bad daughters. We didn't help out enough at home. We made her feel like a servant instead of pulling our weight.'

'What the fuck is he on about?'

'Yep. Anyway, I have to go and fax a two-hundred-page document now. That's my lunch break gone. Oh well. We'll talk properly later. I just wanted you to know before you phoned them, so you didn't get a shock.'

I stood staring at the phone when we hung up. Was I going to ring Mama now, or was I going to seek counsel and comfort from the other two first? Hugs and hair stroking from Michael, my not-a-boyfriend; candid advice from my friend Amy.

'Excuse me,' said a high, wispy voice behind me. 'Have you finished with the phone?' A speaker of Nicely. Thin, pale face, blonde hair in a bun, smiling awkwardly as I turned around. A waif. How old was she and what was she doing at a university? Probably a child prodigy, a precocious chess player who'd be on crack by the time she reached twenty-one. She was an irritant in any case.

'Umm, do I look like I've finished?' I repackaged all the hardness from Sherine's voice into mine. The waif's smile snuffed out. She took a step backwards, muttering, 'Sorry.' It was a thing Amy and I had joked about, how we had this effect on some people at university. 'These posh wankers from the Home Counties think we're well 'ard just because we're from London,' she'd said gleefully. 'Watch this,' I'd whispered once when we were in the queue for the toilets at a Jamiroquai concert and a braying donkey had tried to push in front of us. 'Excuse me,' I'd said, tapping her on the shoulder. 'There's a queue here.' Then I'd faced her down and kissed my teeth and she'd gone skulking off to the back. 'She's probably never met an ethnic minority before in all her life!' I said to Amy, cracking up when we got out of the toilets, feeling safe enough to say this because I knew her best friend back in Hounslow was Nigerian.

But now that I'd driven the waif away, what excuse did I have not to use the phone? Hands shaking, I dialled the 081 number.

'Phone me back,' I said as soon as Mama picked up. No way was this was going to be a fifty pence kind of call.

'Your sister's told you, hasn't she?' she said, her voice swimming in tears. 'I can tell from your voice…'

'Why, Mama?' I started to cry again too. 'I don't understand… and why didn't you tell me yourself?'

'You know why, *hbibti*. You know I can't stand this country – and now you're gone, what reason do I have to stay here?'

Did it cross my mind to point out that she had another daughter too? If it did, the thought was too flimsy to stick.

'But why didn't you tell me?'

'I was going to, *hbibti*, but it was hard. I knew you'd be upset, and I'm so upset too, believe me. I couldn't do it if you were here in front of me, if I was looking at your precious face, *ma perle…*'

'I'll come! I'll come down to London tonight, as soon as I can get a train, and we'll talk properly—'

'No! Please…'

And now her rising voice had woken another from its slumber, the rumble growing to a roar as it approached the phone.

'Nesrine! Come home immediately and tell your mother you're sorry! Tell her you're sorry for leaving her like that and running away… God curse the day I ever gave in to your sister and let you go. Tell her you want her to stay!'

'Why isn't he at work?' I said, but she was already warming up for her response: 'You son of a dog, don't you dare blame her for this – why is nothing ever your fault?'

And off they went, all the old names they called each other, dogs and donkeys and bitches, skipping down the phone and into my ears. I listened for a few seconds before I hung up, breathing in that choking way you do when you're crying.

The waif was in the library when I walked through it on the way to the lift. Suddenly, the urge to apologise swept over me, as if I'd stuck my finger into a socket connecting me to all the world's sorrow. A wave of shame surged through me as I looked at her lank, stringy hair, her spindly frame and fast-blinking lashes, her shoulders that barely occupied the space of one of my thighs, her hands that twitched nervously like a rabbit's nose. Why had I lashed out at this helpless little runt whose only crime was to want to make a phone call? What kind of evil bitch was I to bring darkness into someone else's life just because of my fucked-up family? I slowed down as I approached her table, keeping my tear-streaked face pinned to hers, willing her to look up as I got the 'Sorry' ready on my lips... but her eyes stayed glued to her notebook as she fumbled with her biros and highlighter pens.

Could adulthood be peeled off you, like a painful, involuntary leg-wax? It seemed possible as I shuffled past her, wiping my dripping nose on the back of my hand. What was I but an imposter? A pathetic child beneath my veneer of independence.

*

Mama left the following Thursday. I cried for two months. It felt so physical, the loss of her. A hard lump crept into my throat during tutorials, making me sound like a spluttering idiot when I tried to speak. A shared laughing fit with Amy ended with me rolling round sobbing on the floor. 'What's wrong?' she said.

'What's wrong with you?' and I said, 'Nothing, nothing,' lying weak and wrung out on the scratchy brown carpet. I was too ashamed to tell her I was crying for my mother. What was I, eighteen or eight?

The nights were easier. I started to dream I was three or four again, lying next to her, burrowing into her skin, inhaling the smell that could only belong to her. Transported back into babyhood, I started licking Michael's nose when we went to bed, drooling slightly at this delicious, long-forgotten sensation. Why didn't the experts tell you the skin on a loved one's nose contained everything you needed to keep you alive? 'This is weird,' he'd say sometimes, but he let me do it, propped semi-upright on one of our narrow beds, holding the pose with intense concentration as I went about my business.

Without really noticing, I looked for her everywhere. In the rows of faces in lecture halls. In the student union bar. On sticky dance floors when I went out with Amy – those nights when we split up and prowled around with our drinks in our hands. Sometimes I found her. A hint of her smile in Dan, a laconic geography student from Runcorn. A strong resemblance to her eyes in Andrew, a nervy engineering student from Egypt via Worksop. An almost identical replica of her nose in Khaled, a garrulous builder from Barnsley. They thought I was weird, those guys, because all I wanted to do was hug them. They didn't know that anything else would've been incest. It was enough just to have them in my arms for those precious few moments, letting her presence drift over me again.

I went to Tunis to see her in September, laden with gifts: Jaffa cakes, Encona hot sauce, tandoori chicken paste, cosmetics from The Body Shop, a grey silk scarf Sherine had bought her from Selfridges; it cost nearly as much as my plane ticket, which she'd paid for too.

'Tell her I'm sorry I can't come this time,' she said. 'It's just the timing... I can't go on holiday just after I start.'

She'd finally been offered a place on a graduate training scheme.

'My oldest daughter is a management consultant!' That Man went round telling the world, revived from the shell-shocked state he'd been in since Mama left. 'Business,' he said, waving his hand like a Jedi mind-trickster in the face of the toothless old bloke next door who asked what that meant.

Mama hugged me like a boa constrictor when she came to meet me at the airport in Tunis.

'Have you shrunk?' I said, laughing and crying, when we finally let go of each other.

'No, *hbibti*, you've grown!' She stepped back to look at me, making me feel like a nine-year-old.

She looked older than I remembered, as if months had turned into years unnoticed. Her hair was longer and thinner, worn in a low bun that dragged her face down. Her neck was thinner too and her waist was fatter.

We got back to her flat and I said how nice it was. Was it nice? It was big. It had a balcony, giving her the space to pace around in her long white nighty, a restless, unsettled air about her.

'Did you used to smoke, Mama?' I said, suddenly seeing her with different eyes, and she clapped her hand to her heart and said, 'How did you know? I gave up when you were a baby... I didn't want you to pick it up too.'

Her flat had two sofas: one for family and one for guests. The guest sofa stayed permanently covered in the plastic wrapper it came in. No pictures on the walls. That Man didn't have any either, and neither did I in my room at university. A hangover from living in places where scarring the walls could get you in deep shit, or so they'd believed. What were immigrants, after all, but guests in someone else's house? My best effort was a Giorgio de Chirico postcard Blu-Tacked onto my wardrobe door. Sherine was the first to pick up a hammer and nails and defile her walls with art, just like an English person would, without fear of eviction or deportation.

We only got our British passports because of you, remember. He was too scared to try and she didn't care.

Mama made a sound like a child on Christmas Day when she unfolded the silk scarf. 'Your sister has such a good eye! She should've been a fashion designer.'

The Body Shop lipsticks sent a procession of frowns across her face as she puckered her lips in the mirror. 'Why did you choose this shade of pink, *azizti*? It's too bright.' 'Why such a brown colour? It makes me look so grubby and dark.' 'Sorry *hbibti*, you keep them for yourself – I don't want to waste them.'

Like a five-year-old, I hated Sherine for a few seconds then. Her with her flawless, impeccable taste.

It was strange seeing Mama in this new place of hers. Even though it was hers, she occupied it like a diffident stranger. But hadn't she always done that? Made everywhere feel like a hotel where she was part of the staff, not the management. I watched her with different eyes, feeling like she wasn't really my mother but someone else: someone I loved dearly but didn't know very well.

'Tell me all your news,' she said, and I smiled blankly – what could I tell her about my life that didn't need a thick black line crossed through it? I asked her about her work instead.

'It's good to work,' she said, with pride. 'It gives you purpose. The boss knows I'm serious, not like those ones who gossip all day and bring their salad vegetables in to chop at their desks.'

We sat quietly for most of those three weeks. Watching TV, nibbling on pumpkin seeds, eating grapes, flicking through the magazines I'd brought, ones with lots of pictures. Routine stepped into the breach where news had failed. She started to feel like my mother again. I cried for a week when I went back to England.

*

Sherine came with me the next summer. They circled each other warily. Leopards don't change their spots. In honour of the special guest, Mama pulled out all the stops. Djellabas shoved nighties to one side, pumpkin seeds stayed put in their packets, the nice Turkish tea set came out to play at night. Polite conversation was in order. Wasn't work the obvious candidate, now that they were both working women?

'Do you have to wear a uniform to work?' said Mama. 'Do you work behind the till at this bank of yours?' 'What time do you start and finish every day?'

'No,' said Sherine and 'It's not exactly a bank' and 'I stay until the work gets done.' 'Oh, and you're a dipshit,' said her crisp, formal tone.

My face grew hot at this voice, and at the interrogation that had provoked it. Why wasn't 'management consultant' good enough for Mama, like it was for That Man? Why did she have to look a gift horse in the mouth and pull the seeds of her own humiliation out through its teeth? And why was her jaw twitching like that? Hands tugging at her djellaba – a fancy, bright-pink one – she turned away from Sherine and said to me: 'Why are you wearing your hair in a big bush like that? It looks horrible, like a bird's nest – let me brush it for you.'

'No,' I said. 'Leave me alone. You know I can't brush my hair unless it's wet!' Throwing my hand up in her face like a five-year-old again. Sitting on the guest sofa with *Marie Claire* on her lap, Sherine said quietly, 'Her hair looks nice. Leave her alone.'

There was a picture of sorts in Mama's living room now. An inscription from the Koran, chunky gold calligraphy embossed on an expanse of black velvet, framed in a baroque monstrosity that matched the gilded arms of the red Louis Farouk guest sofa. A harbinger of the hijab she'd start wearing the following year.

'Classy,' muttered Sherine, casting her eyes up at the wall, making a stabbing motion through her chest when Mama went to the kitchen. I had to put my hand over my mouth to squash the splutter that came out.

'When did you two become such good friends?' said Mama later, when it was just me and her. I shrugged my shoulders and fidgeted. My turn to pick up *Marie Claire*.

Sherine and I got drunk on the flight home to England, giggling over the velvet inscription, the perma-plastic sofa, the china shepherdess in Mama's display cabinet, the way she'd started pinching the pennies when she didn't need to, now she was earning her own money.

'Did you hear her arguing with Tante Ghalia about the money for that chicken she bought her from the market?' Sherine said, crying with laughter. 'I was half expecting her to get the scales out and weigh it herself!'

I laughed too. Yes, Mama was right, her daughters were friends now. Partly it had crept up on us. Partly it was because Sherine had fought tooth and claw for my right to go drinking and whoring up north and sleep in a bed that wasn't my own. Tooth: 'Let her go to university where she wants,' she'd said to That Man, stabbing her finger in his face. 'Don't you dare ruin her life like you ruined mine!' When he'd lunged at her, she'd grabbed his hand and sunk her teeth into it. Claw: when Mama chimed in, sobbing, 'Why are you trying to take my daughter away from me?' Sherine had laid her hand on her arm. I only realised she'd dug her nails in when Mama screamed and snatched her arm away.

At some point on the flight back to London, I got up and went to the toilet, where I cried too, over the velvet picture, Mama's thinning hair that showed patches of her scalp, the china shepherdess. Her bright, frantic eyes, and the way she'd questioned Sherine like a child asking *Why is the sky blue?* or *What's rain?*

My tears lasted as long as it takes to have a piss, wash your hands and wipe the sink down for the next passenger.

Leopards don't change their spots, but humans do. 'People change,' you said the last time I saw you, a catch-all for the inexplicable reasons why I didn't miss her any more. All the aching sadness of the world seemed contained in the word 'change'; in that single devastating syllable that died in the air as you exhaled.

Singed eyebrows

When I was a child, was I naive to think you were one of the few adults who possessed the wisdom they claimed? It was the way you said things – quiet, understated. The message itself was nothing radical: it was the kind of thing we heard in assembly as we slouched cross-legged on the floor, picking at the plastic covers on our *Come and Praise!* hymnbooks like scabs. Be nice to people. Think of others less fortunate than yourselves. Treat each moment with the people you love as if it might be the last. Give small cans of baked beans instead of big ones at harvest festival so old people don't stick the other half in the fridge and die of oxidisation.

But your voice elevated these homilies into something fit for real life, not an afterthought to 'He Who Would Valiant Be'. Like when I was nine and Mariana kept flirting with a girl called Sharon, a transplant to our junior school who talked like *Brookside* and had a bubble perm like Kevin Keegan's but flame-red, and, appropriately, a fireman dad.

'I hate that girl Sharon,' I said to you. 'I wish she'd go back to Liverpool.'

To which you replied, 'You have to let people be free, Nessie. No one belongs to anyone else. If Mariana's really your friend, she won't like you any less just because she's got a new friend.'

'But she didn't wait for me to walk home with her yesterday,' I said, my voice all over the place as I looked out of your car window, everything a blur. 'And she swapped her Asterix stickers with Sharon instead of me...'

With your usual tact, you let me compose myself, swiping away at my eyes, before you reached over and touched my shoulder, briefly taking your hand off the wheel. 'I know it's hard,' you said.

The downward cadence of your voice told me you did know; that it wasn't just a platitude.

Who were you thinking of, I wonder, when you talked about this need to let others be free? Was it the mysterious Mr Brown? Or perhaps you had someone closer to home – my home – in mind when your voice inflected in that gloomy way.

It's hard to reconcile your air of wistful, bitterly gained experience with the recklessness that drove you out of our lives. You once told me, 'Always count to ten before making important decisions, Nessie.' Did you count to ten before you went to the theatre with That Man? And again before you married someone else, two minutes after your escape from the carnage? Surely you were too old for that kind of madness when you finally succumbed to it. Turning the world into your science lab just to see what happened. Heedless of the loose wires that might electrocute your friend as she stood holding a crumpled piece of paper saying, 'What's this?' Aren't actions like that best left to the unthinking young? To people who still have time to recover if an experiment goes wrong and gives someone third-degree burns, or singed eyebrows at least.

*

Here's a picture of me, Amy and Michael, my not-a-boyfriend. It was taken a few hours before the singed eyebrows. Our smiles are as extravagantly theatrical as our makeup, our eyes gleaming with an alcoholic sheen. We think we are adults.

Here I am with my hair sticking up in two plaits like the devil's horns. Amy looks like a Celtic rose with her smooth pale skin, her sleek black hair recently cut in a 1920s bob. Michael's light-brown hair is fluffed up, his face caked in cheap cosmetics from Boots. His makeup was my and Amy's handiwork, done in swipes between swigs of perry, £1.23 a bottle from the Co-op up the road.

'More, more,' said Michael as we trowelled on the blue eyeshadow, scarlet lipstick and hectic pink blusher. Amy helped him stuff two tennis balls into a bra strapped to the outside of his T-shirt.

'Twins!' said Amy and I in unison as we stood next to each other looking at our reflections in the mirror: matching blue and white striped pyjama tops, boxer shorts borrowed from Michael, fishnet tights bought from the covered market in town. Other people called us twins all the time, even though we looked nothing alike. We were joined at the hip. We laughed at jokes only we understood. We could talk about things we'd never dream of sharing with our real sisters.

Who was it who took the picture of the three of us? Could it have been Tom, the elderly ex-factory foreman from next door, or his wife, Val? Unlikely. Amy is frozen in time standing behind Michael cupping his tennis balls and pretending to dry-hump him. I'm standing behind Amy doing the same. Ironically, of course. No, the photographer must've been a friend, a Cinderella who didn't manage to get a ticket to the ball – a fancy dress party for charity snaking across the nightclubs and pubs of this northern city that was in whatever comes after post-industrial decline.

'Come on, you slags, let's go!' said Michael, slapping someone on the arse and getting slapped in return. It seemed almost obligatory, dressed the way we all were.

As we left the house, I whispered to him, 'I bet not many people tonight are going out on the pull with their...'

'With their *boyfriends*,' he said, poking me in the ribs. I still refused to use that word though we'd been together nearly three years.

Several hours later, lips wet with alcohol and unfamiliar saliva, the three of us staggered home and went up to Amy's room in the attic. I called her Mrs Rochester sometimes. Michael didn't know what we were on about.

'I'm going to bed,' said Amy, flopping backwards onto the bed, pyjama top flying up to show her milky midriff. 'You two wankers can do what you want.'

'Let's all go to bed,' said Michael, collapsing next to her.

I wedged myself between them and put my hand on Amy's stomach. Feeling no resistance, I started stroking it slowly, cautiously. Amy squirmed like a cat in front of a fire, lifting her arms up, revealing more of her skin. Michael sat up, watching as I kissed Amy first on each temple, then on her neck, then on her lips, keeping my hand on her stomach.

At some point, I lay sideways on my elbow and stuck my back in Michael's face, blocking his view. His arm crept over my waist, trying to touch us both. It earned him a donkey-kick in the shins. The next attempt won him an elbow in the ribs.

'Fuck off, wankface, you can shag a woman any time you want,' I hissed, shoving my face in his. 'Stop being so selfish.'

Michael jumped up, stomped downstairs and slammed the bedroom door, unironically.

Was Amy falling asleep? Those tiny jerking movements, not quite in sync with anything I was doing...

'Amy? Amy, you awake?'

'YEAH!' She shuddered upright for a second.

When she started snoring, I gathered my clothes, tiptoed out of the room and went downstairs to mine and Michael's room. The door was locked.

For a while, things took an awkward turn between the three of us. Isms and schisms. Sharp edges. 1950s northern kitchen sink drama.

'I'm not a lesbian you know,' said Amy, walking into the kitchen with her shopping a few days later, continuing an argument that never began. She flounced over to the fridge and started hurling her food in.

'Kippers? Again?' I was standing at the hob boiling noodles.

A sniff, a flick of the flapper bob and off she stomped to her attic, shaking the tiny terrace with the thud of her Doc Martens on the stairs.

'Fucking white girls and their hair-flicking,' I said to the noodles. 'Ohh, did I "violate" you, little princess Amy?' I sang quietly into the steam, cracking egg yolk all over my fingers instead of into the pot.

*

Something got wrenched out of place with me and Amy that night. We never really managed to put it back where it should be. Things seemed normal on the surface, but we never called each other 'bitch' or 'fucking cow' or 'stupid slapper' again. There was a risk the other might think we really meant it.

As for Michael, he remained my not-a-boyfriend until we graduated – we both knew that was the expiry date for our relationship. Or so I thought. He caught me by surprise the day before my final exam, saying, 'How about we get married, and I'll come to Japan with you? I'll convert, so you can tell your parents you're marrying a Muslim. I'll even change my name. What's the Arabic for Michael? Mahmoud?'

'Stop fucking around.' I swiped at his legs with a tea towel, my heart thudding at the suspicion that he was being deadly serious. 'Can you imagine what your mum and dad would say? They'd get the priest around to beat the devil out of you before your head started spinning three hundred and sixty degrees like the girl in *The Exorcist.*'

A year after I moved to Japan, when I made a trip back to London for the summer, Michael came and met me at Sherine's place. She'd always liked him, though she didn't know he was my not-a-boyfriend. Just a friend. She said, 'Bring him to my flat, you can ask him to take a look at the boiler.'

When he was done, we sat on the red sofa in Sherine's new flat in Wimbledon, surrounded by boxes of books and the smell of fresh paint. Even though I'd started seeing another guy by then, it still felt natural for me to put my feet up on Michael's legs. When he tried to kiss me, I pulled away and said, 'No, no, I can't, my new boyfriend wouldn't like it.'

'How come you were never such a goody-two-shoes with me?' he said. 'And how come you can suddenly say the word "boyfriend" when you never could with me?'

'I'm older now,' I replied, putting quote marks around the word 'older' to give it a touch of irony, putting my feet back on his legs. 'I'm trying out monogamy.'

My new boyfriend in Japan had told me that he didn't share. Compliance with this policy was a condition of us being together. The politics of possession were new and exciting to me. Goody-two-shoes, I said proudly to him when the summer was over and I was back in Japan. I neglected to mention what exactly the feet wearing those shoes had been doing on Sherine's sofa.

Prison break

In case you were wondering, it was That Man's weariness that allowed me to plant the idea of me moving to Japan to teach English right after I graduated.

'Booming economy,' I'd said in my brightest voice when I went down to London from university to deliver my sales pitch. 'Good money in Japan'... 'chance to learn another language while I teach'... My stomach churned as I waited for the obligatory explosion.

But he'd just mumbled, 'Okay, my love,' head hanging down as we picked at his chicken tagine. 'But only for a year, and then you must come home, to your family... You've been away too long already. I've lost your mother and sister – I can't lose you as well.'

Nearly three years had passed since Mama's prison break, but Sherine's was still recent and raw. All these abandonments had left him heavier, slower, less nimble in the boxing ring. At least my official reason for running away absolved him of any blame.

'You crack me up,' said Mariana as we sat in the Burger King in Turnpike Lane the next day, my appetite restored now that the ordeal of telling him was over. 'Why stop at Japan? Why not go to New Zealand, to really make your point?'

'Shut up, bitch,' I'd said, cracking up too. 'You know I can't go back and live with him after college – I'd end up slitting my wrists. And I can't be arsed to go through what Sherine did. This is the easiest way.'

Sherine's efforts to do things the normal way, like an English person, had ended in tears. She'd left home in a minicab at 2am, raking her nail down That Man's face when he'd tried to stop her. None of this surprised Mariana. She came from a milieu that understood why it was easier to concoct a burning desire to share the spoils of Japan's 'booming economy' than it was to simply tell your parents you were leaving home. Her own escape eventually came via the standard template for our 'set': marriage to a guy she'd been seeing on the sly for two years before she finally sprang him – ta-da! – onto her ostensibly unsuspecting parents. He was Greek-Cypriot too, so what could they say? Everyone knew the drill.

'Yeah yeah,' she said. 'I know. But you can't put it off forever. You can run away from your problems, but they'll still be waiting for you when you get back.'

I knew she was right. I knew it was only a holiday away from reality. But it was a holiday I was determined to drag out for as long as possible.

My need to run away to another hemisphere couldn't be pinned entirely on my family. London itself had to take its share of the blame. The feelings and associations it induced in me... the sadness that enveloped me each time my train or coach pulled into its shabby suburbs on my trips back from university. I thought those feelings belonged to me, Pavlovian echoes of my childhood. I didn't realise then who they really belonged to, or the role you'd played in creating them. That understanding came later, when I'd left a trail of destruction on the other side of the world, and when London's calls grew too insistent for me to keep hanging up.

Part 3: Mistakes

1997–2004

Language lessons

When I first moved to Tokyo, I made an effort to learn Japanese. I didn't want to be *that* kind of *gaijin*. Arrogant. Insular. The type who only wanted to hang around with other foreigners.

Full of good intentions, I bought books on *hiragana* and *katakana* – *kanji* was a step too far – and flung my newly acquired baby babble at anyone who would listen. A wine-tasting event at a little bar near the language school where I worked provided the perfect victim: a sweet-faced woman who made the fatal mistake of smiling at me as we queued for top-ups of red wine.

'First time Japan wine drink me,' I said. 'Reddy wine don't drink. Me make...' Cue jazz-hands, the new international symbol for 'drunk', and everything else in the abyss where words should've been. My hands deserved to be paid overtime for all the work they were doing while my mouth sat idle, crying out for new equipment. 'Is it *aka-wain*, or *akai-wain*?'

'*Aka*. It's my first time to go to a wine-tasting event too. Yes, red wine is very strong.' Putting me out of my misery, she switched to English.

'Where did you learn such good English?' I said, wiping the sweat off my forehead. Even in September, I was a melting waxwork in Japan; makeup was out of the question.

'In England.'

Sussex, some town I'd never heard of. We talked about homestay families and language schools, cricket and warm beer, mists and mellow fruitfulness. All the Englands I didn't know, apart from in the Mr Kipling adverts. I nodded until my head felt like it was about to roll off, smiled until my lips were poised to crack and bleed. It felt important to give her the version of England she wanted. Something to make up for the flicker of surprise that passed over people's faces in Japan when I told them I was 'English'.

Being a 'good' *gaijin* was too much effort. Gradually, I stopped trying and allowed myself to sink into the comforting arms of the expats I worked with; in particular those of Kieran, an Irish guy my own age, who became my new, official boyfriend. Despite having parachuted myself into the heart of Japan, I ended up spending all my free time with other English speakers.

I hadn't realised how exhausting it was to rebuild yourself from scratch in a language you barely speak. Your life story, your jokes, the thin line between flippancy and truth.

'It's so stressful,' I complained to Sherine on the phone. 'Even when I'm speaking English, I have to talk like a newsreader, otherwise Japanese people don't understand me. The Americans can be themselves because everyone thinks they speak the "real" English.'

'Oh, cry me a river,' she replied, making me tug at the telephone cord while imagining it was her hair. 'Please don't tell me you'll end up being one of these people who lives in another country for seventy years and never gets beyond "hello"? Even Mama managed more than that.'

'I can say more than "hello"!' I replied, not bothering to hide my offence. 'But it's hard, you know. You try learning Japanese...'

'Well, you won't get very far if you spend all your time with other foreigners, or with Japanese people who speak fluent English, will you?'

Even Mama gave me short shrift when I offloaded to her, thinking she of all people would understand. 'What's the problem?'

like it: Ayako, an admin assistant with an inane giggle and feet that never mustered the energy to pick themselves off the ground when she walked.

She's at it again, I typed in an email to Lilia. *That laugh... it's drilling right through my head. What's he saying that can possibly be so funny?*

You don't even sit as close to her as I do! Lilia replied. *She's wearing her fluffy pink hooker's toilet-slippers – maybe John will get lucky tonight.*

Don't ever use the words 'John' and 'get lucky' to me in the same sentence again, I wrote.

When we went out for drinks that night, John said he'd give Ayako an English lesson. '*Ureshii!*' she said, clapping her hands like a little girl. Happy. They were sitting at a small table on their own, next to the big one occupied by the rest of us.

'Listen,' I said, nudging Lilia after the first round. 'Can you hear what he's saying to her?'

'It's the way we say hello in English,' he was saying. 'In Manchester. Now say it after me: "Please touch my tits and my arse".'

Ayako dissolved into giggles.

'Don't say it, Ayako.' I turned round to their table. 'He's trying to make you say bad things.'

'Keep your big nose out of it, Lilia,' said John. 'Who involved you in this conversation?'

'I'm Nessie, not Lilia. Not all brown people are interchangeable, you know.'

'Ah, shut up!' The redness in his face cranked up a notch. 'You know it was just a slip of the tongue. Why do you have to drag racism into everything?'

Lilia chimed in: 'Ayako-san, he's making you say...' She translated the sentence into Japanese.

'Heeeeeh!' said Ayako, gasping and leaning backwards as she clapped her hands over her face. 'Is this true, John-san?'

'She knew what he was saying,' I said to Lilia as we walked to the station afterwards. 'I can't believe what she lets him get away with. I sometimes wonder if that girl's all there.'

'Yeah, it's true. I think she has low self-esteem.'

We talked about John a bit too: 'One of those white guys who thinks he's God because of the way women fall at their feet here – he couldn't get someone to sit next to him on a bus back at home.'

But mostly we talked about Ayako, our voices rising and falling in animation as we picked over her annoying walk, her tarty shoes, her stupid laugh. That girl who had no self-respect. That girl who let men play her for a fool. That girl who acted like she hadn't got a brain in her head. That girl... that girl... that girl.

*

Something funny happened with Ayako soon after this. I heard two Japanese voices talking in the women's toilets while I was in one of the cubicles. One belonged to Misako, a translator Lilia and I were friendly with. The other I didn't recognise. Deep, firm, assertive: a PE teacher's voice. The kind of voice I tried to turn mine into whenever I caught it rising to a girly squeak under stress.

It was a shock when I came out of the cubicle to find Ayako standing at the sink with Misako.

'Nessie-san!' said Ayako in that same voice, smiling, followed by a stream of Japanese. In response to my blank expression, she repeated, in English, 'I like your...' – gesturing at my dress. I was wearing a psychedelic sixties print I'd bought from a second-hand shop in Yoyogi.

'Oh... oh, thanks.' I found myself stammering and turning red as I washed my hands. 'I forgot the Japanese word for dress.' My mouth emitted a nervous giggle, which my wet hand flew up to smother. I wanted to get back to my desk and eat my tuna sandwich, not be subjected to an impromptu Japanese test in the toilets by Ayako, of all people.

She smiled and said something in Japanese to Misako. The two of them started laughing. Not in a bitchy way; just quietly raucous, slightly dirty. The way Lilia and I laughed together. As I scuttled away, I caught Ayako looking at me with an expression of something like pity. As if she would have been more than happy to share the joke, if only my Japanese was good enough to understand it.

Home

It felt weird going home to London for a holiday every year. Shuttling between two lives that seemed to belong to different people. The first time I did it, I had an upset stomach in both directions. My bacteria was all out of whack, unsure if it was supposed to freak out at fish and chips from the chip shop I'd been going to since I was four, or convenience store *makizushi*.

Sherine kept up a running commentary on the bizarre new habits I had developed. 'Why do you do that bowing and running thing when you're crossing the road at zebra crossings? You look like you're having a fit.' 'Why do you flush the toilet while you're having a wee? What a waste of water! Do you think anyone really cares if they can hear your urine hitting the bowl?' 'Stop covering your mouth like that when you laugh – you look like a freak.'

I met up with Amy from university for a pizza in Soho, and she regaled me with questions about Japan. My enthusiasm for these conversations had ebbed rapidly after the first couple of times. Since when did living in another country make you an unpaid representative of its tourist board?

'I've got a new boyfriend,' I said, trying to steer the topic in a more interesting direction. 'His name's Kieran.'

'Yeah, you said.'

I waited for breathless questions about what he was like, the way people kept asking me if it was true that middle-aged

Japanese businessmen could buy schoolgirls' knickers from vending machines (how the hell was I supposed to know? I wasn't close enough to any Japanese people to ask, and the foreigners I hung around with had a tendency to ham these stories up with salacious glee).

'He's Irish,' I added, when no enquiries came.

'Yeah, you told me. Still got your Catholic-boy fetish, then?'

'Huh? Oh! Oh yeah.' I laughed, playing with a bit of congealed cheese on my plate.

'Don't tell me you've forgotten about Michael already?'

'No! Course not.'

'He was so upset when you left, Ness. You never told me he'd asked you to marry him.'

'When did he tell you that?'

'After you left. He said he wanted to get married so you could come clean to your parents and live together openly, and that he'd been ready to become a Muslim and everything.'

'He was only pissing about. He didn't really mean it.'

'I think he did.'

As I gazed out of the window, I thought of how much like Sherine she sounded. Words digging and twisting into my skin like nails. Was this what sisters were for? Well, I already had one and I didn't need another.

We talked about other things. 'I might come and visit you in Japan,' she said. 'When I've saved up. Make a change from summer holidays in Canvey Island, wouldn't it?'

'Yeah, yeah, sounds good. Let's sort something out.'

I thought it was just one of those things people say, but she wrote to me about it a couple of months later: *I'm gonna take the plunge and go backpacking before teacher training. I think I can get all the way to Japan if I'm careful. What do you reckon? Shall I come and swoon on your futon like a delicate Edwardian laydee?*

Really sorry, Ame, I replied. *They don't give much holiday over here and I don't think I can make the days work...*

Our letters dwindled to birthday cards and the odd postcard every once in a while. Then they dried up altogether.

I never really noticed I had lost her.

Spectre at the feast

My memory of the fish reared its head again when I got engaged to Kieran in July 2000, shortly before my twenty-fifth birthday.

The engagement itself was a matter-of-fact affair. We'd been together two years by then, and had two foreign holidays under our belt – India and Thailand – each of which had felt like a honeymoon. Our engagement was arranged one Sunday, as we were having lunch at an Indian restaurant in Shinjuku, and he said, 'I guess we should get married some time if we want to be together properly in London or wherever. Given that we can't just live together there. Because of your family situation, I mean.'

'Yeah,' I said. 'I suppose that makes sense.'

'Only if you want to...'

'Yes!' I said. 'I do.' And then in a silly, swooning-lady voice: 'I do!'

We both laughed. For an instant, I thought about the last time someone had raised the topic of marriage with me. With a jolt, I remembered I still owed Michael a reply to a letter he'd sent me eighteen months ago. It hardly seemed worth it now. What could I possibly give as an excuse? The truth was that I'd been too busy reinventing myself in Japan, far away from anyone who'd known me in my raw, unfinished state. The kind of state where I had gone to parties with one guy – Michael – and left with random strangers, turning my head away so I wouldn't have to see the look on his face. I didn't do that kind of thing any more.

'What about… you know?' I said to Kieran.

'Converting? That's fine. It's not a big deal, from what I've read about it. We can get pissed afterwards, once I've done it.'

'Are you sure your mum won't get upset about it?'

'Nah, she'll be all right. She's a collapsed Catholic too. She'll think it's funny. When do you think we should do it?'

'How about in two years' time? We'll be twenty-seven then. That's a good age to get married. Still enough time for children.'

'I thought you didn't want children?'

'I don't know. Maybe. I keep changing my mind.'

He made a funny little clicking noise with his tongue, like something in a Miriam Makeba song, which he did when he was pleased. He'd told me before that he wouldn't mind having children. He was the oldest of five. Looking after other people was normal for him.

He took a small blue velvet box out of his pocket and said, 'It's not a proper engagement ring, but I hope it'll do until we sort out the real one?'

It was a silver Claddagh ring. Irish, like him.

'It's lovely,' I said. 'I don't want anything else.'

Every day had felt like my birthday since we'd moved in together. Our one-bedroom flat was finally fully furnished after months of procrastination over whether to get a sofa or a sofa-bed, buy a proper bed or stick with the futon. We'd installed two separate phone lines to get around the problem of him never being able to answer the phone in case it was one of my parents calling. A disaster contingency plan had been worked out for the slim eventuality that one of them decided to visit: he'd move out to a friend's place and we'd clear the flat of any evidence of his existence. The day before our engagement, we'd had a big double bed delivered.

'I feel like a grown-up,' we'd said at the same time as we stood looking at it and then burst out laughing and wrapped our arms around each other, a position we couldn't seem to stay away from for too long.

The night of our engagement, Kieran had to shake me awake.

'What's wrong, baby? You were whining like a lost dog.'

'The fish...' I told him about the big silver fish lying on the chopping board, the trail of blood leading across the floor to Mama as she cradled her hand. The doctor dragging her along by her hair as she screamed, you whispering with That Man in the living room, Sherine covering my eyes and ears, trying to protect me.

'I don't think it's just a recurring dream,' I said. 'It feels too real. I feel like something really bad or sad happened that day. The way my dad's face looked when Genevieve was comforting him...'

He stroked my head and said, 'Why don't you ask your mum? Maybe it happened, but not in the way you think. Maybe she just cut her finger or something and all the other stuff got layered on top, in your imagination, because you were so young then.'

'I don't know... It doesn't feel right to ask her. It feels intrusive somehow. I don't know what can of worms it might open up.'

'Don't miss your chance, Nessie,' he said with a wobble in his voice. 'You never know when it might not be there any more.'

I squeezed his hand and kissed his forehead. He was fourteen when his father died suddenly of a heart attack.

'Why don't you ask Sherine, then, if you don't want to ask your mum? She's what, nearly four years older than you? She might remember what really happened.'

'Yes,' I said. 'Yeah, why not? I'll do that next time I see her.'

Two minutes later, I had my head in my hands, sobbing.

'What?' he said. 'What is it, sweetheart?'

I only knew what it was myself when the words came out: 'I don't want to end up like them. I don't know what I'm more scared of, turning into him or her.'

'Shhh,' he said, hugging me tight. 'Shhh. That's not going to happen. You're nothing like them. You're brave and honest, Nessie. You won't make the bad decisions they made. You're nothing like them.'

Brave and honest. I went back to sleep feeling I was those things; that he'd given me those two qualities just as he'd given me the Claddagh ring.

I didn't need to go blabbing to the world about the ring, but I didn't mind when people noticed.

'Something you're not telling me, missy?' said Lilia, grabbing my hand in the work canteen a couple of days later as we deposited our trays at our usual corner table. Like an army scout, she was constantly on the lookout for new recruits into the ranks of the practically married: she'd been with her girlfriend, Nicky, since they met at college at the age of eighteen.

Laughing coyly, I replied, 'Not exactly, but we've talked about it – we'll probably do it in a couple of years.'

The warmth I felt when she yelped and hugged me flooded my whole body. It felt good to be doing something other people approved of. Swimming with the tide for once, instead of against it.

Mariana made me feel good too, when I told her on the phone.

'Oh my God, Ness, I'm so happy for you! We could have a double wedding if you do it this summer instead...'

Being normal was like a kind of club, it seemed. A welcoming, non-exclusive one, where people found safety in numbers; in doing things just like everyone else.

'What does Sherine think?' said Mariana.

'I don't know – I haven't exactly told her.'

'How come? She likes Kieran, doesn't she? She'll be happy for you!'

'Oh yeah, but... you know.' I laughed it off. 'Telling her always makes things into a big drama, and I don't need that right now. I'll mention it nearer the time.'

For all my reluctance to go flashing the Claddagh ring in people's faces, I loved the feel of it on my finger. It was something I could stroke for reassurance, whenever I needed it. I was getting married, which meant I was normal. I might have children, which was a family-sized KFC bucket of normal. And I was brave and honest too.

That feeling lasted all of three weeks.

*

You know, Genevieve, I thought of you occasionally in my waking hours, in that brief interval when I was brave and honest.

The leaps and bounds of technology had nudged you into my brain again: 'I wonder...' 'Where does she...?' 'Is she...?' The blindingly obvious didn't occur to me, as I scrolled with bated breath past your alternate realities: Genevieve Brown the pharmacist from Orange County; Genevieve Brown the pastor of the Southern Valley Baptist Church in Sacramento; Genevieve Brown the chiropractor from San Diego. When my moment of realisation came, it hit a raw nerve, one freshly exposed by my entry into that liminal state known as 'engagement'.

The question had come up early between me and Kieran, well before he'd given me the Claddagh ring. He'd said, 'But I don't get it – you've always said you hate your surname, so why wouldn't you change it to something else?'

'Because...' I said. 'Because it's weird – how can you go from being one person all your life to suddenly being someone else?'

'But didn't your mum change her name when she married your dad?'

'No! She kept her own name. My grandad's name, I mean. Hassan.'

So why wasn't I jumping at the chance to lose the phlegmy collection of consonants that had clogged my throat my whole life? Kieran had a good surname – Stevens. A name that would serve us well in London. Not too Irish. Nothing that English people would butcher with their phonetic literal-mindedness. Was it a fear of losing my identity that explained my reluctance to change my name – a sense that ditching Boughanmi would sever a connection that was already stretched to its limits? Partly, partly, but it wasn't just that. I couldn't explain to Kieran how my stomach lurched at the thought of this vanishing act. I couldn't tell him that you had to have solid, unshakable foundations before you let yourself perform a shape-shifting act of that magnitude. My own trickery and sleight of hand were subtle, elaborate, performed behind the scenes almost unconsciously – not executed with the smiling bravado of a woman in a sequinned leotard climbing into a wooden box and letting a man in a black tuxedo saw her in half.

It gave me the creeps when I realised I didn't know your name. That I never really had known it. And that you'd disposed of the woman I'd thought you were just a few months after you vanished, shrugging her off like a costume borrowed for a fancy-dress party.

On the rare occasions I let myself think about you, knowing you'd slipped out of my reach in that way, the questions seemed to chase themselves in circles: 'Who is she?' 'Who was she?' 'Was she?'

I could've done it the old-fashioned way. I could've opened the letter you'd sent me all those years ago and looked at the address written on it. Gone after you in earnest. But I didn't – I preferred you as a concept, an enigma of the virtual world. Not a real, physical presence who might have some questions of her own for the detective who'd decided to hunt her down.

'Home'

Both Mama in Tunis and That Man in London seemed to experience a reverse growth spurt after I moved to Japan. An accelerated shrinking process, each trip home marking a new strain on my back muscles as I bent down to hug them. I say 'home'... It wasn't just Tunisia that had quotation marks around it now. London had acquired them too. Tokyo was different: it was the dream of a life always slipping away from me, tinged with melancholy from the start. Even on the days I hated it, when the dense air and low, heavy sky felt like a prison blanket thrown over my head, I wallowed in nostalgia for this city I still lived in. Each season in Tokyo brought an aching sense of loss, as if I was already at the end of my life looking back on it, because I knew the autumn leaves in Inokashira Park and the cherry blossoms in Yoyogi Park were transient for me in more than the seasonal sense. My life in Japan had an expiry date, but I didn't know when it was – and how could I think of it as my choice when two people on two different continents were counting down the minutes until my return? The clock was ticking for me to create a life I could pack up and take home.

At a party thrown by a rich American couple at their penthouse flat in Roppongi, an Australian woman said to me, as we stood shoeless on the thick cream carpet sipping champagne, 'Don't you think that when you live abroad, you feel like you're permanently on holiday because nothing seems completely real?'

'Yes!' I said. 'That's so true.'

I looked out of the floor-length window at the glittering night sky that left a vapour trail across my heart in a way nothing real or permanent could ever do. If That Man and Mama hadn't realised they were on holiday in London, that was their own fault – they should've been different people. Expats, not immigrants. People who went to parties in penthouses, not wholesalers off Hendon Road. People who could live in another country without learning the language, unbothered by speeches denouncing their 'ghetto mentality' on TV.

The two small, shrunken people waited for me in their respective homes. When I visited, they thrust food into my face like an offensive weapon, refusing to take no for an answer.

'I've baked a tarte tatin for you,' from That Man.

'I've made shakshouka how you like it,' from Mama.

Anything less than three helpings would trigger hurt expressions and enquiries about my health.

They bombarded me with oblique questions and odd conjectures, futile attempts to understand what had led me down this perverse path in life.

'I suppose you like Japan because it's clean,' Mama said once, as if cleanliness had always dictated my decisions. 'It must be clean because they don't have many immigrants,' she added, prompting me to fire off a half-hour lecture about hypocrisy.

They showered me with worry and concern:

'Aren't you lonely over there?' That Man kept saying. 'I don't want you to get old and sad on your own... I don't want you to miss your chances and realise life's moved on without you.'

How was he supposed to know my bed was warm with another body more often than it was cold and lonely? Maybe he was only worried about mortgages and unemployment rates and house prices. I responded with flippancy – my newly acquired weapon – saying, 'Don't worry – if no one wants to give me a job when I come back, I'll come and work in the shop with *you*.'

He laughed as if I'd said something hilarious, and I realised that was the first time I could ever remember making him laugh.

Neither of them gave up on the emotional blackmail, which earned them hollow victories. He lobbed an 'I might die while you're away' into my ears at the Burger King in Heathrow airport when I was waiting to fly back to Tokyo. I retaliated by walking through security an hour earlier than I was supposed to. Invoking death at an airport was a breach of the Geneva Convention.

Fizzing grenades came flying out of Mama's mouth too: 'You and your sister don't care about either of us – you both do what you want as if you don't even have any parents!'

That one blew up in her face when I spent the next two nights of my ten days in Tunis at my cousin Amani's place.

I attacked them back, using my own arsenal, which consisted mostly of gifts. Clothes from Uniqlo that didn't fit them properly. Savoury snacks bought at the airport, which they examined with polite interest and left to languish in the cupboard until I ate them myself the following year. Money sent to them in amounts some might call flashy. (Look! Hasn't something good come out of Japan after all?) A new microwave for That Man and a massive TV for Mama. More tat for his mantelpiece and her display cabinet – miniature screens, beckoning cats, lucky deer shit from Nara, framed calligraphy of their names in *kanji* – which they devoured with prodigious appetites.

'Thank you, thank you, *ya hbibti*!' That Man said, and Mama hugged me until I could hardly breathe.

But most of all, I attacked them with physical affection. With a hand laid on the back of his neck, encountering unexpectedly soft skin; I'd never touched his neck before, that I remembered. A touch that made him turn around and lift my hand to his lips or place it onto his heart, closing his eyes as if he was praying for me, or for himself. I bore down on her with a light stroke of her earlobes like I used to do when I was eight, which made her giggle and squirm, relaxing with sensuous abandon into my touch. They clung like children when I touched them, starved of physical contact, desperate to hang on to it when it came.

I let them cling. It was the least I could do before I removed myself from their lives again. I did it because I had to look away each time I saw how thin Mama's hair was getting and how That Man shuffled in his new furry slippers. I did it so I wouldn't have to talk to them too much, because there was so much we couldn't talk about. Their shrinking frames and hungry eyes saddened and scared me, and made it hard for me to stick around. I knew they were just as temporary as the leaves in Inokashira Park, but I still didn't want to stay with them.

Magic mushrooms

'Brave and honest' – that's what Kieran had said I was.

My bravery and honesty disintegrated on 18 August, the day before my twenty-fifth birthday. People at work were calling it my birthday Christmas Eve – any excuse for debauchery. They decided to combine it with a farewell do for another copy editor, Paul, who was moving back to Canada.

'Let's get some magic mushrooms,' said my boss as we got off the train at Roppongi. 'To celebrate Nessie getting old and Paul fucking off back to Tim Horton-land.'

My boss was an Australian, in his early forties. He'd come to Japan to sell jewellery, and ended up marrying a Japanese woman and getting a job at the paper.

He divided the mushrooms up between me, him and Paul. 'I've given you a smaller share, Nessie, because it's your first time.'

I lost the other two and the rest of the work gang when we got to the club, which was an icebox of blue – blue walls, blue sofas, blue lights, blue smoke. The music was dreamy and low-key, ambient jazz and trip-hop.

The mushrooms started to take effect. As I'd read about in Aldous Huxley, I felt most of myself falling away, receding into the background, but it wasn't pleasant. What was left was something I didn't like the taste of. A small, hard pebble of amoral self-interest. I wished Lilia was there so I could cry on her shoulder, but she was on holiday in Thailand with her girlfriend. Of all my foreign friends in Japan, Lilia sometimes felt like the only one who was actually real. A solid, reassuring presence whose fluent Japanese gave her a foothold in this country that most of us didn't possess. Right now I felt as vague and ephemeral as a fragment of someone else's dream.

'Mate!' said Boss-man, finding me a couple of hours later whimpering in a ball on the sofa. 'Why are you crying? There's nothing to cry about! Everything is beautiful! You're among friends.'

He went off to mingle, and I lay on the sofa chatting to Paul, the Canadian copy editor. I was coming back to myself. Shaky but human again.

'What are you smoking?' I said. 'It smells really nice.'

He showed me the packet. Indonesian clove cigarettes.

'Oh!' I said. 'Are you part Indonesian?' I'd often wondered about his background – his colouring was almost exactly like mine and his features hard to pin down.

He laughed. 'Can you only eat sushi if you're Japanese or drink Coke if you're American?'

'Oh. Oh yeah.'

Why was he being so logical when he was supposed to have had his mind blown as well? And why didn't he look like someone who'd been gazing into the void, as I had? He looked as mellow as always, his face serene and friendly under the blue light. Chilled but not cold. 'Handsome,' I thought, a word I didn't normally associate with men. More with women who looked like Benazir Bhutto or Maria Callas. Or you.

We drew closer together on the sofa.

'Did you dress to match this place?' he said, hooking his finger inside the neck of my top.

I'd forgotten I was wearing a light-blue T-shirt that day.

'You don't normally wear things like this,' he said, pulling me closer still. 'You're normally all buttoned-up.'

I found myself in something like the recovery position, more than ready to receive mouth-to-mouth resuscitation. Perhaps it was that which made me say three times in quick succession, 'I don't smoke, but I like the taste. I don't smoke, but I like the taste. I don't smoke, but I like the *taste*.'

Obligingly, he pressed his mouth against mine and blew a hot gust of cloves into my lungs. His mouth tasted good beneath the cigarettes. I felt a rush of relief at the foreignness of it. A reminder that a whole world of mouths existed outside Kieran's, and that I could still press my lips to those mouths. The next thing I remember, we were in Paul's flat, on his bed.

'I can't get undressed, I'm engaged,' I said, waving the Claddagh ring in his face, ignoring the insistent vibrations of the phone in my bag.

I kissed him goodbye an hour later and got the train home.

*

'For fuck's sake, where've you been?' said Kieran, opening the door as soon as I put my key to the lock. 'I was just about to start trying to figure out how to report you missing in Japanese.'

'I'm really sorry...' Dazed and numb, I told him about the magic mushrooms. Not about the sofa or the clove cigarettes or the visit to Paul's flat.

'I wish you hadn't done that.' He sounded sad. 'Not without someone there to look after you.'

'I was with the others,' I said weakly.

'Hmm,' he replied, and for a second I wanted to ask him, 'What do you think of Paul?' They'd met once, at a party.

'Ah well,' he sighed. 'You're safe and well, and that's all that matters.' Then he hugged me and put me to bed, like a mother would.

I tried to sparkle for my birthday dinner at a Cajun restaurant, just the two of us, but it was difficult. My heart was pounding with tiredness and I felt sick. Also, I kept thinking about Paul. How good it had felt to touch him. Someone different, someone new. A world of possibility that was closed off to me now. Officially, at least. It hadn't hit me yet that this was something I'd never be able to talk about to the person I talked to about everything.

When we went to bed that night, he said, 'Are you too tired?' and I said, 'No, no, let's.' He kissed me as usual and I tried to kiss him back, but the movement felt all wrong. Wooden. Jerky and stiff, like a Thunderbirds puppet. As if I'd suddenly forgotten the mechanics of kissing. As if my mouth wouldn't work properly with his any more.

*

I can't lie, Nessie, said Mariana's email when I told her what I'd done. *I didn't expect to hear that so soon after you got engaged. I really thought Kieran was the one for you. You sounded so happy.*

I was, I replied. *I don't know what made me do it. I feel so guilty and I wish I could tell him, but I'm scared of what he'll do. If we break up, that's my whole life gone. It's not like being at home where there's always someone there to help you pick up the pieces.*

Try and put it behind you then, Ness. Make sure it never happens again, and you'll forget about it soon enough. It's not like you actually shagged Paul, is it? Just think of it as a slip of the lips!

Yeah, I said, *you're right. I'll do that.*

But I knew it was already too late. I'd gone and got myself turfed out of that clubhouse called Normality. As usual, it was my own fault: my inability to follow simple rules; my greedy, grasping nature that could never just pick one option and stick with it. Once again, I found myself exiled on the threshold, gazing with envy at the cosy groups huddled inside.

Heaven lies at the feet of the mother

To my surprise, children – those already in existence, not the hypothetical ones I might have one day – seemed to like me. Mariana's baby daughter did, at least.

They'd moved out to the suburbs. Rows of immaculate houses stationed like a vigilante army repelling intruders.

'Go on, go on, hold her,' Mariana said when I went to visit on a trip back to London. 'Look how she's smiling at you! She never does that. She's usually a moody little cow with new people.'

'Hmm,' I said. 'I don't wanna drop her...'

'You won't. And don't worry if you do. I only had her as practice for getting a dog.'

It didn't feel as awkward holding a baby at the age of twenty-six as it did when I was eleven. The increased size differential between us made it easier. My arms were stronger now, able to hang on to her without incident as she clung to me like a young macaque and deposited drool on my shoulder. We adopted that same position when Mariana and I wheeled her out to the park, and I took it one step further, jogging her up and down on the spot, walking her around to look at stuff. 'Look!' I said. 'Grass!'

Obligingly, she turned her head as Mariana looked on from the bench, beaming: 'You're a natural. Maybe it's a sign.'

I felt something I'd rarely felt before – the sensation that I was a real person at last, a serious contender. An athlete on the field, not a spectator criticising from the sidelines.

But dabbling in amateur athletics wasn't the same as being a professional, was it? Dedicating your life to the sport. Giving up your free time. No hours left to read books or watch films or put earphones on and blank the world out. Suffering public opprobrium if you made a tactical error and fucked things up. And how many times a day could you say 'Look!' before the urge to ram something sharp into your own jugular vein overcame you? Having children rekindled the wonder of childhood, people said, but what if you didn't want it rekindled? What if you preferred the clarity of adulthood to the sinister undercurrents of the unknown that plague the world of children, if that's what they meant by 'wonder'?

The only thing that might make it worthwhile was the smiles. The smiles that rained down on us as I held the baby. They seemed to leap off her happy, yapping little face and onto the faces of the people around us, bouncing back at her and onto me as I held her. They made me smile back as I basked in this rosy, dazzling reflection of myself as a woman holding a smiling child, smiling at the people smiling at her. The giddying effect of this hall of smiles brought out a circus performer in me, someone I didn't know existed, who tipped the baby backwards and spun her around, squeezing gleeful giggles out of her. The idea of tossing her into the air and catching her even crossed my mind, but I decided against it. My hand–eye coordination hadn't improved that much since I was eleven.

The world smiled upon mothers, it seemed. They were doing something good, something normal, something that women were put on this earth to do. I had a vague memory of a Hadith about heaven and the feet of the mother, and I knew the Catholics loved their mothers too. If only there was a way to be a mother without all the hassle of having a child...

But did the mothers themselves know that heaven lay beneath their feet, if that was what the Hadith meant? Had Mama registered this fact? You wouldn't think it from the way her feet shuffled and twitched as she sat on her hard sofa watching Turkish soap operas in the dark, the blue light from the TV flickering over her face. You wouldn't guess it from the way her toes curled into fists that gave painful-sounding clicks, and how her feet tap-tap-tapped away like someone waiting for a bus they were starting to suspect would never come.

*

People sometimes thought *you* were our mother. I'd forgotten that. How you took ownership of us, when we were alone with you.

'Oh, did you have another one?' said an old friend of yours once when we ran into her at Bejam in Muswell Hill. She looked at me curiously as if trying to match my features to the ones of the children she already knew about. 'It shows how long it's been, doesn't it!'

'She's a kind of adopted daughter,' you said, putting your arm round me. Just you and me that day. No Sherine. I was about seven then.

Soon after this, an older girl called Lucy who hung around your library all the time asked me: 'Is Mrs Brown your mum?'

'Adopted,' I said, copying you, not really sure what the word meant.

'Really?' Her voice rose to a squeak. 'How come? Who adopted her? What about your real parents?'

I tried to mumble my way out of it, feeling annoyed with you in some obscure, illogical way. As if you'd set me up to say something wrong. Something disloyal to That Man and Mama.

For some reason we had a minor argument about Lucy once. I told you her name was Lucy Ball but you insisted it was Lucy Bull.

'Her name can't be Lucy Ball,' you said dismissively, a touch of a jeer in your voice. 'Lucy Ball is an actress. Why would her parents have called her that?'

What could I say? Lucy Ball the actress was something I didn't know, just like the word 'adopted'. You expected too much of me sometimes. You expected me to be an adult when I was only a child.

*

It was an unsettling experience when one of your real children jumped out at me from the pages of a magazine.

I was on a trip back to London, sitting in the reception room at the dentist's waiting for my annual clean and polish. The receptionist kept trying to make conversation: 'Oh, wow! You live in Japan? What's it like over there?'

I picked up a magazine to deflect her, and there was Amanda smiling up at me – she looked exactly the same as the last time I'd seen her, apart from a few grey streaks in her hair, which she was wearing in locs rather than the plaits I remembered, and a slight blurring around her chin.

I skimmed the article quickly, my heart pounding, bracing myself for words that would trigger a shock: mother, death, brother, that kind of thing. When I saw it was all about her job as an art therapist, I went back to the beginning and read it properly, feeling my face burning up and my breath coming fast.

Now that the receptionist had taken the hint and was ignoring me, I wanted her to look up and talk to me again. I fidgeted in my chair and laughed softly to myself, hoping she'd look up with an enquiring expression so I could say, 'So weird – I know this woman!' and wave Amanda's picture in her face. But she picked up the phone and started talking quietly to someone else, giggling into the receiver: 'Oh you never... Oh shut up... Oh shut *up!*'

'You're a bit flinchy today, Nesrine,' said the hygienist when I sat in her chair a few minutes later. 'Shall we take a quick break?

Wasn't it you who told me you like having your teeth cleaned the way other people like having their nails done?'

'Yeah, I know, sorry.' I swilled and spat. 'I don't know what's up with me today.'

She looked down at me, her eyes smiling from above her face mask. 'Never mind. We all have our sensitive days.'

She was a blonde Scottish woman with a soft voice and the kind of accent that makes words sound like a log fire on a chilly day.

'I just saw a woman I know in a magazine downstairs,' I said.

'Oh, really?'

'Yeah. She's an art therapist. I don't think I knew that when I was young. Maybe she became one later. Her mum was a really good friend of our family, back then. I haven't seen her for years.'

Her eyes smiled down at me, waiting for the rest of the story.

'Are you going anywhere nice on holiday this year?' I said to fill the pause as she got another implement ready to stick in my mouth.

I was meeting Sherine after my appointment. I knew Amanda wouldn't come up in our conversation then or at any other time. How could I mention her without mentioning you?

I left the dentist with a bad taste in my mouth beneath the medicinal mouthwash. The bitter, familiar taste of festering secrets.

Fish scales

I decided to ask Sherine about the fish on a flying visit back to London in December 2001. It was New Year's Eve, and she'd booked us a table at a posh restaurant.

'Modern British,' she'd told me on the phone before I left Tokyo. 'Bring something nice to wear, not that skanky brown cardigan with the fur-balls.'

She interrogated the waiter about the wine list while I zoned out, jetlagged and spacey, happy to be a clueless tourist and let her take charge.

'Châteauneuf-du-Pape,' she told me in her schoolteacher voice when the bottle came, swilling the wine around her glass, sniffing in a way she must've learned from the Tristans and Jeremys she worked with.

'Neufff di Bap,' I said, pinching my fingers in the air, enunciating how That Man would. He'd gone to Tunisia for a winter break, which solved the problem of who to stay with in London.

Sherine spat a mist of fine wine over the white tablecloth. We shook with silent laughter as the waiter passed petri dishes of shrivelled mushrooms over our shoulders.

'Can we go to Burger King after this?' I whispered, and her shoulders shook even harder.

The stars felt aligned for a perfect evening. New Year's Eve, the cusp of fresh beginnings. Why shouldn't I ask her questions about our childhood? She was my friend now, a development that still gave me a warm feeling in my stomach. Hadn't she come to see me three times in Japan, the last trip culminating in a damp squib of a firework display at a nothingy temple in Hiroshima to usher in the new millennium?

'It was fun,' she'd said bravely afterwards, as we watched other people's more combustible celebrations on the TV in our hotel room.

Hadn't I lapped up vicarious compliments as people in Japan cooed over how *kirei* she was? Her big eyes! Her velvety lashes! Her lustrous hair! Years ago, I would've been spitting with jealousy, especially over the hair – hers being the good kind that grew downwards, not up and outwards. But now I was proud of her. Proud to be related to her.

And hadn't we just spent Christmas Day together at her flat, lounging around in our pyjamas all day, stuffing our faces with food from Marks & Spencer's and drinking champagne from 10am, feasting our eyes on the Christmas tree decked out in the corner of her living room, the first one either of us had ever had?

'I always wanted a Christmas tree,' she'd kept saying. 'Ever since I can remember. I can't believe it took me so long to actually go out and get one!'

I'd laughed hysterically and said, 'I know, I know,' drunk on the knowledge that someone else understood what it meant to have a Christmas tree, that symbol of the normality we'd craved as children.

We had so much in common, didn't we? The places where we'd grown up. The parents we shared, who we could talk about at last, though it had taken us long enough. The weirdnesses we'd experienced as children, which were hard to explain to other people. Our habit of saying 'inshallah' when we wanted to keep our options open or avoid jinxing ourselves. The tut-tut noise we made to mean 'no'. Our shared hatred of raisins and love of spaghetti with marmite. Last time she came to Japan, I had to run away without lingering when I put her on the Narita Express at the end of her trip because the tears that were stabbing at my eyes seemed like the kind that could turn into a flood.

So why didn't all those things give me the right to say, as she sat eating her profiteroles, 'Do you remember when Mama hurt herself when she was doing something with a fish?'

'What fish?' She broke off a tiny piece of pastry and swirled it round in the chocolate sauce before lifting it daintily to her mouth. I'd dispatched my whole plate in three bites.

'It was in Oakfield Road,' I said. 'In Mrs Kowalski's house. We were little. Mama must've cut herself because there were drops of blood on the floor and a doctor came.'

Pick pick, went Sherine's fork. Another square millimetre of chocolate and choux pastry inched its way into her mouth. How could anyone eat a dessert so slowly?

'Don't you like your profiteroles?' I said.

'You know I do! Get your greedy eyes off my pudding, you've had yours.'

'All right, all right, I was just checking cos you're not making much of a dent in it.'

'Some of us like to savour our desserts.'

'The doctor dragged her along by her hair,' I said. 'It was really horrible to watch.'

'What doctor?'

'The one who came when Mama cut herself.'

'I don't know what you're talking about.'

'Yes you do, you were there. You tried to cover my eyes so I wouldn't see.'

'You dreamt it,' she said. 'It's a figment of your imagination. I don't remember anything like that.'

Her fork ploughed and hoed at the profiteroles, dropping each tiny chunk back onto her plate and then starting again.

'Here,' she said, pushing her plate towards me. 'I'm too full to finish these. You can have them.'

'No thanks.' I pushed it back at her. 'You shouldn't bother ordering a dessert if you can only ever manage two bites.'

It lasted about two minutes, the boiling urge to swing my fist across the table and into her jaw.

'How's Kieran?' she said eventually, her words falling into the silence like pellets from a constipated arse.

'Fine.'

She gave a small, conspiratorial laugh. 'What's the story with you two, anyway? Are you actually engaged or what?'

'I told you ages ago.'

'You said "kind of". What does "kind of" engaged mean? That you'll be half-married one day?' She laughed at her own joke.

I gave a big sigh.

'Sorry,' she said. 'I should've remembered you hate telling me anything about your life, though you'll always tell Mariana or whoever. Anyway. Do you think he'll like living in London when you move back?'

'Don't know. We'll see.'

She wanted to punch me too, I could tell. Something in the air.

It settled and simmered. We drank the rest of the wine then ran down to Trafalgar Square, swept up in a crowd of revellers. Linking arms so we didn't get separated. Trampling the fish under our feet like sour, rancid grapes.

Rut

I don't know if Kieran would've liked London. The carriage transporting us there turned into a pumpkin before we could find out.

I closed my mind to what was happening until the evening he put an unwanted gift into my hand. He'd bought it from a sex shop in Roppongi.

'I got this...' he said. 'Just... you know. I thought we might try it sometime. To liven things up. To stop us getting into a rut.'

'Oh. Thanks.'

I took it from him and looked at it, hating the dense, unforgiving weight of it in my hand. What were you supposed to say when receiving a gift of this nature? I think I made an indeterminate noise of approval – a hmm or mmm – before I shoved it into the chest of drawers. It went into one of the small drawers at the top that didn't belong to either of us. Receptacles for the bits and pieces we didn't know what else to do with. Somewhere I wouldn't have to look at it too often.

'You don't have to use it,' he said, watching me put it away. 'It was just an idea.'

'It's fine,' I said. 'We'll try it sometime.'

'Okay.' He made his clicking noise. I'd come to realise that this wasn't always a mark of pleasure. Sometimes it indicated resignation. An acceptance of whatever life was about to spring on him. An *oh well, can't be helped.*

The irony of the word 'rut' didn't occur to me then. That came later, once the rut had resolved itself, to the extent these things ever can.

The object in the drawer proved to be as weak and impotent as we were. It was too late for all that. My betrayal the night of the magic mushrooms had plunged us straight into a rut.

What did rut mean for us? Not Jilly Cooper. Not the *Rutshire Chronicles*. For us, it meant that once a day had dwindled to once every two weeks, or even three if I could arrange it that way. It meant us going on holiday to Singapore and me silently celebrating the arrival of my period because it gave me a legitimate excuse; and then locking myself in the bathroom to cry when I remembered how once, that wouldn't have been any kind of excuse. On the days I couldn't get out of it, rut meant me lying rigid with my eyes shut, thinking about someone else. No one in particular. Almost anyone would do. The guy with the nice smile who worked in Seven-Eleven. A Brazilian man I'd flirted with in a Roppongi bar (but that was it, because I'd already started seeing Kieran, and don't you know I was so monogamous it hurt?). Canadian Paul, my partner in mushroom crime. Even my old science teacher, Slaphead. Anyone who wasn't Kieran, my fiancé, this person who trusted me and thought I was worthy of his trust. Anyone but the owner of those sunny blue eyes and equally sunny nature. God save us from life's optimists – making everyone else do the worrying they selfishly refuse to do.

'Life always works out, one way or another,' he'd say.

'But what if it doesn't?'

'What's the point of thinking like that?'

Rut meant having a panic attack on the underground the day after he said, 'Shall we start thinking about dates, for the wedding? Or at least when you're going to tell your parents?'

It meant phoning Mariana and having a rant about the institution of monogamy, which seemed like the biggest act of self-sabotage ever perpetrated by the human race: 'It's just like Ramadan!' I said. 'People doing something they really don't want to do, but pretending to do it with a happy face.'

I thought she'd laugh, but her voice was quiet, sympathetic. 'I know how you feel, hon, and I don't know what to tell you... You have to weigh up the nightmare of being with the same person for the rest of your life against the nightmare of losing them.' She'd already made that choice. Married by then, with an eighteen-month-old daughter. 'Why don't you talk to him?' she said.

'I can't. It makes me feel sick. I don't wanna hurt him. And I love him so much. The other night, we went out for dinner and I realised he's one of the few people in the world I always have something to say to, without thinking.'

Rut meant other things too. It meant waking up with a craving for the smell of his skin – so clean and innocent – and wanting to sniff around his nose, where that smell was concentrated, without giving him the idea that this was a prelude to a passionate kiss, the way we used to. A dry peck was the most I wanted.

I wanted to protect him from the reality of the rut we were in. That's why I would invent haikus to amuse him as he drifted off to sleep. He'd laugh drowsily and say things like: 'Do you think anyone else is as happy as we are?' I'd reply, 'I doubt it.' Then I'd roll to the other side of the bed and cry silently, doing my best to contain my muscle spasms so I wouldn't wake him.

*

I wonder if optimists are just born that way. Is there such a thing as a happiness gene? If there is, the girl on *Top of the Pops* back in 1982 seemed to have it. Happiness oozed out of her every pore as she skipped across the screen, pink-ribboned blonde ponytail flying around her head: *I could be happy.*

I was six then. I was trying to swallow her happiness when you caught me licking your TV screen.

'Nessie! What are you up to now?' You had that little twist in your voice that told me you were suppressing a laugh.

'Tasting...'

'Is this about the dog?'

I'd started pretending to be a dog, which was the next best thing to having one.

Sensing some sort of dog-related treat, I went along with your interpretation, which secured me half an hour of *Shadow, the Sheep-Dog* before you took me home. I loved it when you read to me – the way you made each character sound different. The emotion you injected into sentences that looked limp on the page but came alive in your voice. The way you sometimes went off on flights of fancy of your own, inventing additional plots and subplots, encouraging me to join in. Was it a natural talent, this storytelling, or something you learned from your mother who was On The Stage? Reading aloud never happened at home – Mama and That Man only ever read Arabic newspapers and magazines. Reading was for information, not pleasure. Whenever I asked Mama to make up a story for me, she got embarrassed and impatient. Being other people didn't come naturally to her. Was that why she always looked so drained and exhausted in England, where acting was a constant requirement, one way or another?

As for why my tongue was pressed against the TV, that was harder to explain than why I wanted to be a dog. It was a feeling, an intuition. I knew the girl on *Top of the Pops* had happiness flowing through her veins in a way that I didn't – neither did Mama, or Sherine, or That Man. It was part of her, not something that came and went like fleeting patches of sunlight. I wanted that quality too. Seeing this girl with her halo of happiness brought a realisation that not everyone lived how I lived – not everyone woke up with a heaviness in their stomach, a feeling that something horrible was about to happen. Some people wore pink ribbons in their hair and danced and skipped and didn't care.

Did you have the happiness gene? You weren't a skipper. You weren't light like candyfloss, not like that girl. But you gave the impression of having something even better than happiness, an older, wiser cousin of it – peace.

When everything fell apart and I learned that you were acting about that too, buried among all the other emotions was a small, grudging flicker of admiration. I only registered it much later, when I'd taken a hammer to my own life. Who knew that you were so talented? Why did you end up being a librarian, ignored and invisible, rather than an actress like your mother? Up there on the stage, frozen in adoration under dust-flecked spotlights, shining for all the world to see.

Act of destruction

I decided to detonate my bomb in October 2002, when the clock started ticking in earnest. Kieran and I had settled on moving back to London in the spring. We'd go to a mosque and get him turned into a Muslim, then I'd tell my parents, and then we'd get married.

One Friday night that October, I went out drinking with work people. My manager was there – Boss-man's boss. He seemed much older than me, but he was only thirty-four. German-American, very tall, with the whitest, straightest teeth I'd ever seen. He had his own office, on the other side of the floor from us. Lilia said he had a soft spot for me because he'd said I was 'sharp' in my performance review, though she'd put it more bluntly. 'He wants to bone you,' she'd said. 'No one else got "sharp" – I've asked around – and let's face it, you're really not the sharpest tool in the box, Ness—'

'Shut up, bitchface!' I'd smacked her on the bum with a rolled-up copy of our newly produced guide to the best bars in Tokyo. 'He probably just said it because I'm the only one who ever laughs at his jokes.'

The special relationship between me and my manager had begun without me really noticing. He'd been on a business trip to New York on 11 September the year before, and I'd found myself worrying about him to an extent that had taken me by surprise.

As if he was a friend, not my manager. From conversations with other people, I realised he'd replied to my email asking if he was okay much earlier than he'd replied to others. There was a tragic backstory in his life – his wife had died suddenly a few years ago, aged twenty-seven, three months pregnant. I was wary of him in the office – he could be cold and scathing; he'd once told me off for letting through a restaurant review where every paragraph started with a 'the' – but I liked to sit next to him at social events and try to make him laugh, feeling I'd scored some kind of victory. One time, he used the adjective 'fly', ironically, and I shoehorned in a joke about Spanish Fly.

'What's up with Matt?' someone said. 'He's giggling like a five-year-old girl.'

On that Friday in October, I said 'Can I see your watch?', leaning close to him, brushing my fingers against his forearm in a way that could've been accidental.

'Let me see yours,' he said, after I'd pretended to look. It was a silver watch Sherine had bought me from Next, which looked like a bracelet. He held onto the elasticated metal strap for what seemed like ages, examining the watch intently, assiduously avoiding touching my skin. That was the last physical contact we had until 3.30am, when we held hands as we walked back to his flat.

This time, the clothes came off. That was in the nature of this act of destruction. When I manoeuvred myself into the right position on top of him, I said, 'Oh Jesus Christ,' at the electric shock to my stomach. At the miracle of feeling again, at last.

'Jesus Christ is my lord, not yours,' he whispered in the semi-darkness, and I said, 'Shut up,' whispering back, putting my hand over his mouth. Laughing because I knew we were both atheists.

*

I got home around 6.30am, turning my minidisc player off when I reached the door. 'Laundry Service' by Shakira. She escorted me home on my walks of shame in those months. Kieran was in bed, fast asleep. My Friday nights didn't keep him up any more. He'd got used to them. He went out with his workmates too, although he was always home before me. I had a shower and put on a T-shirt and a pair of his boxer shorts, then I crept under the sheets beside him. He put his arm around me and we slept like that for a few hours.

That Saturday was peaceful, unhurried, as if we were both convalescing from an illness. We went shopping then came home and watched videos. He laid his head on my lap and I stroked his hair. We were watching *The Sopranos*, resuming halfway through an episode where Tony becomes haunted by a fantasy of a beautiful, voluptuous woman in a white dress. Something to do with his mother, who hated him. The last time we'd watched it, I couldn't sit still – I had to keep getting up to fill the kettle, check the washing, do anything to get rid of the tight, heavy feeling in my chest. This time was different: I sat still, breathing easily, enjoying the storyline and the feel of the soft hair between my fingers.

The pile of magazines that Sherine had sent over from London had lost their bite too. I picked one up from the coffee table later and read it from cover to cover, even the articles about orgasms and g-spots, which would've had me flicking hurriedly past only a day earlier, anxious to avoid seeing those words. They didn't bother me now.

*

When I told Mariana what I'd done, it was a German expression that hovered, unspoken, over our telephone conversation.

'Are you sure?' she said. 'You can still stop this – you can still sort things out with Kieran, if you want to.'

'I can't. It's too late. It's all ruined.'

'It doesn't have to be ruined, Ness. You could put it all behind you – a last fling before you settle down. He doesn't have to know. It was only the once. Anyway, how do you know he hasn't done the same?'

'He hasn't! Stop trying to make out this is anyone's fault but mine!'

'Sorry,' I said into the offended silence on the other end of the phone. 'But I honestly don't think he would. He's not that sort of person.'

The pause that followed gave time for reflection. For thinking about what sort of a person it was, who would do the thing I'd just done.

What I didn't bother explaining to Mariana was that everything had been ruined two years ago – the night of the magic mushrooms. The night I'd lied to Kieran for the first time. So what if nothing much had happened with Canadian Paul? It was the principle of the thing and the thoughts that had followed. Thought crimes were the worst, weren't they? Ever since then, my mind had been cast in a role it didn't like – the role of a furtive, weasel-faced villain. The only way to fix it was to walk out of this play and start again, as a new character, one true to the ideals I'd always preached; one worthy of the crown my victim had placed upon my head just before I'd knifed him in the back. The role of someone brave and honest.

(Did the thought of taking a break from the drama and razzmatazz of relationships altogether cross my mind? I can't say it did. If a seemingly self-contained woman of the world like you could leap out of the frying pan and into a Californian whirlwind – pouf! – what chance did I have?)

The German expression Mariana had unconsciously paraphrased was '*einmal ist keinmal*', which means 'something that happens only once might as well have not happened at all'. I'd read that in *The Unbearable Lightness of Being*. It didn't apply to my situation now, though: whatever the Germans might say, *einmal* had proven once too many in my particular case.

Two years after this conversation, when I was getting ready to move back to England for good, the expression cropped up again, in a different context. I was recovering from a bout of the flu that had knocked me out for a week. It had come on during another telephone call, one that brought a revelation which kicked off the series of events that culminated in me sitting at your bedside. The layers of wilful ignorance wrapped around me since childhood had peeled off during that phone call, leaving me with no choice but to join the dots. Finally, I understood the true nature of the catastrophe that had blasted you out of our lives and all the way to California. Finally, I understood why the situation you'd found yourself in was untenable. Why something had to blow the lid off the pressure cooker in which you'd slowly been roasting alive. Was it a coincidence that I was struck down by illness just then, an easy target for the bacteria that circle like vultures, in my raw, unprotected state?

But one piece of the puzzle remained unsolved, encapsulated in those German words. The expression kept buzzing around my head as I lay shivering and sweating on my sickbed. When I'd shaken off the fever and stood on the platform waiting for the train to take me to work, still woozy from my illness, it continued. *Einmal ist keinmal.* It seemed to skate around my brain in a graceful figure of eight as I sat on the bench in the little park opposite my office, chewing on the tuna onigiri I bought for lunch every day until my stomach could handle something more substantial, not tasting it, barely noticing it. *Einmal ist keinmal.* What I needed to know was this: was it just *einmal* for you, Genevieve?

Brave and honest

Kieran and I tried our best to split everything in half when we broke up in January 2003. The maths was easier with some things than others.

Books were straightforward. He didn't want my Margaret Atwoods and Paul Bowleses and Graham Greenes, and I didn't want his Iain M. Bankses and Neil Gaimans and Terry Pratchetts.

'Maybe we should've made more of an effort,' he said, watching me pick clumps of books off the bookcase. 'Instead of slobbing round reading and watching videos at the weekend. We should've gone out more, done things. I should've tried harder. I shouldn't have taken you for granted.'

'Don't,' I said. 'You know this is nothing to do with anything you did, or didn't do. Please don't say that.'

We took another break to hug each other and cry.

CDs required more thought because we'd bought lots of them together. Some caused minor arguments.

'You take the Nick Cave...'

'No, you take it – you listen to it more than I do.'

'Please, Nessie, you take it... It would make me too sad, listening to those songs without you.'

'All right, then,' I said meekly, accepting that I should be the one to bear the burden of Nick Cave, because this whole thing was, after all, only happening because I'd said it should.

Practicalities dictated our decisions about the furniture. I'd take the chest of drawers and he'd keep the bed. There'd be a single bed at the place I was moving to, a partly furnished studio apartment in Minami-Asagaya where you didn't have to pay key money and you could leave with only a month's notice. It was an apartment block for people who didn't know if they were coming or going, leaving Japan or just arriving. In the meantime, our routine continued more or less as usual.

'Gareth says he thinks it's weird that we're still sharing a bed,' Kieran had said, a few days earlier. 'He says I should move onto the sofa and let you have the bed... He says it's not healthy for us to keep living as if nothing's changed.'

'Gareth can go fuck himself.' I felt the tip of my nose turn hot and red. How dare people stick their beaks in like carrion crows, picking over the entrails of other people's relationships? What made 'Gareth', whose name didn't even have the courtesy to attach itself to a face, the arbiter of what was 'healthy'? Didn't Gareth, whoever he was, understand that breakup or no breakup, I still needed that body beside me in the bed? I needed to lie behind it at night and bury my head in the warm, broad expanse of its back. I needed to position myself in a spot where my nose could touch the nape of its neck, another wellspring of that clean, innocent smell of his. I needed to be able to reach around and stroke its stomach, which he'd started patting ruefully, saying, 'Gotta cut out the snacks, I'm starting to look seven months pregnant,' and which I used to kiss, saying, 'Don't be so stupid – of course you don't.' A kiss was a step too far now, but I still needed to stroke it.

I needed all those things, but I also had to be careful, because a confusion had embedded itself in my subconscious ever since my double life began; since I'd started going to my manager's place two or three times a week in the evenings, saying I had to work late.

On the morning we started dividing our things up, Kieran had said, 'Do you remember what you did last night?' and I said, 'No. What?'

'You took off your T-shirt. You sat up out of the blue and took off your T-shirt and put my hand on you... You were making a sound, like you wanted to...'

Unable to keep my eyes pinned to his face with its smile lines that had flipped the wrong way around and its agonised question marks and its quivering, tentative expression of hope, I looked at the bed instead, as if the events were about to replay themselves there in holographic form.

'I don't know, baby,' I said. 'I was asleep. Maybe I was just too hot, or cold.'

And on we went, dividing things into two lots. Cutlery, pillowcases, condoms. 'Take your share,' he said firmly. 'I want you to be all right when the time comes. I want you to look after yourself.'

Then we came across the gift he'd bought me, in the top drawer on the right of the chest. 'Well?' His tone was flat and defeated as he held the object out to me.

'Ummm...'

'Let's just throw it away. Let's just get rid of it.'

'Okay. But where do we throw it? Does it go into the burnable or non-burnable rubbish?'

'I don't know. What's it made of?' When I made no effort to touch it, he squeezed it gingerly and said, 'It feels like rubber, I think.'

'So it can go into the burnable rubbish? Can you burn rubber?'

'I don't think so. I think rubber is non-burnable.'

'Why do people talk about burning rubber, then?'

'That means something else.'

'Oh. Well, we'd better get it right if we're gonna throw it away. The last thing we want is the Komodo Dragon fishing it out of the bag and leaving it outside our door, like she did with the milk carton.'

The previous caretaker of our building, a sweet, smiling woman in her sixties, had recently been disappeared after a small fire broke out in one of the flats. Her replacement was made of sterner stuff. Steel wool rather than the fluffy cotton variety. She scowled and muttered things under her breath when she passed us in the stairwell.

'Imagine what the neighbours would say if they saw a vibrator outside our door!' I said.

He didn't reply.

Suddenly, there was a whiff of blame in the air. Something intruding on all the sad, tender goodbyes, like the smell of decaying organic matter wafting out of the rubbish room downstairs. Why had I never made the effort to acquaint myself with this appendage? Why hadn't I formed an association with it that might've made all the difference, might've averted this disaster and prevented the need for us to be where we were now, breaking our lives in two?

That's when he said, in a preamble I'd been dreading, 'Nessie, I have to ask you something.'

'What?' My breath caught in my chest.

'I know you've explained what this is about... I know our sex life's gone down the toilet, and we can't condemn each other to a lifetime of that. I understand where you're coming from, and I respect your decision, but I have to ask you: is there anyone else? Because if there is and you're not being honest with me, I don't think I'll be able to stay friends with you.'

'No.' I looked him straight in the eye. 'Of course there's no one else. You know I'd never do that to you.'

'Thank you,' he said, exhaling with a sound that gave me permission to release my own breath. 'I didn't think you would, but I just had to ask.'

As it turned out, I ended up keeping the gift Kieran had given me. Some intuition told me it might come in useful, and it did. The day I moved into my short-term let, I opened the chest of drawers that had moved with me and finally laid my hand on the object. Transporting it to my bed, I curled up in a ball and wept as I ran my fingers along its jaunty, unequivocal hardness. Who knew that this stick could serve a purpose so different from the one it was designed for? Who knew that it could be a device for converting the grief and shame that lay trapped in the pit of a stomach into a steady, cleansing rain of tears?

Nick Cave did his bit too, cranked up as loud as he'd go on my headphones, howling like a mournful dog at the moon. I was nobody's baby now.

Performance review

At first, it was my misery that gave my manager cause to question my performance.

'I'm worried I've ruined your life. You don't seem very sure you've made the right decision.' Eyes cast down, he swilled his whisky around his glass.

It was a Saturday night in February and we were in a small, dimly lit bar near his flat, just me, him and the barman. We confined our outings to the dark hours and a tiny patch of streets where no one was likely to see us. He lived in a fancy apartment block in Ebisu, where none of the plebs from English editorial were likely to be hanging around.

'No, I think I have,' I said, welling up again. 'I just hate myself for all the lying... but you understand why I couldn't tell him, don't you?'

'Yes, of course. We couldn't run the risk of a scene at work – that wouldn't be good for either of us.'

His words stopped the tears from spiralling into the kind that would've required me to slide off my stool and take a trip to the toilet to blow my nose. He was right. Of course telling the truth wasn't an option. Of course I'd had no choice but to lie.

'Yeah,' I said. 'Although I don't think he would've done that. He's not that kind of person. I've never really known him blow up like that. But then, you never know, right?'

'Right.'

It hadn't escaped my attention that each 'he' or 'him' that came out of my mouth seemed to make my manager's mouth creep downwards.

'Sorry,' I said. 'I know I keep going on about him. I'll get over it, I promise.'

I put my hand on his leg and gave it a squeeze. We ordered two more drinks: another whisky for him, a Cointreau for me. The barman poured them with one hand thrown up in front of his face as if he was shielding his eyes from some dazzling light only he could see.

'Did I tell you I'm going to London for work next week?' said my manager as we watched, mesmerised.

'I can't believe you'll be in my hood! So weird to think of you there.'

'I like London. Maybe I'll pay a little visit to your dad's shop on Edgware Road and introduce myself.' Putting on what he called his Hearty Dave from Kansas voice: 'Well hi there, Mr Boughanmi! You don't know me but I'm uh, Nessie's boyfriend! Just thought I'd uh, pop by and introduce myself!'

'Jesus,' I said. 'Don't!'

It wasn't just the Cointreau warming my stomach. It was the word 'boyfriend'. My manager was my boyfriend. How had that happened? It was what I'd dreamt of for months, and yet it seemed more of a concept than a reality. Something from a film. It was easy to imagine yourself in a film when you lived on the other side of the world, and went to moody bars where solitary barmen did strange things with their hands, and everything was softened by a lack of understanding. Had my parents ever felt like this in London? I doubted it. They had me and Sherine to worry about, and other concerns: money, landladies, rent, a limited supply of hot water. Things like that have a habit of bringing your surroundings into sharp focus.

My manager did more of this imaginary dialogue with That Man, and I laughed and wiped my eyes and said, 'Don't! Don't!'

Of course, it wasn't just my 'him' and 'he' that kept cropping up. My manager had a pronoun of his own to contend with. 'I didn't think I could ever be with anyone again, after she died,' he'd said. 'It was so sudden... I felt like, why should I still be alive when she was dead?'

'I'm so, so sorry, sweetie,' I'd said, cradling his head. 'It must've been so awful – I can't imagine.'

'The funny thing is,' he said to me once when we were talking on the phone, 'I don't know if our marriage would've lasted if she was still alive. She could be a difficult person. We didn't bring out the best in each other sometimes. She always seemed to have the upper hand.'

'Oh?'

'Yeah. I didn't always like her, but she had something... I think it was her intelligence. I'd never met anyone with a brain like hers. Such an unbelievably fierce, uncompromising intelligence.'

'Oh.' Suddenly, the 'sharp' I'd got in my performance review didn't seem all that. It seemed mediocre. Below par. A poor relation to that fierce, uncompromising intelligence. And she was stunning too. Her picture sat on the top shelf of the bookcase in his living room. She was from Shanghai, and had studied with him at Harvard. She had a pointy, elfin face and long, perfect hair. I saw smugness and malice in her expression, though. She didn't seem like someone I would've liked, if I'd met her. She'd already made me feel ungainly, frazzle-headed and ugly, and now she was making me feel stupid too. And then there was the pregnancy... She was sanctified in perpetuity by her uncontrollable fecundity – he'd told me it was an accident, they'd been planning to wait a couple more years – and by her selfless desire to bring another being into the world and look after it. Like an unbelievably, fiercely, uncompromisingly intelligent Virgin Mary. The bitch. I was frosty to him for the rest of the conversation and we didn't speak again for two days.

'Did I say something wrong?' he said when he eventually phoned me. 'Things got a bit weird between us, didn't they? Did I put my big foot in it somehow?'

Laughing in relief that he'd ended the silence and that he'd noticed my *froideur*, I said, 'No, no! I was being silly. I guess I just resented the implication that I wasn't intelligent enough for you.'

'What do you mean?'

'Well, you know, when you were saying how intelligent she was... it made me feel like you were saying I was stupid.'

'What do you mean? Why would you think that? I was talking about her, not you. I didn't say anything about you.'

'Yes, I know,' I said, making sure my voice told him that was the problem.

'I'm sorry, Nessie. I really don't know where this is coming from, but I can assure you I don't think you're stupid. I'm not the kind of guy who goes for stupid women!'

And that was the best I could get out of him. I nearly said, 'I bet you like her hair better than mine too, don't you?' but I bit my tongue, congratulating myself on my self-restraint. A narrow swerve away from a fatal crash into indignity.

We batted those pronouns back and forth between us over the next few months. I cried over my him and clenched my teeth over his her. He brooded over his her and did a downward dog pose with his mouth over my him.

'He's still your best friend, and that's difficult for me to deal with. You're the only person I'm close to in this country, but your best friend is someone else...'

'I didn't want to marry him, but I miss him so much...'

'It's hard for me to let myself be happy. She never had the chance to live properly... why should I?'

'You have to stop blaming yourself. I'm sure she wouldn't want you to live like this, like a bystander in your own life...'

Him and her, her and him. They just wouldn't leave us alone, those pronouns. They just wouldn't get on with their lives and leave us to get on with ours.

Best friends

My manager was right – he wasn't my best friend, even though he'd witnessed the striptease of the soul that's part of any courtship. The problem was that each layer I revealed in our intimate conversations became something other than what it was – like when your Stephen lifted up the carpet in your living room and, with the help of a noisy, juddering machine, transformed the shabby floorboards into something lustrous and glowing, their imperfections polished into beauty. When my manager eventually saw me at my worst – my real worst, not the prettified version I presented as we lay whispering bedtime stories about ourselves – it was too late. Too much had happened for us to be friends of any kind.

'But I told you,' I was tempted to say to his pale, shaken face after I'd thrown crockery at his head and smashed his dead wife's smile to smithereens. 'I told you I'd thrown scissors at people and I used to tear out clumps of my own hair in a rage, and you just laughed at what a "wilful" child I was.'

'What right do you have,' I wanted to say, 'to claim to be "disturbed" by the fact that I sent you twenty emails, phoned you thirty times, and hand-delivered a letter to you all in one day after you refused to hear my apology? Don't you remember me telling you how I once stood in a phone box on Wood Green High Road with Mariana, dialling and hanging up on a floppy-haired boy I fancied for a solid half hour until she said, "Come on Ness, let's go before this turns into *Fatal Attraction*"?'

But my manager wasn't to blame. It was my fault. I'd made my flaws sound funny. I'd dressed them up for an audience I wanted to impress, rather than displaying them in all their nakedness to someone who claimed to want to be my best friend.

What about you, Genevieve? Did you ever have a best friend? Was your best friend the woman sitting next to you in this rare instance of your entrapment by camera? The two of you are perched on the bench outside our flat in Cranfield Gardens, photographed from an odd, low angle, as if by a child. Perhaps it was a child. Perhaps the child was me. Was it spring or summer? It must've been warm, warm enough not to need a coat. You're wearing a pale green dress that comes almost down to your ankles, a light swirl of chiffon and silk. Mama is wearing a tight, emerald-green T-shirt and a bright yellow knee-length skirt with a butterfly print, an outfit I hated. I liked her in the flowing djellabas she wore at home or the smart skirts and blazers she wore when we went out to meet other Arabs. Not these clothes that looked like something I would wear, containing a body too big for them. A body the wrong shape for them. She was denser than you, more compact. Your slimness disguised the larger space you occupied. I always knew you were taller than her, taller than both of them, but I'd forgotten how you dwarfed us all, being built to a different scale.

How old was I when I asked Mama who her best friend was? Eight or nine, of an age when these things are a pressing concern, and she'd said, smiling: '*You're* my best friend, *ma perle*.'

'No!' This adult prevarication annoyed me. 'Who's your real best friend – like Mariana?'

'I don't have a best friend.' She sounded tired and sulky.

'What about Aunty Amira?'

'I only see her once a year now, during Ramadan.'

I thought for a moment, then said, 'Aunty Noura?'

'She's always busy with her husband and children. She's got no time for anyone else. You can't rely on anyone but your sisters or brothers to be your best friends, but what can you do when you're so far away from them?'

I hesitated before offering up the next name, already sensing something unbefitting about it – something awkward and inappropriate in attaching it to those two words, just as there was in Mama forcing her grown-up body into girlish clothes.

'Mrs Brown?' I said in an offhand kind of way.

She looked at me with a startled expression, her eyes opening wide, as if she'd never considered this possibility. Then she said, in a seeming non-sequitur, 'But she's English.'

'But she speaks French,' I replied, taking us further down the rabbit hole.

We stood looking at each other, her face retaining its perplexed expression, before I changed the subject. She'd given me what I needed. She'd confirmed what I'd suspected in the split second before I'd said your name.

I never asked you if you had a best friend. Something told me that you operated outside this framework, just as Mama did. Your reasons were different, though; I knew that too. Don't ask me how or why.

Saddam pulls it off again

When our benefactor, Saddam Hussein, popped up again more than twelve years after the first time, everything had changed. Mama had gone back to Tunisia, I was living in Japan and Sherine was in her own flat in Wimbledon. That Man was alone in his house – no family shawarma in front of the TV this time around. But true to the traditions of Arab hospitality, Saddam didn't show up empty-handed. Our patron still pulled a rabbit of sorts out of a hat for us.

'Did you go on the march?' said Sherine, phoning me the day after the world had tried to Stop the War. 'I saw they had one in Tokyo too.'

'No, I had to work yesterday. Big deadline on Tuesday.'

The truth was that I'd spent the day with my manager. It was the first full day we'd ever spent together. He'd made us breakfast in his flat, granola with hot soya milk followed by French toast, then we'd watched videos – *The Enigma of Kaspar Hauser*, *Paris, Texas* and *ER* – and had sex on the sofa until it was time for dinner, which I'd made: a tagine based heavily around carrots, a vegetable I usually found bland and uncompelling but had bought in the absence of other root vegetables in the supermarket that morning. When I took a mouthful of the tagine, the rich earthiness of the flavour made me exclaim: 'The carrots!'

'What's wrong with them?'

'They taste of carrots.'

'And that, folks,' he said, gesturing to an imaginary audience, 'is why I hired this woman.'

This was the golden thread running through that day. Everything I ate or touched or smelt – the parsley and honey and carrots in the tagine, the rough cotton of the sofa cover, the black tar soap in the bathroom – had an intensity that seemed to erupt from its very essence, as if the dulling layers of familiarity that characterise everyday life had peeled off, revealing the wondrous nature of all organisms.

But Sherine wasn't really interested in whether or not I'd gone on the march. She wanted to tell me about her own Saturday, spent marching in London with That Man.

'We met at Oxford Circus,' she said. 'I went to the hairdressers early so we'd get there on time... half a head, caramel highlights... fitted in my nails quickly too... You wouldn't believe the crowd... I thought he'd moan about all the walking with his bunions but he wore comfortable shoes for once... We ran into Uncle Ali and his kids, pure coincidence, then we went for a coffee with them afterwards...'

Her voice was infused with a warmth I'd rarely heard in connection to an experience involving That Man. But maybe that wasn't as unexpected as it seemed. Time had passed. Their landmark moments had circled various anniversaries by then. Perhaps that turbulent river had run its course and was content to be a still, placid lake.

Fourteen years had passed, for example, since he'd forced her to give up her place at Bristol University so she could stay in London and sleep in her own bed.

Nine years had passed since she'd told me she'd considered spraying antifreeze onto his rice as it boiled on the stove after she'd worked a fourteen-hour day and then come home to a breezy 'What are you making for dinner tonight?'

'He even made Mama cook dinner the first night we arrived in London,' she told me, her voice shaking with anger. 'She got confused and tried to fry burgers in ice cream because she thought it was butter. Never any rest for anyone but him…'

'The lazy fucker!' I said. 'Couldn't he be arsed to make dinner just that one time?'

'I know, I know. And he wonders why she left him.'

Seven years had passed since he'd watched Sherine stagger out of a taxi wearing a coat splattered with red wine and vomit, and lurch up the path to the house, swaying from side to side.

'What did he say, what did he say?' I said when she told me.

'Nothing. He just looked at me without saying anything, then I said, "I'm off to bed" and that was that.'

Seven years had passed since he'd told her she'd burn in hell if she followed through on her plan to leave home, at the age of twenty-four, intercepting the brochures that had come for her from the estate agents and throwing them in the kitchen bin without bothering to hide the evidence. She rang me at university and said, 'I'm gonna fucking kill him if I don't get out of there.' I don't know what shocked me the most: her use of a swear word or of 'gonna'.

Six years had passed since I went to see him after Sherine had gone, bundling her stuff into a minicab at 2am, dragging her nail down his face when he'd tried to block her way. He'd said to me, looking old and broken, beads of drying blood running from his forehead to the tip of his nose, 'I've got no one now. No one.' Then he'd said, 'Please phone her and check she's okay. I need to know she's okay.'

Five years and six months had passed since they'd started speaking again after they both came to see me off at the airport when I left for Japan. This reconciliation almost allowed me to convince myself I had more noble motives for running away to the other side of the world than cowardice at the prospect of enduring the same exhausting battle myself.

All those milestones had passed, and now Sherine sounded ready for something else. She sounded ready for times spent doing things with That Man voluntarily, on a Saturday afternoon no less, fitting him in around highlights and nail appointments. Times spent walking side by side in a common cause, wearing sensible shoes that precluded frayed tempers and bickering caused by pinched, aching feet. Times spent having coffee with friends, family friends, safe in the knowledge that family no longer meant a boulder strapped permanently to your back, but something you could pick up and put down as you needed. I watched these developments from six thousand miles away, my pleasure shot through with a generous dollop of relief that I wasn't the one who had to spend those times with him.

'I'm pleased you had fun!' I said, and she said: 'Yes!' before we both seemed to recall the reason for the excursion. But even as we chatted about the criminality and the injustice and the endless pummelling of the Iraqi people, our voices were bright, bubbling with the realisation that new emotions could spring from unexpected sources.

'I know it sounds funny,' she said, 'but I almost feel like he's part of my life now.'

For a second I thought she meant Saddam Hussein, and then I realised she was talking about the other one – the tricky, moustachioed man who seemed to have decided to stop being a tyrant, reviled and ostracised by all right-thinking people, and finally build bridges with the civilised world.

After dark, Tia Maria

Kieran got engaged to someone else six months after we broke up. I cried when he told me, and he took both my hands in his, looking a little bit pleased. I didn't begrudge him his pleasure. He deserved it.

'She said she'd always liked me,' he said as we sat at our usual table in the Indian restaurant in Shinjuku where we'd got engaged. 'I'd never thought of her that way, but then you think, well why not… I didn't tell you I was seeing anyone so soon because I didn't want to upset you… didn't want you to think I'd moved on too quickly. I would've waited if I'd thought there was any chance of you changing your mind, but, you know, you have to make your own happiness, don't you?'

'You do, you do.' I dabbed at my eyes with my fingers when he released them. 'I'm really happy for you.'

I'd met his new fiancée a couple of times before. She was Irish too, a workmate of his, the captain of a women's hurling team in Tokyo. Her hair was a nondescript shade of brown, neither straight nor curly. No one had ever described her as having a fiercely uncompromising intelligence. Not in my earshot anyway. He'd always said she was 'gas', one of those Irishisms I used to tease him about, like 'bold' instead of naughty and 'messages' instead of shopping. Gas was fine; I was gas too. He used to say he'd never laughed as hard with anyone as he had with me. She might be gas, but I'd been his helium canister.

'What about you?' he said suddenly. 'Are you seeing anyone?'

As if it knew my mind better than I did, my mouth opened and said, 'Yes. Yes, I am.'

'Oh really?' He raised his eyebrows, smiling: 'You never said anything either!'

'Yeah, I know... It's really early days still. I'll tell you about it when things are more definite, if that's okay? You know I don't like jinxing myself.'

I ran my fingers along the neckline of my sleeveless polo neck to check it was pulled all the way up. It was July and sweltering, but I'd taken to wearing polo necks whenever I met him in case awkward questions arose. The kind preceded by 'Nessie, I have to ask you something.' The kind that would cause a rash to erupt all over my upper torso as if I'd been rolling around half-naked in a bed of nettles. Redness in the face could be blamed on simple girlish embarrassment, but tie-dye blotches on the neck and chest screamed of a more serious disorder.

'Sure, sure,' he said. 'Whenever you like.' After a pause, he said, 'He must be someone really special for you not to want to jinx it.' And for a second we both had to look away because of the tears that had jumped to his eyes.

*

My manager had asked me to go to his place around 12pm the next day. I went to Shinjuku Park in the morning and lay on the grass reading P.G. Wodehouse, enjoying the solitude because I knew it would end soon. All this time alone was something I had to get used to again. My manager was often busy with work dinners, conference calls, trips abroad; the business of managing people, me among them.

'I don't know what to say about you in your performance review,' he'd grumbled a couple of months ago. 'Of course, I want to say you're wonderful, but now I don't know if that's because you're my girlfriend or my subordinate.'

I'd sat astride him and pretended to strangle him because of the 'subordinate', but my heart had leapt again at the word 'girlfriend'; at the recurring sensation that I – or rather, a more glamorous, more luminous, infinitely more enchanting version of myself – was starring in a film of my own life. Not a Hollywood blockbuster, but something dreamlike and drenched in sadness, like *Mulholland Drive*, which we'd watched together on video, hitting pause once to have sex when the main characters did. The kind of sadness that doesn't weigh on you too heavily because film sadness is different from real sadness.

When he opened the door to his flat, I flung my arms around his neck and kissed him before I took off my shoes in the *genkan*. I was wearing wedge-heeled sandals that made me feel nearly as tall as he was. Kissing him from that vantage point reinforced the idea of me as a super-charged version of myself.

'Hi, hi,' he said, pulling away, looking distracted. 'The aircon's not working and I've been trying to get someone to fix it, but we've been having non-stop miscommunication so God knows when they'll actually come.'

'Jesus Christ,' I said as I stepped into the hallway. 'It's like an oven in here.' I didn't offer to call the aircon people myself. My Japanese was no better than his. Words went into my ears and coalesced into some kind of meaning, but my attempts to reverse the process were met with the same blank stares that had followed Mama around like a bad smell in England. My Arabic was beginning to crumble too for lack of practice. I was starting to inhabit a linguistic no-man's land, unlike the dead wife, who'd spoken four languages, fluently.

'Yeah, I know it's hotter than Hades,' he said, snappily. 'But as I said, I've been trying to call them—'

'I know, I know.' I raised my hands placatingly. 'Don't worry, it'll get sorted.'

'Sorry, sweetie. It just feels like one thing after another at the moment...'

He ran on for a while about his boss who hated him – my manager squared, a diminutive former Broadway pianist from Iowa renowned for his spite and his polka dot bow ties. People called him The Pinprick. When he'd finished, I told him about my dinner with Kieran last night:

'It feels like such a relief. For the first time in months, I slept properly... Now I know he's okay, and that I've been honest with him too, sort of. I really thought I was gonna lie and say no when he asked if I was seeing anyone, but then it just kind of came out.'

'But you didn't tell him it was me, right?' This was the second time he'd asked.

'No, I told you I didn't. I thought I'd wait a while until everything settles. Tread carefully.'

'Yeah, yeah, good. Because The Pinprick would hang my ass out to dry if he found out about us right now.'

'Why, though? There's no law against it. It's not in our contracts or anything that you can't covet thy neighbour's ass. And we wouldn't be the only ones...'

One of the Japanese line managers had just married his own subordinate.

He snorted, darkly. 'Yeah, but they don't report to pricks like him.'

'Well. We'll both have to get other jobs anyway, when we move to London. Did you ask your friend Emma about that marketing job you said you might go for?'

'Not yet.'

There was a pause. The stuffy air of the living room was making me open and close my mouth like a goldfish. He held an ice pack to his forehead.

'Be nice if we could go for a walk,' I said. 'Go and sit in the air-conditioning in Freshness Burger and have a mango smoothie...'

'You know we can't do that, Nessie. Not right now, okay? Once I sort out all this work crap and get The Pinprick off my back, we can come clean and go out like a regular couple, Ted and Marsha from Missouri, but for now, daylight is dead to us. It's after dark only.'

'Tia Maria.'

'What?'

'It was an advert,' I said. 'Back at home. "After dark, Tia Maria".'

'You people are weird,' he said, with no discernible hint of laughter in his voice. And from her pedestal on the bookcase, his dead wife looked on, her smile seeming to have grown another inch since I last saw it.

*

As if he had a sixth sense for knowing exactly when I didn't need this shit, That Man phoned me out of the blue that night, back on his old form.

'When are you coming home, madam?'... 'What's keeping you over there?'... 'I'm an old man now but you don't care'... 'You think you're an English person, you think your life is yours to play with, but you've got responsibilities...'

Sherine told me afterwards that he'd been looking at old pictures and it had put him in a sentimental mood.

'Couldn't he just say "I miss you"?' I said.

As he ranted on, I held the phone away from my ear and let him continue until he ran out of steam. When we'd said our goodbyes, I sank my teeth into the fleshy part of my palm, then walked over to the bathroom door and slammed it as hard as I could, three times, the word 'home' ringing in my ears. A chunk of plasterboard came crumbling to the floor, and the door wouldn't close properly after that. When I finally left Japan I had to pay for it out of my deposit, conceding defeat to those four letters that always had to have the last word.

Once more,
with feeling

Sherine took the news of my former fiancé's engagement much worse than I did. I mentioned it on the phone, slipping it in after an anecdote about an Italian restaurant in Ginza that I'd been to with Lilia: '...The best arrabbiata I've ever had – by the way, Kieran got engaged to Noirin, you met her at the Christmas party at Will's flat when you came to Tokyo.'

'Already?' she squeaked. 'He didn't waste any time!'

'It's been six months.'

'I'll never understand that kind of fickle behaviour. How can you can go from wanting to marry one person to wanting to marry someone else in the blink of an eye?'

'Well, it was me who broke up with him...' My pulse had ratcheted up with each do-re-mi of her voice. Why did she always have to sound like this – like a teacher telling the whole world off? And why had I even bothered telling her? Because it was one of those things that normal people shared, with normal sisters.

She made a sound like a heavy breather down the phone. 'I know it was you who broke up with him, but I never really understood why.'

My silence elicited another sigh. 'Are you sure you didn't make a mistake, Susu? You've sounded so down ever since it happened. I'm worried about you.'

'I'm fine.' I suddenly wanted to cry in the way you do when someone says they're worried about you.

'I know it sounds selfish, but it was easier for me knowing you were with Kieran. I didn't have to worry about you being so far away, on your own, because I knew you were with someone who cared about you.'

Now her concern felt like yet another burden to bear. Why was it down to me to provide the model family we'd never had? Mother, father and their 2.4 children tossing out sickly grins like frisbees from behind a white picket fence. If she was gagging for a happily ever after, why didn't she arrange one for herself, instead of settling for what she called her 'little flings'?

'I just don't like to think of you being miserable,' she said. 'If you've made a mistake, you should tell him. He can still get unengaged and get back with you!'

'Your faith in my irresistibility is touching,' I said, trying to laugh her out of it, but she made another one of her blowhole sounds.

Finally, grudgingly, I said, 'Actually, I'm seeing someone too.'

'Oh yes?' She sounded more surprised than seemed necessary.

'Yes. A guy I work with. I'll tell you about it later if that's okay? It's still early days and you know I don't like to jinx myself.'

The words came out lifeless and robotic, from a mouth that was sulky and recalcitrant now. Stripped of its earlier ease and spontaneity. Fed up with this script and ready for a new one.

*

A year or so later, on my next trip to London, I was having cocktails and nachos at TGI Fridays in Covent Garden with Sherine, and she said, 'It's a shame it didn't work out with you and Kieran.'

'I know.'

'He was such a great guy. He reminded me a bit of Michael.'

'Oh.' I took a sip of my mint julep.

'Michael was your boyfriend at university, wasn't he?'

For Christ's sake, there she went again, digging into my private life as if it was any of her business. How did she know, anyway? I'd always told her he was just a friend.

'Yes,' I said. 'You could say that.'

'I haven't heard you mention him for years. Or Amy, actually. Wasn't she your best friend at university? You lost touch with her too, didn't you?'

It wasn't just the jabbing tone in her voice that got me; it was the words themselves. I looked down at my plate and willed the hot, prickling sensation behind my eyes to go away.

'Amy was lovely, wasn't she? And Michael and Kieran were so kind and genuine, both of them. You seem to have a knack for attracting people like that, but you don't realise how rare they are. They all adored you.'

'Well, I loved them too.' My voice came out all hoarse. 'Always will. And I won't lose touch with Kieran the way I did with Michael and Amy.'

'Not loved,' she said. 'Adored.' And then, in a voice devoid of bitterness, as if she was merely reciting the dictionary definitions of red and blue or dog and cat, she said, 'There's a difference between being loved and being adored. But it's probably not obvious to someone who's been adored since the day they were born.'

I suppose that was my cue to say, 'What do you mean?', but I didn't. I knew what she meant. And I knew she knew that I knew.

That funny old
suffocating sensation

My body knew what was going on before I did. It tried to tell me, but I played dumb, pretending I couldn't understand.

'I woke up feeling really odd today,' I told my manager over the phone that Saturday morning. 'Like I can't breathe. Like I've suddenly developed asthma.'

We discussed the combination of heat and pollution that might be causing these symptoms. It was mid-September, and the Tokyo summer showed no signs of going on its annual holiday.

'Stay indoors if you can, sweetie,' he said. 'Don't go breathing in that dirty air.'

'Yeah. I'll see. Don't think I can bear being cooped up in here all day.'

Hearing a note of what could be construed as resentment creep into my voice, I added hastily, 'Though even that sounds better than the barbecue of doom!'

He was off to a managerial shindig at The Pinprick's house out in Machida.

He sighed. 'I can think of so many things I'd rather be doing than picking at shrivelled sushi and schmoozing with desiccated husks of human beings.'

'Oh yeah?' My tone was nakedly suggestive. 'What would you rather be doing?'

'I could've gone for a bike ride, or gone hiking, or started reading *Long Walk to Freedom,* or, I don't know, put a gun to my head and blown my brains out. Anything but this.'

I let a silence build.

'Or seen you, sweetie,' he said.

'We could meet in the evening?'

'I'd love to, but I don't think I'll be up for much after ten hours of being a corporate lizard. Maybe tomorrow evening once I've caught up on my real work?'

'Sure. Let me know when you know.'

I put my hand to my chest when I hung up, trying to massage away the tightness. Never mind the pollution, I couldn't stay indoors all day. I was going to lie out in the sun, in the park, and try to chase this sensation away with the help of my chums Jeeves and Wooster.

But P.G. Wodehouse let me down that day. Page after page and not a single smile bothered my face. Really? Was this really the same book I'd read so many times before? It might as well have been a textbook on agrarian reform in Maoist China. Why had I ever thought this book was funny? It was shit. Classist, outdated shit. Why did everyone rave about P.G. Wodehouse anyway? He was a twat – a childish one at that, and, in the space of a few hours, I'd put away childish, twattish things.

I drifted aimlessly around Shinjuku, Shibuya and Ebisu for the rest of the afternoon, giving loved-up couples dirty looks, scowling at the foreigners selling jewellery, kissing my teeth at a couple of people who accidentally bumped into me, relishing the taken-aback looks on their faces. Fuck them, fuck all of them, fuck this country with its people scurrying everywhere like ants, putting up a glass wall around themselves to exclude everyone else, to exclude people like me. So what if I could barely speak Japanese? Shouldn't human connection transcend mundane barriers like language? The sight of a dachshund in a frilly white collar, which normally would've made me smile, only seemed to symbolise the moral vacuum at the heart of this city, this place where you could wander like a ghost for days, talking to no one, touching no one, as if you'd died and no one had had the decency to tell you. For the love of God, what kind of diseased society was it that thought it was okay to dress a dog up like a prostitute or a vicar in a French maid's outfit?

My phone buzzed. I pounced. It was Lilia, asking if I wanted to go out for dinner with her and her girlfriend, Nicky. 'Yes!' I said. 'Yes! Where?'

Nicky was Sicilian-American, with a predilection for calling people cunt-hairs.

'Nicky!' Lilia would say. 'That's disgusting.' While putting her arm round her and winking.

Nicky and I took a seat at a wooden table outside a *yakitoriya* in Ginza, sending Lilia inside to order our chicken skewers – she was the only one who could read the menu properly. We fanned ourselves with our hands and moaned about how hot it was, pausing to smother our giggles when a middle-aged salaryman in a grey suit lurched up the alley and stopped for a piss two feet away.

'Nice,' muttered Lilia, plonking three mugs of beer down on the table. She smiled sweetly at the man as he did his zip back up and swayed past us on his way to the station.

Seven o'clock and already dark. The humid air enveloped us, carrying the smell of smoke and grilled meat; a faint undertone of sewage. That hot-country smell, so different from the vague, indecisive smell of England. Safe among friends, I felt the old nostalgia pierce me: the wish that I still lived in Tokyo, even though I *did* live in Tokyo. The need to grab hold of something permanent and pin it to me.

The conversation turned to plans, a word I had come to dread. Nicky planned to go to film school somewhere in Europe once the two of them had had enough of Japan. Lilia planned to keep expanding her repertoire of languages, adding German and Italian to her already fluent Spanish and Japanese.

'What about you, Nessie?' she said. 'What are you gonna do when your Japan bubble bursts?'

'Don't know. I'll have to go back to England soon enough. My family are getting fed up with me being so far away, but...'

Two pairs of sympathetic eyes alighted on me before flickering at each other. They thought I was still licking my wounds from the breakup with Kieran. My relationship with my manager was a secret in Japan, even from Lilia. Too risky; no one was allowed to know until he was ready. Truth was imprisoned in this world I had created for myself.

Lilia stroked Nicky's wrist-bone. 'So delicate,' she said. 'My little sparrow. I could skewer you. What do you think, Ness? Two hundred yen a piece?'

I laughed, washing down the lump in my throat with a big gulp of beer. Nicky was a real person, a real girlfriend, not someone from a film. Their life together was happening in real-time, right here, as we sat in the *yakitoriya* laughing and eating chicken skewers and drinking beer. It wasn't sitting in the cutting room waiting for the director's sign-off before general release. It wasn't suspended in some milky, cloudy fluid as mine was, waiting for a bottle to break and send it rushing out into the world.

For a couple of hours, basking in their kindness, I almost forgot I was suffocating. When I got home I took a melatonin from the stash Lilia had brought me back from America and passed out.

*

The buzzing of my phone woke me up at 11am the next day. 'Where've you been?' my manager said. 'I've phoned you like five times since yesterday.'

'Sorry, sorry. I took a melatonin… I was out with Lilia and Nicky last night.'

Gradually, I came to as he told me funny anecdotes about the lunch yesterday.

'…This friend of theirs from California, talks like the guy out of *The Matrix*: How. Can. You. Scream. If you don't. Have. A mouth.'

His accents always made me laugh. 'Stop it,' I said. 'My jaw's still slack from the melatonin. I just drooled all over the sheet.'

'And that's what I love about you. Your ladylike, refined qualities.'

We arranged to meet that evening at six o'clock.

I'd pretty much forgotten about the feeling, but it descended on me again after I'd had my shower, as I stood by the sink chopping a banana onto my granola. I cranked the aircon up to the max and stood under it with my mouth open, swallowing the air in hungry gulps as if that would get my lungs working properly again, get them pumping like bellows to blow this thing out of my chest. I'd had enough of this perverse feeling that all the light and joy and goodness in the world had been extinguished in the space of two days.

I went swimming and then I phoned Mariana.

'Something's bothering you,' she said, when I described my symptoms. 'That's what happens when something's wrong.'

'I don't think there is – nothing's changed since I last spoke to you.'

'How's things with Matt?'

'Good, I think. Although…'

When I'd finished, she was quiet for a moment, and then she said: 'I think you know why you're feeling depressed, Ness.'

'I know.'

'You need to talk to him. Ask him if he still feels the same about you. Ask him if he still intends to move to London with you. And then deal with it.'

'But what if he says he doesn't want to be with me?' My legs were starting to shake. 'I'll have blown up my whole life for nothing... All that lying and cheating, all that pain for nothing. You don't understand – I have to make this thing work. It's the only way I can justify what I did to Kieran. And if it's broken, how am I gonna fix it? I've got no time... I've got no time to make anything work over here, in this limbo, when I know I have to go back to London.'

'You have to ask him,' she said. 'Whatever happens, just keep your dignity.'

Those last three syllables bounced around my head for the next couple of hours as I lay scrunched on my bed. They zinged from one bit of my brain to another when I got up and got dressed, pulling on the clothes I'd worn yesterday, cargo pants and a black vest, no makeup, no earrings, hair any old how. They chimed in an echo of his doorbell as I stood outside his flat. When we were inside, sitting stiffly side by side on his sofa like a pair of old maiden aunts, they commanded me to stay calm, no tears, as I said, 'Do you still want to be with me?' and then to say 'Okay, I understand,' when he bit his lip and looked down at the floor. Perhaps they went a step too far when they made me say, twenty-five minutes later, 'So long,' an expression I'd neither uttered nor heard anyone else utter in all my life, and stick my hand out to shake his as I put my sandals on by the door. Then they performed one final act of mercy, smothering the whimper that tried to break out of my throat when he looked at my hand and said, 'What are you doing?' He pulled me into a tight hug and said, 'I'm really sorry, Nessie.' And I got one last hit of that intense, dark, musky smell of his, so different from the baby-clean innocence of my former life. A smell that represented everything I'd come to think of as adulthood.

Cultural differences

Dignity was soon drowned out by the clamour of louder, needier voices. By searching questions, heated rebuttals and thinly disguised pleas. Without actually saying, 'You mustn't do this to me,' that's what I told my manager each time we spoke on the phone. After five days of shuffling round the office ashen-faced and red-eyed, I went back to his flat on Saturday morning. Food had become an irrelevance; my cargo pants were hanging off me even with a belt on. For the first time in nearly fifteen years, I had cheekbones to rival those of his dead wife, but I was too upset to enjoy them.

'You're fading away, girly-girl,' Lilia had said one afternoon, sneaking up behind me, pretending to lift me up by my belt-hook as I stood at the tea-point.

'Oh, am I?' I couldn't hide the flatness in my voice.

'What's wrong, Ness? You don't look yourself...'

Before I could help it, my eyes were welling up.

'Hey...' She ushered me into a quiet corner. 'What's up, hon?'

'Oh, you know... just life.'

A look of understanding came over her face. 'I'm sorry, Ness. It must've been so hard for you breaking up with Kieran. I know you don't mention it much now, but it's still gotta hurt. Do you want to talk about it?'

I cried even harder at how little I deserved her sympathy. How I always had to hide the real reason for my tears, because it was something secret or shameful or a killer combination of both. She took me out for a walk and bought me a frozen yogurt to quash my tears. Not for the first time, I wondered how Lilia and I could possibly be the same age: she seemed about twenty years older than me sometimes. A real grown-up, not someone pretending to be one.

My manager looked like he'd been on holiday when he opened the door to me on Saturday. Youthful, fresh, carefree. The cornflower blue of his eyes shining through, no longer upstaged by the dark circles that continually plagued him. When we'd talked the previous night, he said he'd had his first proper sleep in weeks; he could breathe easier now he'd been honest with me. Not realising she was twisting the knife in, even Lilia had remarked on his revitalised appearance: 'Did Matt finally get laid? He actually smiled at me today. I didn't need to put on an extra layer when I entered the Arctic zone to discuss the proofs with him this morning...'

'What did you mean by "cultural differences"?' I said to him, diving into the first item on my agenda as we sat opposite each other at his dining table, adopting the formal posture we used at work meetings, minus the footsie we used to sometimes play under the table. 'Is this about the Muslim thing? About the ridiculousness of you having to convert when we're both atheists?'

'No, I didn't care about that. I kinda liked the idea of Burt and Sherri from Olympia representing at the local mosque.'

When I didn't laugh or attempt to disguise my impatience for the real answer, he said, slowly, 'No, I guess it was... things you say sometimes... maybe it's because you're British... this idea that you have to be blasé and give the impression you don't care too much about anything.'

'What do you mean? You know I care about things... about you.'

'Yeah, but what about that time when we were making love and you said something like "I know it's not cool to say I love you during sex, but I love you."'

'Oh. Yes.'

Why had I said that? Probably because I'd heard someone else say it. Not a real person. Someone from a book or a film.

'I'm sorry,' I said. 'I didn't really mean it.'

'All right, but can you understand why I thought it was weird? There I was, letting myself love someone else at last, and then she starts laying out guidelines for when it's "cool" and "not cool" to say I love you.'

'Sorry,' I said again.

'I don't love easily, even if it hadn't been for... what happened. I'm not like you in that way.'

'Sorry.' That seemed to be the only word left in my vocabulary. But a protesting voice asked: why wasn't he sorry too? Was this really all about me and my crass British need to coat my feelings in a brittle, protective layer of irreverence? What about him and his made-up entourage of small-town American oddballs who travelled everywhere with us like a dedicated security outfit? Dave from Kansas who'd insisted on accompanying him to meet my father. Ted and Marsha from Missouri, our chaperones on our hypothetical daylight excursion to Freshness Burger. Burt and Sherri from Olympia, the would-be witnesses to his conversion at the mosque. Had this motley crew gone everywhere with him and the dead pregnant wife?

Something told me they hadn't. Once again, my eyes jerked miserably up to her photo, as if she had them on a leash.

'I'm sorry too, Nessie,' he said, reaching his hand across the table. 'Please don't think I'm blaming you. This is probably mostly because of me... because I'm finding it harder than I thought to let go.'

I took his hand and we stayed quiet for a while, stroking each other's fingers.

'I think you should get help,' I said eventually. 'I think you should go and see someone who can help you get over this guilt you feel at still being alive. Not because of me or us or anything, but because of you. You deserve better than to live your life like this.'

When he gripped my hand tightly, he had tears in his eyes, something I'd never seen before. He was one of those people who boasts they haven't cried since they were three and their lollipop fell into a puddle. He came round to my side of the table and put his arms around me from behind, and I let my tears come out too. I'd earned it. Under the serene, malevolent gaze of his wife, I'd proved I could be a saint too, when the occasion called for it.

*

Like an injured athlete delivering a pale imitation of former glories, my heart gave a hop rather than a leap when an email came through from my manager's Hotmail to mine on Monday afternoon. He was convinced The Pinprick monitored his work account for evidence of misdemeanours to use against him. Such was the world of court intrigue inhabited by senior management.

Thank you for our talk on Saturday. I was thinking about what you said, and you're right – something has to change if I'm ever going to get on with my life. I've found a guy who does English-language counselling. He's one of my countrymen, unfortunately, but let's not hold that against him. I explained the situation and he says he does couples' counselling as well as individual. What do you think?

Couples. Couples' counselling. There it was in writing. Not quite the same as boyfriend and girlfriend, but still. A scrap to seize on. A glimmer of hope that the tournament wasn't over yet.

On Wednesday evening, we sat side by side on a navy sofa facing a grey-haired, bearded, WASPish American man with the kind of glasses that magnify the wearer's eyes to cartoonish proportions. A bush baby with gravitas. He took notes as he listened, the movement of his hands giving the impression he was drawing lines and circles, perhaps devising a flowchart or a formula – the type that used to intimidate me when I caught sight of them in Sherine's A-level maths textbooks – to tell us exactly where we stood.

'Well,' he said, after a thoughtful pause. 'You're both showing a great deal of concern for each other. You're talking a lot about each other's feelings, which is a positive sign.'

I found myself exhaling with the relief of someone who'd gone to the doctor to be told a suspected case of cancer might be only a cold after all. Our homework, he said, was to draw our respective family trees. I did it the next day with a diligence I'd rarely applied to real homework, the kind that wasn't about yourself.

When the session was over, we got a taxi from outside the counsellor's office, standing a few feet apart until it arrived in case anyone saw us.

Sitting with his knee touching mine, my manager said, 'I just realised counselling was the only thing we've ever done openly together.'

'I know,' I said. 'It was...' I hesitated, not wanting to frighten him away with the wrong choice of word.

'It was good,' he said, taking my hand. 'It was good to see you holding your own, being an adult, talking without letting your emotions run away with you.'

What did he mean by 'being an adult'? I was the only person allowed to observe my charlatan status in that regard. And since when did I let my emotions 'run away with me'?

'What do you mean?' I moved my leg away to make my point.

'Nothing, nothing. I just meant you were so calm and poised, when I know things haven't been easy for you this last week... easy for us.'

This was the first time anyone had ever described me as calm and poised. Even in the days when 'sharp' had grown wings and burst into its new incarnation as 'wonderful', he'd never ascribed those two particular attributes to me. This renewed validation of my performance made me rest my knee back against his, emboldened enough to put my other hand on his knee.

'Pretty in pink,' I said, nudging his shirt with my shoulder. By spooky coincidence, we'd both worn pink that day, the first time I'd worn anything but black or grey since the previous week. Surely this was a sign?

'Call me Molly Ringwald,' he said, pulling me towards him with a fervour I hadn't witnessed since the early days. I responded in kind. Was there really another human being sitting less than two feet away from us, presumably one with functioning eyesight and hearing, driving the vehicle in which we lolled on the back seat, heavy-petting like hormonal teenagers? What did it matter that there was no screen dividing the driver from the passengers like there was in London cabs? Our foreignness, or the driver's Japaneseness, fulfilled this function all on its own, providing a protective layer between us like the white cotton gloves that preserved the driver's hands from direct contact with the wheel. So what if the language of groping and fumbling, gasping and moaning was the same the world over? Somehow it didn't matter. Our brains had tricked themselves into thinking only we could understand. Once again, I was on holiday; an expat, not an immigrant, living a life that wasn't real, sharing this unreality with the man whose flies I'd just undone in full mirror-view of a head that might as well have belonged to a statue. My sense of floating above my surroundings, the effects of the pushing and pressing of hands and tongues, the better-late-than-never corroboration of our status as a couple – because a couple in counselling was a couple no less – all those things combined to make me pull my mouth away from his and say, 'Shall we do something different tonight? Have you ever been to a love hotel?'

Family tree

You didn't appear in the family tree I produced for the counsellor's homework. How could you, when you were still buried in the spot I'd left you fourteen years earlier? Isolated and contained in the blue airmail envelope tucked into the diary I'd kept when I was thirteen, a lurid pink thing with 'Keep Out' embossed in the seven colours of the rainbow on the front.

Only the officially recognised planets inhabited the familial solar system I presented at the next session – mother, father and sister. The convenient archetypes of bullying patriarch, downtrodden wife and dutiful older sibling, huddled together under the self-explanatory blankets of 'immigrant' and 'Muslim'. Did I feel any guilt at reducing these individuals, with all their contradictions and complexities, to stock figures from a psychology textbook? If I did, it was a small price to pay for gaining a unit of currency in which to denominate certain aspects of my own behaviour... the ones that caused alarm bells to ring in my manager's ears and detracted from my overall performance score. My 'tendency to fly off the handle at perceived insults'? That was the bullying patriarch. My 'jumpiness and habit of leaping to the worst possible conclusion'? That was the downtrodden wife.

'Why did she put up with it for so long?' said my manager as we picked over the respective elements that had produced us. 'Why didn't she walk away years earlier, or at least right after what happened?'

His own father, a wealthy insurance executive, had been cold and violent – he used to hold his and his two younger brothers' hands under freezing water to punish them when they were little; his mother had stayed because of the money, he said.

'I don't know. I don't know what she thought would change or get better.'

Even the dutiful older sibling didn't get off lightly – her alternative protectiveness and disapproval added up to my 'need to constantly seek reassurance from others rather than trusting my own judgement'. As for my 'cynical attitude to monogamy', that was obviously the sum of the bullying patriarch and the downtrodden wife.

'What do you mean, "cynical attitude to monogamy"?' I said when my manager raised it in one of the sessions. 'I know I had a problem with monogamy when I was young, and I know I lied and cheated in my last relationship, but people can change...'

'It's the things you say,' he replied. 'Like when you said' – and here he put on a voice that was supposed to be an imitation of my accent, all lilting diphthongs and lightly clipped consonants, a cross between the Queen and Eliza Doolittle – '"What's the point of anyone ever getting married? You get three years of good sex, top whack, and then all of that goes down the drain."'

Denial was my automatic response, but the 'top whack' gave it a credence that was hard to wriggle out of. If it was an expression I used rarely, it was one he had no reason to have ever heard.

'You never had a role model,' he said. 'I didn't either, so I had to figure it out on my own, when I grew up and got out.'

Of course, you had to feature somewhere in all this – how else would I have explained the cynical attitude to monogamy? But something prevented me from pouncing on any of the templates put forward to define you: duplicitous friend, lonely middle-aged woman, socially superior temptress. None of those things explained you, but then what did? It was too much to think about on top of more pressing matters, like was my manager ever going to get over his dead saint and move to London with me? In the face of my immediate concerns, I downplayed your relevance and made you a bit player, passing up the chance to exhume you from the small patch of my consciousness that you occupied and examine the reality of who you were.

'My parents were just incompatible,' I said. 'They shouldn't have got married in the first place. Something else would've happened if not that.'

Some things went unmentioned to the counsellor. The fish. Other things that occupied that dubious territory between dream and reality. I told him about the time I threw scissors at you, which I knew was a fact, and he presented theories to try to interpret this piece of history that I'd always thought of as mine, unsettled by his suggestion that it might be yours as well. Sitting opposite us in his leather armchair, with his grey hair and matching beard and thoughtful, professionally sympathetic expression, and eyes that wandered to the clock only a couple of times each session, he sifted through the various options and offered them up like a medium reading a pack of tarot cards. 'Instability in your home environment'... 'Agitation'... 'A sense of threat to your parents' marriage'... 'An interloper in your family life'... 'Anger in the air around you'...

'Yes,' I said, and 'Maybe,' and 'I don't know,' and 'There might be something in that,' knowing he wasn't really a medium at all, because if he was, how come he couldn't hear them? I mean the forces that were starting to push at the barrier that had restrained them for all this time; a procession of revenants bearing your name and your secrets, tapping softly on the underside of the table as he summoned them forth.

Overactive amygdala

A different scene played out in the rear-view mirror of the taxi that ferried us away from the counsellor's couch two months after the first session. We sat without touching, my manager wearing a dark-grey shirt, me clinging on to the pink top I'd worn the very first time. Knees kept themselves to themselves. Zips stayed upright and unmolested.

'Why don't you want to see him any more?' I said.

'I've told you... we're going over the same ground again and again, and we're not getting anywhere. I'm not going to keep paying some guy with a beard twenty thousand yen a pop to tell me I'm still grieving. I know I'm still grieving!'

I let my silence encourage him to correct his error. When it didn't work, I said: 'Ten thousand yen.'

'Huh?'

'You've been paying ten thousand yen. I've been paying the other half.'

He raised his hands in an impatient gesture. 'What does it matter? The point is that this isn't working.'

My stomach lurched at the open-endedness of the word 'this'. Why was he being like this? How could he be on the verge of turning his back on the sessions, on the yeast that had made our relationship rise again? A relationship renaissance – that's what he'd called it himself in those heady first few weeks. Popped into the oven with this active ingredient as our catalyst, we'd emerged bigger, bolder, imbued with new textures and depths. He'd sat beside me and held my hand while I cried about my childhood and I'd done the same for him while he spoke haltingly about his wife:

'I don't miss the reality of being with her, but I miss the person I was before I realised life can be gone like that, in an instant.'

I'd snatched my hand away once during one of these conversations, but that was because he'd said, 'Nessie seems younger than her... I can't imagine Nessie being ready to become a parent any time soon.'

When we got back to his place, I'd said, 'How fucking dare you say I'm immature? Are you just another arsehole who measures a woman's worth by whether or not she wants to have kids?'

When he'd said nothing, picking up his phone and looking at it instead of me, I'd thrown the mug I was holding at the wall behind him, sending shrapnel flying around his horrified face.

'Oh my God, oh my God,' I'd said, covering my head with my hands as if I was the one at risk of being blinded. 'I'm so sorry...'

Then there was the time I'd got the hump when he'd said, 'Her family were opposed to our marriage at first – they wanted her to marry a Chinese man – but she stood firm and they came round in the end.'

The complacent, didactic tone in his voice made my ears flare up like someone had struck a match on them.

I said, 'And of course the fact that you come from money and you're a white American had nothing to do with it – I'm sure she would've stood just as firm if you'd been a penniless labourer from the Philippines, right?'

When we got back to his place, he'd drifted silent and grim-lipped from room to room as I tagged behind him saying, 'For fuck's sake, talk to me.' Ignored, I dragged a chair over to the bookshelf, climbed onto it, grabbed his wife's picture and held it up in the air. When that didn't prise his mouth open, I sent the photo smashing to the floor, overcome by the same breathless urgency that used to course through my veins each time I took something sharp to my own skin. If you don't have time to fix something, why not just break it beyond all repair? Then I ran out of his flat to get away from his blanched, panicky face and his shallow, raspy breaths as he stood surveying the wreckage.

And now here we were, a week after this last incident, sitting in the taxi that he'd instructed to drop me off at my place before depositing him at his. He had a conference call that evening. He'd come along to the counselling session reluctantly, after I'd sent him a series of pleading emails throughout the day.

'So are you saying you don't want to go and see him again, ever?' I said.

'I don't know. Not right now. But that doesn't mean you should stop going. I think you'd benefit from it more than I would.'

'What do you mean?'

He began plucking words out of the air and fashioning them into a corsage that stabbed thorns into my chest: 'Your fear of commitment'... 'Your double life'... 'Your secrets and lies'... 'Your unresolved childhood issues'... 'Your overactive amygdala'...

Overactive amygdala, eh? What the fuck was an amygdala anyway? After 'calm' and 'poised' had crawled back into hibernation, he'd bought me a book about the mechanisms of the brain to help me 'manage my emotions'. But all the labels on the diagram had already blurred into one big blob of scientific tedium. As for my double life, he obviously hadn't been paying attention when I'd made my keynote speech to him and the counsellor:

'Everyone I knew lied and sneaked around!' I'd said. 'All the ethnic minorities did – the Asians and the Mediterraneans and the Africans at least. Truth is a luxury for people who only have one identity. If you have to be one thing at home and another thing at school, or work, or college, how the hell are you supposed to have any life at all if you don't have a double life? It doesn't mean you're a pathological liar in general.'

I was only slightly deflated when the counsellor said, 'I understand that, Nessie, but how many of your friends are still living a double life now, as they approach the end of their twenties?'

'You don't know what it's like!' I'd said. 'Neither of you knows what it's like to feel your life isn't your own, and every choice you make has to be one that will keep your family happy, and the only way to live your life is to get as far away from them as possible, but you always know the clock's ticking and you'll have to go back. Most of my friends gave in to the pressure! They lied and had their fun when they were young, then the Greeks married Greeks, the Sikhs married Sikhs, the Hindus married Hindus...'

Well, come to think of it, the counsellor could go fuck himself too. Maybe this was partly *his* fault. Maybe, just as counselling had validated our status as a couple, it had validated the status of our problems too – baked them into something bigger and bolder than they would've been if we hadn't introduced a third ingredient into the mix.

'So does this mean it's over?' I said as we drove past the FamilyMart convenience store on the corner of my road. My manager had once gone there to buy condoms at 1am, even though I'd said, 'It doesn't matter, I don't mind risking it, what will be will be.'

He sighed and said, 'I just can't do this any more.'

What would the man behind the wheel have witnessed then, if statues had functioning eyes and ears? He would've heard me saying, 'Please don't do this to me...'. He would've seen my manager touching his fingers to his temples in the gesture of a man tired of everything, tired of life, tired of London though he'd never moved there, keeping his lips stubbornly closed as I seized his head in my hands and frantically tried to give our relationship the kiss of life. He would've heard me say, 'Fine then, fuck off.' And then he would've heard the final death-rattle of dignity as one of my big hoop earrings got caught on the door as I got out, tearing a screech of agony from my already humiliated mouth.

*

I didn't know it, but the clock in my manager's head was ticking faster than mine; he ended up leaving Japan before I did. Before he took a job at a newspaper in Singapore, we broke up four times in total. Once because I said so, thrice because he did, so you could say the final score was 3–1 to him.

I went to see him three months after he left and we went out to a club called Benji's, where I plied him with vodka and lime and tried to get him drunk enough to sleep with me. It didn't work. He removed his hands from my waist halfway through 'Milkshake' by Kelis and kept them tucked behind his back for the remainder of the song, like Lord Kitchener inspecting the troops as he danced. The kiss he gave me at the end of the night when he walked me back to my hotel had a new flavour I struggled to identify. I realised later it was pity.

Still in the dark about our history, Lilia said to me at work a month later, 'Guess what! Nicky and I ran into Matt at the bird sanctuary in Singapore while we were there. He was with his new girlfriend.'

'Oh yeah? What's she like?'

'I took a picture of them.' She reached for her phone.

I heard you have a new girlfriend, my overactive amygdala punched out to him in an email, my hands shaking, when I sat back down at my desk. *Nice of you to tell me. Lilia said she's a bimbo and an airhead. Nice to know that's what you wanted all along. What a surprise that she's the spitting image of your wife. Why did you ever bother pretending you wanted to be with someone different?*

She probably is a bimbo and an airhead, he wrote back. *But at least she lets me breathe.*

That was the last I ever heard from him.

Part 4: Return

2004–2005

Are you still in
touch with her?

The Tokyo counsellor's prodding and poking had disturbed you in your resting place, but that wasn't enough: the universe wanted more. It wanted to wake you up with a bang and get you back on your feet, tearing around my head.

The grenade that exploded you back into my life came out of nowhere. Showing no mercy, Mama hurled it across her balcony on the last night of my trip to Tunis in summer 2004. Fifteen years after you disappeared.

It was August, around 9pm. I'd already packed for my flight back to Tokyo via Paris the next day, and we were sitting outside eating grapes and drinking tea, tilting our heads back to look at the stars, letting the breeze tickle our faces.

Mama said, 'Do you ever hear from *her*?'

My throat constricted. The last grape I'd popped into my mouth took a wrong turn and got lodged somewhere it shouldn't.

I coughed a few times, putting my hand on my chest, before I said, 'Who?'

'You know who.'

'No.' I tried to keep my voice steady. 'No, I haven't heard from her since she left.'

I forced myself to look at Mama. Her face was all lines now. Deep grooves on either side of her mouth, furrows in her forehead, a criss-cross pattern like the ones I used to doodle on my exercise books etched around her eyes. Her mouth was turned downwards. Under the fluorescent light of the balcony, she looked white. A crumpled offcut of the moon. All the colour seemed to have leached out of her since she'd moved back to Tunisia.

'Your arms are so pale now!' I'd said once, holding one of mine next to hers for contrast, and she'd said, 'Yes, it's much better now, isn't it?' And then, 'You'd better be careful in that sun over in Japan – you're starting to look like chocolate.'

'She betrayed me,' she said, her voice brimming with hurt and fury as if it had happened yesterday. 'I trusted her. I thought she was our friend, if you can ever call these people your friends, and she betrayed me.'

'Mama...' I said weakly.

'What?' Her tone was hard, as if this was my fault. As if she was shaking that theatre ticket in my face again, saying 'What's this? What's this?'

'Don't be so angry.' I couldn't stop my voice from trembling. 'For your own sake, for your health – it's not good for you. Your blood pressure...'

'Has anyone ever done that to you?' she shot back, lobbing another grenade, and I blushed and stammered as I said, 'No... what? What? I don't know what you mean. I'm not married—'

'Don't play innocent. You're not a child. I know you choose to live so far away so you can do whatever you want without anyone seeing you. You know what I'm talking about.'

When she said 'You're not a child,' she ran her eyes over me from head to toe. Even though I was wearing a baggy djellaba, I leaned forward and folded my arms, feeling naked. As if she'd caught me in the act of what she was alluding to. As if she'd just been watching me fucking someone on her balcony, under the fluorescent white light, without shame or restraint. Another wave of the hot, blotchy feeling crept up to my hairline from my stomach.

'I'm going in.' I gathered up my plate and glass, my hands shaking.

'What about your sister?' Picking up the tray with the teapot, she followed me inside.

'What about her?' I didn't turn around as I replied.

'Is she in touch with her?'

'No!' I stopped by the arm of the guest sofa and faced her.

'How do you know?'

'Because... because I just do.'

She gave a bitter little laugh. 'You think you know, but your sister's sneaky. She always does what she wants. She only ever thinks of herself.'

'That's not true. How can you even say that? She always thinks of everyone but herself!'

'She left him. She left him to get old and lonely, all alone in that house. Just so she can go and get old and lonely in a different part of London. What for? Why didn't she wait until she got married? The Koran says you have to love and respect your parents—'

'But Mama,' I interrupted. 'You left him too. So did I.'

'That's different. He's not my father. And I suppose you had to go to Japan for your work,' she added, pedalling away from her earlier accusation.

'That's not true – I went because I wanted to. I could've got a job in London, but I didn't want to, and you know I didn't want to because I didn't want to go back and live in that house, with him!'

'*Yezzi.* It doesn't matter. You think you know your sister, but maybe you don't. She's sneaky.'

Sherine looked over at us from her place on the display cabinet, among the congregation of aunts and uncles and grandparents, living and dead. Only I occupied the hallowed spot on Mama's bedside table, eternally eighteen, pudgy and ponytailed. Sherine didn't look sneaky. Even with a mortarboard on her head and a certificate in her hand, she looked put-upon and weary, an expression that came over her face whenever someone pointed a camera at it.

'Ask her,' said Mama as I stood looking at the display cabinet. 'Just ask her and see what she says.'

I didn't speak to her again until I said goodnight. My biggest relief when my head hit the pillow was that my flight was leaving at crazy o'clock in the morning. She wouldn't have time to ambush me again before I went, unless she planned to stand by my bed all night interrogating me. Perhaps she could wear her cream hijab-djellaba combo that always put me in mind of the KKK or a capirote, a sinister Easter ritual of penitence. Torturing me with the red-hot poker of her demands. Prodding me with her accusations and insinuations, her rage and her pain until something in me broke and gave a howl of agony to equal her own.

Swan song

My last few months in Japan were a series of swan songs. Departures were part and parcel of our bubble – don't all holidays come to an end? – but they gathered pace in that interval, each send-off smaller and more raggedy than the last. Voices massacring childhood songs in karaoke booths became thinner and more plaintive as the hardcore contingent dwindled. When a Japanese-Australian copy editor called Kenji moved back just before his thirty-fifth birthday, I flung my arms around his neck at his farewell do and said, 'Why, Kenji? Why are you leaving us?'

'I've had my fun,' he said. 'I can't get old here. The party's over. It's time to go home.'

It wasn't just the foreigners. Some of the Japanese people in our bubble were swept away too, like Misako, a translator who was moving to London for a year to do a flower-arranging course, a concept that made no sense to me. Since when could people in England arrange flowers better than they could in Japan, the home of *ikebana*?

'What about your fiancé?' I said. 'Won't he miss you?'

'It's my last chance before I get married…'

They were the ones I envied – those adventurers leaving Japan to have holidays of their own, not the expats who were going 'home', carrying with them all the resignation and defeat contained in that single syllable. If 'away' was perky, inquisitive, full of possibility and inquiry, 'home' was final and lugubrious. A bell that tolled for all of us, apart from the ones who'd put down roots, like Boss-man with his three children and wife and the house they shared with her parents and sister and ninety-five-year-old grandmother. My time would come too. How much longer could I keep postponing the inevitable?

'Next year,' I'd said to Sherine and Mama and That Man, and then, when next year came, I'd said, 'Next year' again.

'You need to hurry up now,' That Man had said, the last time we'd had the conversation. 'You can't stay away forever. It's not right.'

Even Sherine was running out of patience.

'When do you think you'll come back?' she'd said with a tightness in her voice one Saturday when she phoned to tell me that there'd been a storm in London a couple of days ago, that the bathroom window at That Man's house had been smashed by a branch from next door's pear tree, and that she'd had to take the afternoon off work to get it fixed.

'He went into meltdown and couldn't sort it out,' she'd said. 'He's becoming more and more like that. I don't mean to pressure you, but do you think you'll come home soon? It'd be good not to have to deal with him on my own any more.'

'I know, I will, I promise. But I don't know how I'll cope with going back and living with him again—'

'Don't be ridiculous – of course you won't end up living with him after all this time! He knows that. Just tell him you need to stay with me because Wimbledon's much closer to central London than Bounds Green.'

'But—'

'You can't keep running away just to avoid confrontation, Nessie – all you have to do is open your mouth and tell him. You're an adult now. You have to make him understand that.'

'Okay, okay,' I'd said to her, and then, once she'd put the phone down, I'd said, 'Fuck off and get off my case' into the humming receiver.

What was I waiting for? As unappealing as the prospect of fixing That Man's windows was, what did I have left in Japan? My manager was in Singapore with his new dollybird. Kieran was ensconced with his fiancée in their flat in Roppongi, the two of them extending dinner invitations with a regularity that was rapidly depleting my stash of excuses. All the things that had kept me in Tokyo were, in some form, gone. But had the things that had driven me away from London gone too? Or were they still lurking, ready to pounce and strip me of the trappings of independence the minute I stuck my head around the door?

Experimentally, I started to bandy the word 'home' around, seeing how it tasted on my lips.

'I'll have to think about going home soon,' I said to Boss-man as we stood outside our office block on one of his cigarette breaks. 'My parents aren't getting any younger... you know how it is.'

'I understand, mate,' he'd said, blowing a sympathetic puff of smoke in my direction; he knew I liked it second-hand. He gave me a light tap on the shoulder as if to say I was doing the right thing, and in that moment I felt that I was. Being an adult, facing up to my responsibilities, thinking of someone other than myself: wasn't it time I did all those things? My next birthday would catapult me into a new decade, one that carried the promise of grim obligation and little enjoyment. The party was nearly over for me too.

The final push came when Lilia and Nicky decided to move to Berlin, ready for a new holiday from real life.

'Who am I going to drink margaritas and eat potato skins with on Sunday evenings?' I said, as we sat on the Narita Express. 'Who am I gonna get pissed at the gym with?' – reliving the time we'd gone swimming and then drunk twelve cans of Asahi between us from the vending machine in the changing room.

I kept this litany up all the way to the airport, and they took it in turns to put an arm round me and give me a hug, like parents about to embark on a round-the-world cruise, leaving their only child to fend for herself.

I took a picture of them at the airport before they went through security. We found a quiet corner in the corridor by the toilets and they performed a sort of maypole dance I'd choreographed for them during one of our drinking sessions. The three of us quietly sang an old English folk song I'd taught them, having learned it myself from a CD given away as part of an information pack dispensed by the British Council to teachers in Japan. A United Kingdom of rolling green hills and shepherds with crooks and north country lasses and Lincolnshire poachers, as foreign to me as it was to the people who were supposed to be enticed by this vision. A country where no one looked like me, and which issued the royal seal of approval to the question 'But where are you *really* from?'

'*On yonder hill there stands a creature/Who she is I do not know/I will court her for her beauty/She must answer yes or no/ Oh, no John, no John, no John, no!*'

The three of us sang the song in little more than a whisper, Japan's farewell to them from me via a bucolic England of the past. The two of them were facing each other, Lilia's hand swinging upwards in a blur, Nicky's dark-brown ponytail flying around her head like a tassel on a tarboosh: that's how I caught them. That's the image I studied on the train back to Tokyo, blinking back tears, flipping my phone open every few minutes to check they were still there, as if they'd already entered the realms of the fictional, or the impossible.

They should've been immortalised like that, but I lost them soon afterwards. I dropped my phone down the toilet a few days later, and that's how they vanished from my life for a second time, in a way that somehow felt more permanent.

Ground control

There was something I had to do before I left Japan. Something that could only be done from the safety of another continent.

'Ask your sister,' Mama had said, 'Just ask her.'

Was it me who asked her, or someone else?

It felt like someone else, but I know it was me. Me who made up my mind on a cold Saturday afternoon in March 2005, sitting on my bed surrounded by boxes and suitcases, my brain in a haze. Counting to ten and then doing it again, trying to hit the number that meant courage. No chūhai to give me liquid courage this time: it was getting old, a childish thing that had to be put away. A drink that didn't exist in England, where I would be going soon because people said it was my 'home'. What would I turn into if I transported those habits back with me? Someone who relied on the kindness of vodka, which didn't leave a smell on the breath, or so people said, or on Hooch and Two Dogs if they even still existed.

Instead of a can, I held a belt in my hand. A black, plaited leather belt that a man had given me. A man who used to be my 'manager' and then my 'boyfriend'; those words belonged to a world I didn't inhabit that Saturday afternoon. A man who'd questioned my ability to be what he'd called an 'adult'. Holding the belt in my left hand, I chewed on the tip, giving my chattering teeth something to sink into, tough but yielding, like the skin on a finger. Why was it so cold that afternoon? Afternoon in Tokyo, morning in London. Would Sherine be up yet? No point waking her up like it was life or death, it had waited this long. Was it really cold or was I coming down with something? A silly rhyme in my head: *coming down with flu, coming down with you.* Shivering and gnawing on the belt, I dialled the 0044 number I knew off by heart.

'What's wrong?' she said after the hellos. 'What's happened?'

'Nothing.' I took the belt out of my mouth, disappointing myself with a voice that sounded like a badly strummed guitar. 'I just wanted to ask you about something Mama said when I last saw her.'

'What? What is it now?'

'She said she thought you were still in touch with Mrs Brown.'

What was that noise that erupted from my mouth after your name? A laugh that sounded like a wheeze that sounded like pain.

Sherine's breathing came loud and fast, like an old man who smoked sixty a day, not the fit, sporty person she was. 'What do you mean?' she said at last.

'What do you mean?' I parroted stupidly.

'I am in touch with her, but what... why was she asking... aren't you?'

'Aren't I what?'

'In touch with her too?'

'No, why would I be?'

'But she said she wrote to you too.'

So small and far away, those words. A bad line or was she holding the phone at a weird angle or was it something in my ear? I felt like I was drifting in space. Ground control to Nessie. Perhaps it was the flu, muffling me from what Sherine was saying, all the things she hadn't told me. All the things I'd never asked her. All the years I'd never known what she'd known.

'I never replied,' I said.

'Oh, Nessie...'

Where had I heard that up-and-down intonation before? An echo of another voice that had said 'Oh, Nessie' when I'd done wrong, caused harm, proved I couldn't keep things alive. Shown I couldn't be trusted not to let you down.

'But why not?' she said. 'I always thought you'd stayed in touch with her too... She never told me you'd never written back. And you know she's back in England now? You know she's not well...'

'I don't know.' A vein ticked in my forehead, kicking off a flicker in my eyelid. 'I didn't know what I was supposed to do.'

'Oh, Susu.' Her breath dragged on the last syllable. 'Why do you always have to make such a drama for yourself out of everything?'

'What do you mean?'

'I mean just because she fell out with them, it didn't mean you had to stop talking to her too.'

'I didn't know.' I scrunched my eyes up to stop the world from flickering. How could I ask what she meant by 'not well' when it was a matter of energy, not courage, and I didn't have any energy left? Who was it who'd pulled the plug out, leaving me in this state? Switched off, I floated in space with my eyes shut, stroking the knots on the belt. I listened to Sherine breathing, my own breath inaudible over hers.

'You were young,' she said eventually. 'It would've been better if we'd talked more back then... about everything. But still, this is a thing with you. It's something I've noticed. It's like you panic when you think someone needs you.'

What did she mean? Everything was so distant. The world was spinning and I was too dizzy, too far away to lash out at the judgement of a thin voice that could've come from anywhere, could've belonged to a stranger in another universe.

My mouth opened like it didn't care and said, 'Do you know why she fell out with them?'

'No.' Her voice clicked sharply back into place. 'I had my theories but I never asked her and she never told me.'

'Okay.'

'Why? Do you know?'

There it went again, the tempo of her breath pitted against mine, refusing to find common ground. That was her all over, doing her own thing, knowing her own mind, even the way she breathed.

Coming down with flu, coming down with you. The sound of things half-remembered grew louder, rapping at my brain in tandem with the jerking of my limbs.

'Nessie?' she said. 'What is it?' and I said: 'I'll swap you the mistletoe for the fish.'

'Huh?' A fresh urgency in her voice. Ground control getting antsy. I'd better snap out of my space haze if I knew what was good for me.

'I'm not feeling very well,' I said through chattering teeth, my elbows banging against my ribs. 'I think I'm coming down with flu.'

*

Is this when it began?

Our first Christmas in London. A party at Mrs Kowalski's. Carols on the cassette player. The smell of baking wafting through the house.

Someone held out a Christmas cracker, and I toppled backwards off Mrs Kowalski's sofa trying to pull it. As if I was drunk.

'We used to give you and Sherine sips of our drinks when you were little,' Mama told me once. 'It was funny watching you get giddy and silly.'

We don't drink, of course, That Man always said, but we used to. Before he went to Mecca and started thinking about his own mortality – getting his soul squeaky-clean and heaven-ready at the drop of a hat.

'Ah, she's so sweet!' exclaimed a man as he picked me off the floor. 'Look at those curls. Like a little dog.'

'He called me a dog!' I whispered to Sherine, hurt and embarrassed.

'No, Susu, he said 'doll'. He's being nice to you.'

She wasn't there any more when I needed the toilet and went upstairs, wanting to go on familiar territory. Not sure yet what kind of toilet I needed. Looking for someone to take me in case it wasn't the kind I could manage on my own. Where was everyone? Why had I been left alone like this?

'Your mother's gone to the corner shop to buy lemonade,' said Marjorie, the old Jamaican woman from next door, stroking my neck when I passed her by the stairs and tugged at her dress saying 'Mama?' I felt a moment of panic, as if Mama had gone to the moon and would never come back. Even the word 'lemonade' sounded sinister, clanging in my ears like the *Doctor Who* theme tune that terrified me. Why hadn't she told me she was going, or taken me with her?

Upstairs was quiet and lonely, like a stranger's house. Full of shadows that seemed to have teeth. Footsteps that didn't seem mine. Dark except for one light, in our living room, which doubled up as a bedroom: Sherine and That Man slept there, in twin single beds covered in lemon-yellow blankets. Soft, warm, orange light. Voices talking in English. One talking, one laughing, a low, throbbing laugh that made my heart shake, like music pumping out of a passing car.

'This is how we do it in England,' the talking voice said. 'This is called...' Something. A word beginning with M. A word I didn't know.

I peeped around the door and saw two people sitting on one of the yellow-blanket beds. The way they were sitting stopped me from running forward and jumping between them: they were closer than I had ever seen two adults before, even That Man and Mama. In my confusion, their forms seemed to waver and shift, pixilated by a context I could never have imagined.

I saw a hand holding a bunch of green leaves tied in a red ribbon. Two faces leaning in towards each other, their necks doing something strange – a sinuous, wrapping motion as if they'd joined together, become a snake with two heads, while the hand with the green bunch pressed itself against the wall. Everything snapped into focus. One of those faces was more familiar to me than my own. Every contour, every pore of its skin, the scent that could belong to no one else in the world.

I went back downstairs and wet myself on Mrs Kowalski's sofa.

'Why didn't you get someone to take you to the toilet?' said Mama when she reappeared and found me sitting there, sodden and stinking. 'Why did you just lift your leg and go on yourself like a dog in the street? What kind of people will they think we are?'

'I saw a snake upstairs, Mama,' I said, trying to impress upon her the extenuating circumstances.

'Snake? What snake? Don't be so silly, they don't have snakes in England!'

Is that when it began?

*

Sherine sent me an email three days after our conversation. An address and a phone number. And a new surname for you; three syllables instead of one. I said it out loud to myself three times, as if tasting it, trying to distract myself from the thudding of my heart as I read Sherine's explanation of what 'not well' meant, in this particular case.

There was something else too, which made me press my fingers tightly to my eyes as I thought about who Sherine had been back then. The anvil her poise had been forged on.

You can go and see her when you come home, she'd written. *I've told her we've talked about it. She's looking forward to seeing you. She's weak and she looks as you would expect but she's still herself, if you know what I mean. Don't worry about that.*

You said something about a fish when we talked on the phone. I know you've asked me about it before. I wasn't trying to lie to you, but I honestly don't remember that much. I know Mama cut herself once when she was doing something in the kitchen, and you're right, a doctor did come, but he definitely didn't drag her along by her hair. Why would he have done that? Maybe he had to pull her by the arm. I think she was crouched on the floor and wouldn't budge. She was hysterical that night. She said afterwards that her hand slipped while she was cutting something. I can't remember if it was a fish, specifically. I don't know... She'd been acting weird for a while. Up one minute, down the next. Maybe England was too much for her.

Anyway, Jenny came to help because no one else knew what to do. He fell apart because he was worried Mrs Kowalski was going to evict us. We didn't have a phone upstairs so I went out to the phone box across the road to phone Jenny and she came with the doctor. If you want to know the full story, why don't you ask Mama? You know she'll always tell you whatever you want to know. Or ask Jenny, if it matters that much to you.

PS. We can talk properly when you come home, if you want. It might be good for both of us.

I wrote a reply: explanations and justifications, tap-tapping and backtracking. Then I deleted it all and typed one word instead: *Inshallah.*

Two minutes later I added what might've seemed like a non-sequitur: *But she never even smoked, did she?*

No, replied Sherine. *She's never smoked in her life. How's that for unlucky?*

My turn

I didn't want a send-off but Kieran had insisted.

'No Noirin?' I said to the solitary face that appeared at my door that Saturday morning.

'No, she's got hurling practice. She says to say bye to you.'

'Say bye to her too.'

'I've brought you some of these so you can spread the stench of rotting rubbish around the Narita Express one last time.' He held out a packet of Ebi-Sen prawn-flavoured snacks.

'Oh, bless. Thank you.'

He gave a snort. 'You've infected me with that stupid patronising English expression. I said "bless" to Noirin the other day and she looked at me like I was the spawn of Satan.'

His voice was teetering on the brink of maudlin. I wished he hadn't come. I wasn't going to play this game.

'Well, you've infected me with your Irishisms too. People will think I've been in Dublin, not Tokyo!'

He gave a polite laugh. I talked logistics to distract him as we got my bags out of the flat and lugged them to the station.

On the train to the airport, I initiated a rival game to his – a game called Remember. 'Remember when you got food poisoning in India and I thought you were dying but you were up on your feet and back on the tandoori chicken the next day?'

'Remember when we thought our plane was going to crash in

Thailand, and I was shitting myself that my parents would kill me if I died because they didn't know I was in Thailand?' 'Remember when I panicked because I saw a brown man in a suit looking shifty at Singapore airport after 9/11 and it was you who had to remind me not all brown people are terrorists? Isn't that funny, an Irish person having to tell a Tunisian not to be racist to other possible Muslims?'

Was my gabbling too frantic? Was there something brash and inappropriate in my delivery? It jarred with his quiet, reflective demeanour as he said, 'Yeah' and 'You were in a real state' and 'I remember that too.' His laughter cowered weakly beneath mine.

When my Remembers ran out of steam, he said, in that insistently sentimental voice, 'I can't believe you're leaving.'

'I know.' Why was he doing this to me? Why couldn't he have stayed in bed, or got up and gone to watch Noirin in action down at the athletics field? Anything but this, the tearful farewell he seemed to think was our due. Didn't he know I'd forfeited the right to be sad over him in the way he was fishing for? Clean, innocent, gently moving. I'd thrown that privilege away when I'd looked him in the eye and said, 'Of course there's no one else.'

'I don't even know when I'll see you again,' he persisted after I'd checked my luggage in at the airport.

'Yeah, I know. But I'm sure we'll meet in Ireland when you have your wedding... or whenever.'

'You'd better come to the wedding.'

'Yeah yeah, of course.' I'd already lined up an excuse for why I wouldn't make it. A minor cousin who was getting married in Tunis around the same time.

So why was I hardening my heart against him? Because he wanted something I couldn't give him, not then. Not as he stood blocking my escape route, imprisoning me with false notions of who I was. He wanted closure, a fitting end to the chapter of his life I represented before he moved on to the next one. Neat, sanitised, all nicely wrapped up: we loved each other but it didn't work. Not the gory ending I'd plunge us into if I finally told him the truth. 'By the way, I cheated on you and then I lied about it. Do you still think I'm brave and honest?'

What if I hurled this revelation into his face like acid, right then and there, at the security barrier? Should I? I could. I could if I had the guts – open my mouth and tell the truth. Why not be brave for once and undergo the painful cleansing that was the only way to restore him to his rightful position in my heart – the position of someone I loved, not someone I'd lied to?

But who would benefit from a stunt like that, at the eleventh hour? What was the point, when he was already happy with someone else?

There was no point. There'd be no winners. The window had closed for that kind of catharsis. And closure was a bedtime story for children, anyway. No, the kindest act was to leave him hanging, deprived of the bitter-sweet ending he longed for. As for me, the mourning would come later, from a safe distance, when I could cry without pretence over what I'd thrown away. Not here at the airport as I shifted from one foot to another, looking at my watch while pretending to scratch my wrist.

'Go on,' he said, laughing awkwardly. 'I can tell you're not enjoying this. We don't have to drag it out.'

'Sorry, sorry.'

Emboldened by the prospect of an imminent end to this ordeal, the tears pricked at my eyes at last. When he'd hugged me tightly and I'd taken a step backwards, my leg muscles revving up like a getaway car, I said, 'I really admire you.'

'Admire?' He smiled cautiously, a touch of suspicion in his voice. 'You sound like you're getting ready to give me a golden clock at my retirement dinner.'

'Haha. No, I do.'

'What do you mean?'

'Because you know how to be happy.'

That was the most I could give him. And that, at least, was the truth.

*

The mourning kicked off soon afterwards, as I downed consecutive mini bottles of red wine on the plane. Not just for him – for everything: for my manager, who I'd driven to distraction and then to Singapore. For the dregs of my youth that I was leaving behind in Japan. Nearly thirty summers on this earth and what did I have to show for it? Nothing. A series of goodbyes. A surface where nothing stuck.

I sat in mourning for all the things I'd lost, and those that others had lost before me. Truths surfaced and then sank in my consciousness, part of a broader pattern of futility and loss that seemed to characterise all human relations. Falling in and out of sleep, I dreamt I was living back at the flat in Cranfield Gardens with Mama, Sherine and That Man. You weren't there, but you hovered over us, your absence filling the air with a dark, heavy foreboding.

'I need to take my books back to the library,' I said to Mama, and she said, 'Tell her my red jumper doesn't fit her any more.'

In my waking intervals I watched a film about three young people in Paris in 1968 who spent their time running around streets full of burning tyres and having sex with each other. Two of them appeared to be brother and sister. Why was this supposed to be so shocking? What was the big deal? Why did people make such a song and dance about a basic bodily function, elevating it to the status of a hungry goddess of destruction demanding human sacrifice and giving bloody birth to secrets and lies? If this young woman wanted to have sex with her brother, who was anyone to say she shouldn't?

As for your transgression, calculated or not, was it really worth the loss of you in our lives? I forgave you. Yes, I forgave you. Who the hell was I to judge you? Fuck them, fuck all of them, no one had the right to judge you. Tearful one minute, elated the next, I planned what I would say to you after all these years, knowing that seeing you would make up for the mess I'd made of my own life as I slunk back empty-handed from my hunting expedition into the world of adulthood. Perhaps closure *could* be had, in certain circumstances, whatever cynics like me might think.

The plane passed from sunlight to darkness and back again. I drank and dozed and dreamt and brooded. In that parallel, suspended world above the real one where people fretted and scurried like ants, the boundaries between your life and mine seemed to blur and twist and dissolve until I could no longer remember who was supposed to be seeking forgiveness from who.

Reunion

April 2005

When I saw you the first time, we talked about your time in America, my time in Japan. Your children and their children; the neat symmetry of Amanda's two boys and Stephen's two girls.

'Amanda and Stephen...' I said. 'It's been so long.' I told you about seeing Amanda in the magazine in the dentist's waiting room. And then, just for something to say, I said, 'When I was little, I thought I would marry Stephen.' But the word 'marry' came out all wrong: bitter and raspy.

You smiled in a way that softened the aftertaste and said, 'Look, I'll show you their photos.'

It's funny how people can carry their stories on their faces like passport stamps. Amanda's eyes shone with the light of people who know they're good at life. Stephen still had that bunny-rabbit smile, begging the world to be kind. No wonder you'd always been so protective over him.

'Amanda and Max have been married for nearly fifteen years – you remember Max, don't you? They still seem very happy, as far as I can tell... Amanda never likes to worry me about anything. Stephen hasn't been so lucky, I'm afraid. He's just lost another job and now he's in the middle of his second divorce...'

We talked about other things: Sherine's job, my lack of one, wars, wildfires, earthquakes and climate change. Not the things that had ripped you out of our lives sixteen years ago. My *I forgive yous* crumbled in my mouth. Who did I think I was to forgive you? I was a bystander, not the victim. And anyway, you didn't look like someone who was waiting to be forgiven. Your eyes were calm, steady, observant, in a face that looked like an X-ray of itself. Something unknowable in them. Had it always been there or had time and distance introduced it? You were different from how I'd remembered, or imagined you.

You asked me to remember things for you. The old days. The day we arrived in London.

'I remember the kitchen but not the aeroplane,' I said. 'I remember meeting him for the first time. Not you. You were always just there. I remember you had a sweater with a puppy on it – it said *Hug Me*. I remember you calling me Nessie, when I was just Susu before.'

I didn't say, *I remember you whispering with my father by the windows while Mama trailed blood across the kitchen floor. I remember two people on a bed, at a Christmas party. I remember a snake with two heads.*

'How did it go?' Sherine said with her back to me as she stood making dinner that evening.

'Fine, fine,' I said. 'You know.' As if it was the kind of thing that happened every day. 'We didn't really get a chance to talk properly,' I said. 'Next time.'

*

The second time I came to see you, you looked different again. Slipping out of my reach, you refused to let me get a handle on you. Who were you, really? A person I used to know, small and vulnerable now.

Where had the years gone, for all of you? I thought of the woman you used to be: tall, gentle, kind. Distant and perceptive. Reckless and calculating. Was it possible to be both? You were a mystery, although I didn't know it then, which was part of your mystery. Separate from us but one of us.

I thought of the disappointments you'd hinted at and the ones you'd caused. I thought of the puppy on your sweater who'd said *Hug Me*, and I had to look out of the window. Away from your eyes. I wanted to hold your hand because you looked so alone, but I was too scared to touch you. I felt I might break you. I talked about the view instead.

'Next time,' I told myself as I closed the door of your room behind me and texted Sherine to tell her I was on my way home.

*

When next time came, it was late June. We talked about exile and return, though neither of us used such grandiose terms, and you said, 'I thought I'd stay in California, even after my marriage ended.'

'Your new name...?'

'It's my old name. My maiden name.' And then you made a kind of 'hmm' sound, as if the concept of you as a 'maiden' was too ridiculous for words.

For a second I had the irrational thought that something might've been different if we'd always known you by that name. If our significant other had been Ms Hamilton, not Mrs Brown.

It occurred to me that you'd learned to be alone, after California. Perhaps you'd always wanted that solitude. It's hard to know what you want when other people are busy wanting things for you.

'But it didn't seem fair,' you said. 'Once I was diagnosed with... to Stephen and Amanda, I mean. To make them worry about me, being so far away.'

I made some noise that was supposed to convey my understanding of these things. Your obligation to your children and theirs to you. It didn't seem like a change of subject when you said, 'Do you miss her?'

Her. Her. The name she used to call you ricocheting back at her. I knew who you were talking about. Of course I did. Because it was you, I answered honestly. 'Not really. As long as I know she's all right, I don't feel any burning urge to see her more often than I do.'

'She'. She. My mother with the ruined face. My mother who lived in mourning because of you, and who had indelible scars. She sat between us like a question mark. Heart thudding at my boldness, I spun the question around to face you. 'Did *you* miss her?'

'Yes, very much.' Your voice cracked as you cleared your throat. 'I thought about her all the time.'

Tapping your right index finger on the bed, you said, 'You used to be so close, the two of you...' And then, as if you were worried I'd think this was a judgement or reproof, 'But people change.'

'Yes,' I said. Did it seem like a tangent when I added, 'I've been thinking about what you said. You know, about a "record"?' It wasn't a change of subject to me, lost as I was in charting the progression of this change. The course that takes people from being one thing to something else entirely.

'Good,' you said. 'And how does it feel, thinking about the old days?'

'All right,' I said. 'You know.'

'Sherine thought it might help you. Taking stock of everything, now you're back.'

'So this was all her idea?'

The hacking started again. I swooped for your glass of water.

'A collaboration,' you managed to say, eventually.

Was I surprised? Not really. Of course she'd talked about me to you. How else would she have ushered me back into your life? It worked that way around too. I kept forgetting.

'What about him?' I said. 'Did you miss him too?'

'I missed you all, Nessie.'

It felt like you were holding your breath. Waiting for me to ask you what you were finally ready to answer. *Did you love him? Why did you blow up all our lives if it wasn't even love? Did you do it because you knew you'd never get what you really wanted?*

'The problem is...' I said.

'Yes?'

'The problem is that there's so much I don't know about the old days.'

And that was when my voice fell apart, as if it was this lack of knowledge that was breaking me. Not the talk of mothers and children severed by change. Not my guilty thoughts of *What if it was Mama?* Would I want her back, as Stephen and Amanda had wanted you back? Not your skeletal frame and eyes too big for your face, or your shuddering breaths and cringing posture, or the way you looked like a sad, resigned little girl abandoned in a place where people grow old in the blink of an eye, cursed by something bitter and vengeful and life-hating.

I don't know what I expected you to do. Something like in the old days, perhaps. Me as a child, you as the adult putting your arms around me, saying 'It's all right, Nessie, everything is all right.'

Lying in the bed, your whole body seemed to sigh. As if all this was too much for you. As if I was too much for you. I sat dabbing at my eyes with a crumpled piece of tissue. Waiting.

When you spoke at last, it was in a firm, clear voice that seemed to have come from somewhere else. Travelled there especially. Made the journey just for me.

'I'll tell you anything you want, Nessie. You can ask me anything.' Speaking to an equal, not a child. As if you respected me. As if I'd ever done anything worthy of respect. As if any of it mattered any more.

Against all logic, it was the fish that swam into my brain again. Why was I so obsessed with it? Why did I keep looking for someone else to solve the riddle, when I was the one who knew the answer? Mama had told me the day she'd caught me carving lines into my arm with your bracelet. 'I did it because I was ashamed,' she'd said. 'May God forgive me for what I did.'

Her words had come up against a blocked doorway, but that door was wide open now – your presence and the persistence of memory had finally kicked it in. Did I want to share the burden by saying the words out loud? *I know my mum cut herself deliberately all those years ago, the night the doctor came, and I know it was because of you.* What did it matter? All it would do was hurt you. I might know how her shame had manifested, but you were the one who knew what had caused it. I believed Sherine when she said the doctor hadn't dragged Mama along by her hair – that bit was just a trick of my imagination – but if I was wrong about that, what else was I wrong about?

Too drained to think too much about it, I said, 'I think I saw you on the bed at Mrs Kowalski's house when I was four years old… you had mistletoe in your hand.'

You flinched as if I'd hit you.

'Sorry,' I said after a heartbeat.

You parted your lips. I held my breath. A non-sequitur, whispered, all your certainty gone: 'It was easier, you see… to be loved by some people than others.'

'You weren't loved,' I said. You looked at me, small and afraid.

'You were adored,' I said. 'By those others.'

You closed your eyes. Your voice turned upwards, like a child's. 'I learned French again so we could talk… so we could understand each other.'

That's when I broke down, bending over in my chair, holding the tissue to my nose and letting my tears drip onto the floor as your breathing became ever more fretful and ragged.

I don't know if you heard me when I said, in a voice that could only manage a whisper: 'Was it just the once with him?' I don't know if I imagined it when your head seemed to slide up the pillow in a way that said yes, your eyes begging for peace at last.

'It's okay,' I said eventually, reaching out for your thin, papery hand, stroking the back of it, keeping my face turned away. 'You can tell me about it next time.'

All the bits of England

Was it too much, the way I embraced the project you set me? Flinging myself backwards into the past in the hope that something would catch me. I travelled up and down the Piccadilly Line to all our old places. Mrs Kowalski's house in Oakfield Road and the flat in Cranfield Gardens. Your library and my junior school. The bench in Finsbury Park where you'd sat with Mama while she'd clung to your words as if she was drowning.

Venturing further afield, I went back to my university, to the steel city I'd loved like a passing stranger. Did the sprawling housing estate in the hills behind the station always possess that desolate beauty? Maybe I'd been too dazzled by my freedom to drink Malibu and Coke and grope unfamiliar bodies on sticky dancefloors to notice. Standing outside my hall of residence, the ugly grey block overlooking the hills that lit up at night like a Christmas tree, I remembered meeting Michael, my first boyfriend, and Amy, my twin who I'd kissed and let slip away.

Walking on, I passed the hospital where I'd had my wisdom teeth out, three for free by student dentists. Michael met me afterwards and said, 'Let me take a picture of you.' He took me back to the skinny terraced house where we'd lived with Amy. It was right after we graduated, and she'd already moved back to Hounslow. The house was so quiet then, just the two of us.

'This is what it would be like if we were married,' I'd said, trying to talk with a mouth full of gravel as the anaesthetic wore off. That was my apology for pretending to think he was joking when he'd asked, and for laughing at normality with the callousness of youth.

'Shhh,' he'd said, because all that was in the past, in the days when Amy's Doc Martens had thundered up and down the stairs and no ghosts had moved into her room yet.

He fed me soup then propped a cushion onto his chest so I could rest there semi-slumped to watch *Neighbours*. He lifted his hand to stroke my hair when I whimpered and drooled like a baby as the pain kicked in. When my cheeks grew damp with tears that had nothing to do with wisdom teeth, he touched my face, without looking at me.

As I stood outside the house nearly ten years later, I still felt like an eternal tourist. But I knew I was lucky, because not everyone gets given the gifts I had received along the way.

When I got back to London, I emailed Lilia and asked when I could come and visit her and Nicky in Berlin. Then I emailed Kieran and told him my cousin in Tunisia had called off her wedding, so I could come to his in Ireland after all, if he still wanted me there.

Then I started writing two other emails.

Dear Amy... Dear Michael. It's been ages, hasn't it? Sorry for losing touch. I'm back in England now...

Did you know…?

The end came a week later on 7 July 2005. Your thunder was stolen by other events that reached their natural conclusion that day.

'She didn't see the news,' Amanda said to Sherine when she phoned to tell us her own news. 'She was unconscious by then, thankfully. She would've been so upset if she'd known.'

Sherine and I talked dates and times. 'The funeral's two weeks on Tuesday. I'll get the day off work,' she said.

No work for me yet. My efforts in that regard were half-hearted, derailed by thoughts that kept running off into the past, not the future. Still in limbo in this place called home. Still unable to watch the advert for the new Sony-Ericsson phone without a pang of loss each time I saw the silver train with the red stripe down the side. The Marunouchi line, my daily commute from Minami-Asagaya to Ginza. As for the DVD of *Lost in Translation* that Sherine ordered on Amazon… it sent me slinking off to my room after the first half hour.

'I only got it for you,' she said. 'Why don't you want to watch it?'

Because it hurts, I should've said, which was the truth, but instead I said, 'Lazy stereotypes', 'Cultural insensitivity', 'Too pouty and annoying'.

'I'll tell him we're going to the funeral,' I said, and Sherine looked at me curiously and said, 'Okay.'

You were the latest in a roll-call by then. The diseases of age calling the names of friends and relatives. Uncle Ali summoned by a heart attack as he drove to work in Edgware Road. *Amma* Zeinab by complications from diabetes. When I told That Man about you, he looked sad and said, 'God rest her soul.' That was it. No invoking of the past. No 'How or why do you know this?'

What were you to him, anyway? A schoolboy crush. Someone who made him feel like a *person*. Someone who brought his head down to rest on her shoulder and said, 'I'm so, so sorry, Hamdi,' and who gave him an excuse to wear his best jumpers and pretend he wasn't getting old. Someone who tried to ameliorate all life's disappointments by taking him to the theatre to watch *Cats*.

And what about you, Genevieve? Were you really so taken with him, or was it a moment of madness? Did you ever actually want him, or was he a smokescreen for what you did want? A red herring that ended up cooked on your plate and had to be eaten out of politeness?

Telling Mama was the thing I dreaded.

I called Mariana instead, walking round Wimbledon Common as we talked, my chest tight at the thought of going back to Sherine's flat, being caged indoors with this obstacle confronting me.

'I know it's weird that I'm only telling you this now...' I said, and she listened without interrupting while I told her the story. 'I don't know how to tell my mum,' I said at the end. 'I know I have to phone her and tell her, but I don't know how to bring it up.'

'Why don't you talk to Sherine about it first?'

'I can't...'

'Why can't you? Stop being such a baby.'

'Me! A baby? What do you mean?'

'Yeah, a baby. You tell yourself you want to protect everyone, but really you're just protecting yourself.'

'From what?'

'Difficult conversations. Things that make you feel sick. Talk to Sherine, Ness. Don't do this on your own.'

So I began the conversation that night when she was home from work and we were in the kitchen dishing out the dinner I'd made.

'Did you know...?' I said.

'What?'

'Nothing.'

She started talking about the health benefits of avocados in a voice that sounded like she was telling me off, blaming me for not eating enough avocados. A voice that would normally make me want to punch her. I said 'Mmmm, mmm.'

Without warning, it grabbed me round the middle, sending me off into fits of giggles. How could it be that I was about to say something so ludicrous? It couldn't come down to this, could it, this absurd, ridiculous sentence, with its air of a *Carry On* film or a coyly prurient 1970s sitcom?

'WHAT?' she said in exasperation before she started to laugh too, infected by the tears running down my cheeks. 'What's so funny?'

'Did you know...?'

'What?'

'Did you...?'

Both of us were gripping the sideboard, doubled over in spasms of laughter.

'What?' she said. 'What?'

'Did you know I saw Mama kissing Mrs Brown under the mistletoe one Christmas?' I said at last, all in a rush. Then, more slowly, not looking at her: 'It was during one of Mrs Kowalski's Christmas parties. Mama told everyone she was going out to buy lemonade, but she went upstairs with Mrs Brown. They were sitting on one of the beds in the living room – the one near the mantelpiece.'

I looked up at her. She took off her glasses and wiped them. 'Yes,' she said thoughtfully. 'That was my bed. I think I saw them kissing there too... but where was the mistletoe?'

And off we went again, clutching our sides, gasping for breath, complicit in the pretence that this comedy of a misplaced piece of mistletoe had banished the tragedy of wasted lives; that props had vanquished plot and none of it was really that sad, whatever the characters involved might choose to feel about it.

Your name

London, 1981

It was summer that day. One of those unblemished blue skies that only seems to exist in childhood, when your school uniform comes off. Mama took me to Finsbury Park and left me to play with some children I knew from school. Sherine had gone swimming with Mrs Kowalski's daughter.

'Wait here,' she said. 'I won't be long.'

'Where are you going?'

'Biz-niss, *ya bis-bis*,' she said playfully, talking nonsense, and I laughed as I watched her walk off in the direction of the ice cream van. I waited a few seconds before I started creeping behind her, playing a game on my own.

Her hair was short then. A fluffy cloud of curls reaching for the sky. After the two-headed snake that formed under the mistletoe you held in your hand. After the shame that made her plunge a knife into her hand. She was wearing a sleeveless midi-dress with a belt around the waist. Tight-fitting. Denim. As if she'd dressed to match the blue above.

I darted into the bushes on the edge of the grass and ran quietly alongside her, feeling like an animal. Cunning and stealthy. Tracking her. Peeping out from the foliage every so often, laughing silently to myself. Watching her swing her arms, carefree. Swaying her hips in a way she didn't normally walk. Dangly earrings shaking with each movement of her head. She'd put them on and done her makeup while she listened to the radio, humming along to 'Being With You' by Smokey Robinson.

'I like this song,' she'd said, and I'd said, 'I like it too, Mama,' punching my fist in the air as I pranced around, making her laugh and tease me: 'Are you dancing or fighting, *ma perle?*'

She stopped in a deserted spot by a bench and I stopped too, keeping as still as possible, watching her fidget and look at her watch.

She didn't wait long. Face bright, arms wide open, she stepped forward to greet you, pressing her body against yours.

'*Ya rouh qalbi,*' I heard her say. Soul of my heart. And then, in a voice I'd only ever heard once before, when you'd kissed her under the mistletoe and made my heart shake as I watched you; three times for luck or to conjure you into existence: 'Genevieve, Genevieve, Genevieve.'

About the Author

Ola Mustapha was born in London and spent part of her childhood living in Egypt, before returning to England. She studied economics and Japanese at university and then moved to Japan, where she taught English for several years. She now lives in London and works as an editor. Her short fiction has been published in literary journals including *Aesthetica*, *Storgy* and *Bandit Fiction*. *Other Names, Other Places* is her debut novel.